Soul Dancing

By
Arlene Brathwaite

BRATHWAITE PUBLISHING

www.brathwaitepublishing.com

Books by Arlene Brathwaite are published by

Brathwaite Publishing
P.O. Box 38205
Albany, New York 12203
(800) 476-1522

Copyright © 2011 by Arlene Brathwaite

Library of Congress Number:

ISBN: (10 Digit) #0-9797462-7-2
ISBN: (13 Digit) #978-0-9797462-7-7

This is a work of fiction. Names, characters, places and incidents either are the product of the author's imagination or are used ficti-tiously, and any resemblance to any actual persons, living or dead, events, or locales is entirely coincidental.

This book was printed in the United States of America.

Acknowledgments

It's 2011 and Brathwaite Publishing is growing in numbers and accomplishments with each year that passes. This year we are bringing on a few new authors, and we're opening Albany's first official urban book café called The Book Club. We're hanging tough in an industry that will run you over if you stand still. So, we here at Brathwaite Publishing are steady moving, and are steady coming up with stories that will keep our fans demanding more.

The fans drive us, but it's' the support of fellow comrades in the book industry that guides us and keeps us focused. People such as; Anthony Whyte, Erick S. Gray, Jason Claiborne, Shannon Holmes, Wahida Clark, Nakea Murray, K'wan Foye, and Deborah Cardona, just to name a few.

A special thanks to Jonathan Johnson of Brand Concepts for the book covers. Their works are fresh and eye catching.

And a very special thanks to all the readers and supporters who motivate us to give them the glued-to—the-seat, can't-go-to-sleep-til-I-finish-this-last-page reads. Those are the kinds of stories that we're known for, and that's not going to change. Thank you so much for your support and we hope to see you at future events and at The Book Club.

CHAPTER 1

In the lobby of the Palace Theatre in Albany, New York, Liana and her girlfriends stood together in the swelling crowd of R. Kelly fans awaiting the Prince of R&B.

Liana was an island blend of Panamanian and Puerto Rican. She inherited her father's dark complexion and her mother's long, straight hair. Since she was the tallest of the crew, at five-ten, she was considered by onlookers to be the leader of the four-girl ensemble. The only piece of jewelry she wore was her engagement ring.

Reese was ginger-complexioned with an insatiable appetite for M&Ms (Money and Mens). Being slim and cute gave her the potential to be a high-end fashion model, but her filthy mouth and stink attitude made sure she would never walk down anyone's runway.

Jenna was the shiest of them all, but her exotic facial features handed down to her from her Chinese mother and father, coupled with her thick thighs made her stand out in any crowd. The Chinese wasn't known for their eye catching curves, or tan complexions, which is why many people suspected that Mrs. Ling allowed a brother to take a couple strokes in the gene pool while Mr. Ling worked fifteen hour shifts at the fish market.

Elizabeth, if you let her tell it, had the best of both worlds. She attributed her hazel eyes, straight hair, and refined tastes to her white father, and her five-foot-eight bootyful body and brains to her African-American mother.

"I don't give a damn what the media say," Reese said. "R. Kelly didn't do anything wrong. Anybody who looks at that videotape can see that girl was totally with it."

"That's not the point," Jenna said. "That still doesn't negate the fact that she was underage."

"That's the problem," Reese said, flipping her hand at Jenna. "Everybody wants to be all technical 'n' shit. Home girl is a grown ass woman. You know what they say. You old enough to bleed, you old enough to breed."

"You are so… disgusting," Jenna said, shaking her head.

"And you are so stupid for entertaining her bullshit," Liana said, cutting in. "You know Reese doesn't have the sense she was born with."

"I'm just keeping it real," Reese said, rolling her eyes.

"Yes." Elizabeth nudged Liana. "That's what I'm talking about."

They all looked at the light-skinned brother Elizabeth pointed out. He was wearing a button down shirt and jeans with a pair of black Timbs. Elizabeth didn't care too much for men with hair on their face, but the goatee this brother sported made him a dead ringer for Denzel Washington in the movie *Training Day*.

"Ka ching," Reese said, appraising the two diamond studs in his ears and the square-link bracelet on his wrist.

"Definitely a drug dealer," Liana said.

"Why does every brother who looks like he's got money got to be a drug dealer?" Reese said with a sour look.

"Because they are," Liana shot back.

"Whatever." Reese turned her gaze back to the light-skinned brother. When he looked her way, she winked. He winked back and held eye contact with her long enough to let her know he was down for whatever. Reese blushed and looked away.

"Oh my God," Jenna said. "Is that Wayne?"

"Wayne who?" Elizabeth said with an attitude.

"That *is* Wayne," Jenna said. "What's he doing here?"

"Duh, the same thing we're doing here," Reese said.

"Wayne and R. Kelly don't even sound right in the same sentence," Jenna said, as she started waving at him.

"What the hell are you doing?" Elizabeth said through clenched teeth. "Don't call that lawn boy over here."

Wayne saw Jenna waving and waved back. As he approached them, he casually glanced at Liana, but it was enough to make his belly jump. Liana gave him the quick once over, surprised at what he was wearing. Everyone knew Wayne was so tight with his money that the only way he would let it go was to get a tighter grip on it. But tonight, he was wearing a pair of vanilla knit pants with a matching tank top. His six-foot frame was chiseled and chocolate brown.

He hugged Jenna and kissed her on the cheek. "What a surprise," he said, releasing her and then hugging Reese.

"Who you telling?" Reese said, hugging him back and kissing him on the cheek.

Elizabeth forced herself to smile and gave him a stiff hug. "I didn't take you for an R. Kelly fan."

"I'm not," Wayne said, as he pecked her on the cheek.

"So, what are you doing here?" Liana asked. "You're like a fish out of water."

"I came with someone."

Liana blinked, and was shocked at the jealousy coursing through her veins. *What the hell do I have to be jealous about? He's not my man... anymore.*

"You came with someone?" Jenna said, looking around. "Where are they?"

"Yo, yo, what up, people?" Taz said, as he bopped toward them.

"Oh God." Elizabeth folded her arms and looked away.

"Hello to you, too, with your fine Mariah Carey-looking ass," Taz said, walking up on her.

Elizabeth scrunched up her nose as she looked at his uneven afro and dingy white headband. "You could've at least gotten your hair braided and act like you're not on the block slinging."

Taz licked his lips as he stepped closer to her. "I would love to sit between your legs and let you twist me up like you do your man, Indio, or am I not high enough on the drug totem pole?"

"Nah, ah, I know you didn't take it there," Elizabeth said, snaking her neck. "Number one, Indio would stomp your raggedy ass out for talking to me like that. And number two, my man, unlike your simple ass, had enough sense to get out the game and start his own legit business."

"Legit?" Taz said, almost choking on the word. "You actually believe that—"

"So, how you doing?" Wayne asked Liana, stepping in front of Taz.

Jenna picked up on Wayne's cue. She grabbed Elizabeth and Reese by their arms and started walking off. "We'll see you inside, Liana."

"I'm coming right now, wait up."

"Nah, stay and finish your conversation with Wayne," Jenna said, dragging Elizabeth and Reese away with her.

"I'm going to get me something to drink," Taz mumbled, as he walked off.

Liana watched her friends melt into the crowd and pictured herself wringing Jenna's neck when she got her alone.

"So, how you doing?" Wayne asked for the second time.

"I'm fine. I'm just out with my girls." Liana studied her nails and then looked around as if she was bored.

"You came all the way from California for a night out with your girls?"

"Actually, I've been back for a couple of weeks."

"Everything okay with you and Rob?"

"Ron." Liana quickly corrected him. "And yes, we're just fine."

"Whoa, sorry for asking."

Liana lowered her defenses. "I just came up to spend a few weeks with Nana. You know... to make sure she's okay and what not."

"Your grandmother is still giving everybody hell. As a matter of fact, me and my pops are going to be at her house on Saturday cleaning out her garage and planting flowers."

"When did your father get out?" Liana asked, genuinely interested.

"Three months ago; and he's driving us crazy with that Muslim stuff. My moms can't cook any pork, Alisa can't wear tight clothes, and he tries to drag me to the Mosque with him every Friday. He's gone from hustle man to holy man."

Liana tried not to laugh, but when Wayne got animated, she couldn't help it. "I'm sorry, I don't mean to laugh, but—"

Her smile had always been his Achilles heel. He looked away when he felt his temperature rise. "Well, I'll let you catch up with your girlfriends. I'll probably see you on Saturday at Nana's."

Liana caught herself staring at his lips and looked him in the eyes. "Nice seeing you, Wayne."

"Nice seeing you, too." Wayne examined her like a jeweler would a rare stone. Liana wore a white linen outfit with a midriff top. Wayne stole a glance at her long legs. The long legs Liana loved to wrap around his waist when they used to make love. He shivered at the memory and walked off to find Taz. It was no surprise to find him huddled with two females. They both wore body-hugging outfits that left nothing to the imagination. Wayne could smell the lust emanating from their pores from twenty feet away.

"Hey, here comes my boy," Taz said, pointing the girls in Wayne's direction. "Wayne, this is Caroline and this is Peaches."

Wayne nodded and smiled.

"Me and the girls were just talking about having a private party after the concert. You know... smoke some trees, pop some E's, shoot the breeze, and if we act right, get a little strip tease." The girls laughed at Taz's impromptu rhyme. "So, you with it or what?"

"Yeah," Wayne said with a smile. "We can hang."

Taz grabbed Peaches by the hand. "Let's head in and try to get some seats together."

It wasn't hard to find four vacant seats together. They weren't vacant because the ticket holders didn't show. They were vacant because everybody was crowded by the stage when R. Kelly started to perform. The females held their hands out, hoping he would come to the edge of the stage so they could touch him. Surprisingly, he reached out and grabbed a couple hands.

Wayne had his arm around Caroline, and his eyes around Liana. He studied her as she laughed with her girlfriends and sang along with every R. Kelly song. There were plenty of times he tried to take his eyes off her and focus on Caroline, but his focus kept wandering back to Liana. He tried to take his mind off her by jamming his tongue down Caroline's throat, who was more than willing to tongue wrestle with him.

"Oh shit, look," Taz said, tapping Wayne on the shoulder. R. Kelly grabbed a girl by the hand and led her onto the stage.

"He picked the wrong one," Wayne said, as he watched Reese quickly close the gap between her and the R&B Superstar. Reese turned around and wiggled her butt on his crotch, letting him know she didn't see nothing wrong with a little bump and grind. Everyone in the theater got to their feet when Reese seductively faced him and grabbed a handful of nuts.

"That bitch is crazy, yo," Taz said, jumping up and down.

"I told you he picked the wrong one," Wayne said, laughing and high-fiving Taz.

R. Kelly's security quickly escorted Reese off the stage, but at that point, she didn't care if they were escorting her to jail. She got what she came for. She had a story to tell her kids and her kids' kids.

Wayne felt the hairs on the back of his neck stand up. He looked over at Liana and saw her looking his way. He looked at her nonchalantly and nodded. She rolled her eyes and got back into the show. Caroline slowly danced against him as R. Kelly sang his next song. She shivered as Wayne gave her the cold shoulder.

"You all right, baby?" she asked.

"I'm good," Wayne responded, looking past her.

She followed his line of sight to Liana. Caroline dismissed it and went back to doing her little dance as R. Kelly tore the house down.

***

"R's the best that ever did it," Taz said, walking out the Palace Theater with Wayne, Caroline, and Peaches. "Right or wrong, Wayne?"

"He's okay," Wayne responded in a distracted tone.

"Okay? I bet every female is walking out of here with soaked panties." Taz looked at Caroline and Peaches. "Your panties wet?"

Peaches slapped him on the shoulder. "You stupid, Taz."

"Well, if they ain't, they soon will be, right, Wheezy?"

Wayne looked at his watch. "I have to head home."

"What?" Taz, Caroline, and Peaches seemed to all say at the same time.

"I didn't know the show was going to end this late. I have to work in the morning," Wayne said defensively.

"You call mowing lawns work?" Taz said, twisting up his face.

"It pays the bills." Wayne looked at Caroline. She folded her arms and scanned the people coming out of the theater. She was determined to have a man for the night.

"You're crazy," Taz said, shaking his head. "Well, fuck it. The least you can do is take us to Kenneth's to get something to eat and then drop us off at the Marriot on Central Ave." Taz put his arms around both girls. "One man don't stop the show; there's plenty of Taz to go around."

Caroline and Peaches looked at one another.

"I'm down for whatever," Caroline said.

***

Wayne's cell phone alarm went off at seven o' clock the next morning. He turned it off and rolled over. Two minutes later, his phone rang. *Fuck!* "What up, Dad?"

"What I tell you about having me waiting?"

"I'm on my way." Wayne would never say it aloud, but he liked the landscaping business better when he was doing it by himself. When his father had to do a five-year bid for gun possession a few years back, he left Wayne in charge of the business. Wayne was twenty-one at the time, but he managed to hold it down and even pick up a few more contracts. He also set his own hours and worked at his own pace. When his father came home, it was back to working from seven in the morning until five in the evening.

Wayne walked out his front door and right across the street to his parents' house. People couldn't understand why he chose to live so close by. His father was a hustler long before he was a husband with two kids, which meant that his loyalty was to the streets first. So, that meant prison would become his second home. And when he went up north for years at a time, it was on Wayne to pick up the slack.

Wayne entered his parents's house and walked into the tail end of his sister and father arguing.

"There's nothing wrong with these pants, Daddy."

"They're too tight. If you dress like a slut, men are going to treat you like a slut."

"Mom." Alisa looked toward her mother for support.

"Don't get your mother involved," Nevel huffed. "This is between me and you. I'm your father, and I'm telling you to go upstairs and put on some pants that fit."

Alisa stormed off, knocking Wayne out the way.

"You better talk to your sister," Nevel said to Wayne. "She's going to make me whip her behind."

"You need to stop being so hard on her," Julie, Wayne's mother said.

"You're the reason why she's giving me a hard time," Nevel retorted. "I went away for a couple of years, and you let her do whatever she wanted."

"A couple years?" Julie said, amazed at how Nevel trivialized his jail sentences. "Try five. Alisa needs a daddy, not a dictator. She was twelve when you went back to prison for the umpteenth time. Get to know your daughter first before you start telling her what to do."

Nevel put on his cap and looked at Wayne. "Let's roll. I'm not trying to hear this."

"Well, you're going to keep on hearing it until you start treating your daughter like she's seventeen and not seven," Julie said to her husband's back.

***

Saturday morning, Wayne was up and dressed before his alarm clock went off. He walked into his parents's house just as his father started dialing his number.

"What the hell are you doing here on time?" Nevel asked in shock.

"You got a problem with that?"

"I wish you could be on time every morning."

On the way to their first job of the day, Wayne drove in silence as his father wolfed down his egg McMuffin.

"You think I'm too hard on your sister?" his father asked between bites.

"I think she's used to being one way; and it's hard for her to accept the things you want her to do just because it's in her best interest. I mean, she's seventeen; she's at the age where she's piecing together her identity."

"And I don't want four babies from four different daddies being part of that identity," Nevel shot back. "You're not stupid. You know how these kids think. They act as if they're invincible, like they can't get pregnant or catch AIDS. She may think I'm hard on her now, but she'll thank me in the long run. Allah says in the Holy Quran 'save yourself and your family from the hell fire'. And that's what I'm going to do. Speaking of which, what happened to you yesterday? I didn't see you at the Mosque."

"You're the Muslim, Dad, not me."

"You *need* to come to the Mosque and get some guidance in your life."

"I'm not the one needing guidance." Wayne could feel himself getting upset at his father's holier-than-thou attitude. "I'm not the one going back and forth to prison, leaving my family to fend for themselves."

"I'm having a hard enough time with your mother and sister, don't you start with me."

"I'm saying—"

Nevel balled up the Egg McMuffin wrapper and threw it out the window. "What *are* you saying?"

"I'm twenty-six years old and from as far back as I can remember, I've always known you as a hustler."

"Well, I've changed. I ran the streets all my life. I've been shot, stabbed, beat down... you name it. Instead of these situations slowing me down, I hit the streets even harder. There was only one thing in this world that could slow a fast track hustler like me down—old age. I look at all the years I wasted on the streets and in prison, and I'm full of regrets. I know I haven't been the perfect father, but if there's anything I want you and Alisa to remember me for, it's for all the mistakes I made. Learn from them so you won't have to waste a large part of your life making the same ones."

Wayne stared at his father, speechless. He couldn't remember the last time his father talked to him from the heart.

Nana stood on her porch in her housecoat and slippers, ready to bark orders when Nevel and Wayne pulled up. "I want you to start with the garage," she started. "Then, I got some stuff in the attic that needs to be brought down and carried to the curb for garbage pickup. And I hope you brought enough fertilizer this time."

"Nana," Wayne said, taking his keys out the ignition. "Can we get out of the truck first?"

Wayne had to clear their calendar for the rest of the day. Nana refused to let them leave until they completed every item she had on her list. What started as cleaning out the garage and planting some flowers ended up turning into a full-scale renovation project. Nevel took care of the flower planting and lawn work, while Wayne cleared out the garage, emptied the attic, painted two rooms, and replaced the cracked tiles in the bathroom shower.

Wayne looked at his watch and sighed. It was four-thirty, and Nana was steadily adding on to her list.

"Wayne!" Nana was sitting at the kitchen table. "How much longer are you going to be messing around in that bathroom?"

"I'm on the last tile right now."

"When you get done, I need to talk to you."

Aw, damn! She's bugging. Nah, I'm bugging. Every year I swear that I'm going to charge her full price like everybody else that way she won't have a heap of shit for us to do. But every year I buckle when I see her scraping together coins to pay me.

"You done yet?" Nana called out two minutes later.

"I'm on my way." Wayne walked into the kitchen, massaging his lower back. "What's up?"

"Sit down." She patted the kitchen chair next to her.

Wayne gratefully accepted the seat. "What's up?"

"I need for you to do me a favor."

That was Wayne's cue to hem and haw, but he saw the sadness in her face. "What is it, Nana?"

"It's Liana."

"What about her?" Wayne asked concerned.

"She's back."

"I know. I saw her at the concert Wednesday night. She said she missed you and came all the way up from California to check on you."

"That's what she told you?"

Wayne nodded slowly, hoping he didn't say more than he was supposed to.

"I swear that girl is so full of pride that it's going to be the death of her. She's not visiting me. She moved back in."

"Really?" Wayne said surprised.

"I told her that man wasn't right," Nana said, referring to Ron. "He moved her all the way to California away from her family and friends and then decided to act a fool."

"Acting a fool how?" Wayne asked, his shoulders tensing.

"Liana caught him in their bed with his baby's mama."

Wayne relaxed his shoulders. "That's crazy."

"Humph. What's crazy is he tried to convince Liana that he wasn't doing anything wrong. Talking about 'she's my son's mother, and we're always going to have feelings for each other.' Boy, if that was me, I would've knocked them both out and lit the bed on fire with the both of them still in it. I'm not lying."

"So, what do you need from me?" Wayne asked.

Nana touched his cheek. "She really needs a shoulder to cry on."

"I don't know, Nana—"

Nana silenced him. "You know her better than anyone else, including her friends. All they want to do is take her out and find her another man. What she needs is someone she feels comfortable enough with to talk to."

"Man, Nana. You're really asking for a lot. You know how she feels about me… and the way we broke up…"

"Wayne Dupree. I know you're not telling me no. I changed your diapers, boy. I even—"

"Okay, Nana. All right. I'll talk to her, but only when she's ready. She'll be more forthcoming if she brings it up. Deal?"

"That's the Waynie Wayne I know and love." Nana pinched his cheek.

"Can a brother get something to drink?" Wayne's father said, trudging into the kitchen with his hat turned backwards and the tail of his shirt hanging out his pants.

"Help yourself," Nana said, pointing to the refrigerator. "And when you finish, I got a couple more items on my list I need you to take care of before you go. I thought you were going to be able to finish everything today, but tomorrow's another day."

Wayne and his father both looked at each other.

"We have other jobs to do Nana," Nevel complained.

"Did I ask you about your other jobs? I paid you didn't I?"

"Hardly, Nana, listen—"

"Nevel Dupree. I know you're not about to get fly out the mouth with me. I changed your stinking ass diapers and—"

"All right, Nana, all right," Nevel said, holding his hands up like two stop signs.

Although Nana cared for a lot of children in her lifetime, she only had one child. A daughter who was murdered in 1986.

The murder of her daughter plagued her so that she became overprotective of Liana, not to mention, she was the only family she had left.

"Break time's over," Nana said, clapping her hands. "We don't have time to be lollygagging. It'll be dark soon."

They turned toward the side door when they heard it open.

"What are y'all staring at?" Liana said, as she closed the door.

"Make some noise when you come into my house, girl," Nana said, grabbing the bag of groceries from her. "You didn't forget the Massingil this time, right?"

"Nana!" Liana said embarrassed.

"What? We're all grown here."

"But I didn't need to hear that," Nevel said.

"If you were outside putting down the rest of that fertilizer like you were supposed to be, you wouldn't have heard it," Nana said.

Liana looked at Nevel apprehensively. "Hi, Mr. Dupree."

"Girl, since when you started calling me Mr. Dupree? You better recognize the Ol' G."

Liana walked into his arms and hugged him. "I'm really glad to see you, Pop Pop."

"Ol' G?" Nana said sourly.

"That's my cue to get back to work," Nevel said, releasing Liana.

Nana threw a dishtowel at him as he headed out the door. "Liana, fix Wayne something to drink. I'm going to go put these toiletries in the bathroom." Nana winked at Wayne and left.

Liana opened to the refrigerator. "We got Pepsi, iced tea and your favorite."

Wayne thought back to when they were twelve years old and Liana had dared him to drink a whole bottle of prune juice. He won the dare, but lost control of his bowels and shitted on himself.

"Pepsi's good." He watched her as she handpicked his ice cubes and placed them in the glass. He wanted to walk up behind her and press his body against hers as he did so many times in the past. He looked away when she turned around and placed his drink on the table. Wayne took four gulps before speaking. "Did you enjoy the concert?"

"It was okay. You know I don't like crowds, especially when people are acting a fool, but I toughed it out for my girls. I see you enjoyed yourself. You, Taz, and them two hos."

Wayne chuckled. "It wasn't even like that. I went home alone."

"Yeah, right. That girl was wrapped around you like an Ace bandage. I know she gave it up."

"You know I don't go to concerts. I let Taz talk me into going. I dropped Taz and the two girls off at the Marriot when I realized how late it was. I had to be up the next morning for work."

Liana twisted a lock of her hair as she stared at him and then smiled. "If it were anyone else trying to sell me that story, I would've called them a lying bastard. But I know how much you love your job, and I do know you would put it in front of some pussy any day."

"Still know me like the back of your palm, huh?" Wayne said rhetorically. Hearing Liana using profanity always turned him on, because she was a good girl. So to hear her say pussy or butt crack just did something to him. Something that was about to become real embarrassing if he had to stand up at that moment. *Think fertilizer, deflating balloons, flat tires, air leaks, go down dammit, go down.*

"You okay, Wayne?"

"Just deep in thought. Going over that long-ass list Nana gave me. You know how Nana and her lists can be."

"You know I know. She tells me to pick up two items from the store. Then she gets to writing them down and before you know it, the list is a page and a half."

Wayne agreed with a smile and then changed the subject. "How's Ron?"

"Ron is Ron," Liana said dismissively.

"Okay, that tells me a whole lot."

"Well, there's nothing to tell. He's doing fine, I'm doing fine—"

"But we're not doing fine," Wayne interjected.

"What?" Liana face knotted up.

"You didn't say we're doing fine. You spoke about you two separately."

"We're both fine," Liana snapped. "Fine as can be."

"I was just asking."

"No, you were reading shit into the answer I gave you."

"Whoa, calm down Miss defensive."

"Nobody's getting defensive. You need to stop minding my business and mind your own damn business." Liana stormed out of the kitchen and headed to her room. Wayne jumped when he heard the door slam.

Nana walked into the kitchen and started unpacking the rest of the groceries. "That went really well."

CHAPTER 2

"C'mon, girl, snap out of it," Elizabeth said to Liana. "Here." She placed Liana's hand on a silk blouse. "Feels nice, right? And look at the design, it's different."

"We should've left her love-sick ass home," Reese grumbled.

"So Ron could harass her with his whining phone calls?" Jenna said. "I don't think so. Liana needs therapy and there's no therapy better than shopping."

"Especially when you're spending someone else's money," Reese threw in. "Ron didn't cancel those credit cards for a reason, girl, so you better stop acting like you don't know what to do with them."

"I'm just not feeling it today," Liana said depressed.

"What's there not to feel?" Reese asked. "You're in Crossgates mall with a platinum card. You're going to buy something, fuck that"

An outfit caught Jenna's eye. She grabbed it off the rack. "This is hot."

Liana looked at it and faintly nodded.

"This will definitely look good on you." Jenna held the outfit in front of Liana. "A black wrap around jacket, a long, polka dotted sash, and feel these pants. They're multilayered silk. Now you can wear those black and white Manolos you're always claiming don't match anything in your closet."

Liana inspected the outfit with her shopaholic eye. "It does look nice."

"Hell yeah, it does," Reese said.

"And look at this one," Elizabeth said, handling a low-cut dress.

Liana looked it over; she was slowly coming back to her senses. She turned away from the two outfits and reached for a form fitting dress. "Now, this is what I need to be in."

"That's the Liana I know," Jenna said. "Now, let's do what we do best."

Liana and her girls walked from one end of the mall to the other, and thanks to Ron's platinum card, whatever Liana or one of her girls wanted they got.

"Spending Ron's money is making me hungry," Reese said, rubbing her stomach. "Let's grab something to eat."

"I'm feeling you," Elizabeth said. "You're treating?"

"Huh?"

"Huh? It was your idea. So, it's your turn to spend some money."

Reese stopped rubbing her stomach. "Well, I'm not that hungry. I can wait until I get home."

Elizabeth's mouth fell open. "I can't believe how stingy and inconsiderate you're being right now. Liana bought us outfits, shoes, and makeup; and you can't even spring for lunch?"

"Why don't you spring for lunch?" Reese said with an attitude.

"Cause you brought it up," Elizabeth shot back.

"Well, forget I brought it up."

Elizabeth stared at her for a moment. "I don't know who's stingier; you or the lawn mower man."

"You didn't have to take it there," Jenna said.

Liana was about to come to Wayne's defense, but she knew if she did, they would think she still had feelings for him.

"I'm not disrespecting him or anything," Elizabeth continued, "I'm just stating a fact. The man's tighter than micro-mini braids. Liana couldn't even dream of a day out like this if she was still with him, or driving a Lexus SUV, or—"

"All right, already," Liana said. "Let's just get something to eat, and we'll each pay for our own food."

***

"So, what's the verdict with you and Ron?" Reese said, as they were finishing their meal.

"What kind of question is that?" Jenna asked. "It's over."

"Excuse me, I was talking to the other Liana." Reese looked back to Liana. "So have you decided, yet?"

Liana put her hamburger down. "I don't know. He's calling me every day, all day. He's sending a bouquet of flowers to the house every week—"

"And he's paying your platinum card and car note," Reese squeezed in.

"This isn't about what he's doing for her, financially," Jenna jumped in.

"Why the hell ain't it?" Reese snapped.

"Relationships are about honesty, commitment, and trust. Without those, you have nothing."

"No, Miss China, *you* have nothing. When your parents found out your boyfriend Eric was a brother, they stopped speaking to you. And when you two got engaged, they cut you out of their will. There's no way I'm going to let a man come between me and my family."

"You mean between you and your family's money," Jenna said, daring Reese to dispute it.

"Watch your mouth, Kung fu."

"Please," Elizabeth said, covering her ears. "We're supposed to be hanging out with our girl today; lending her emotional support, and backing her on whatever she decides to do."

"So, What's up with Wayne?" Jenna said, throwing everyone for a loop.

Liana almost choked on her hamburger. "Nothing's up with him."

"Can't you see she's going through enough drama?" Elizabeth said. "That man will not be a part of our conversation today."

"You don't have to bite my head off, I was just asking," Jenna said, rolling her eyes.

"I'd rather have a threesome with Ron, and his baby mama than get back with Wayne," Liana said.

"Girl, I knew you was a freak," Reese said. "Game recognize game."

"No dear," Elizabeth cut in. "There's a difference between being a freak and being... you."

Liana and Jenna hid their grins for a whole two seconds before they busted out laughing.

"Fuck you," Reese said, sticking up her middle finger at Elizabeth. "You're just jealous. You wish you could do the things I do."

"You two can't be in the same airspace for one day without finding something to argue about," Liana said.

"All I'm saying is Ron was your one-way ticket out of Smallbany," Reese said. "He swooped into Albany and swept you off your feet like you were a ghetto Cinderella; and then he took you to his castle in California and gave you everything your heart desired."

"And then he fucked up your happily ever after ending by fucking his skeezer ex," Jenna spat out. "Granted, Wayne is far from a knight in shining armor; and he may never be able to shower you with jewels and credit cards, but at least he was faithful."

"Faithful don't pay the bills," Reese said, smacking her lips.

Elizabeth leaned forward in her chair. "You're wasting your time, Jenna. Liana isn't trying to get back with him. And even if she was, I wouldn't let her. I'm not about to sit back and watch my home girl get back with a loser who shovels my snow in the winter and cuts my grass in the summer—believe that."

Reese's sonar detected a light-skinned hunk strolling by the food court. "Do you see what I see?" she said in a sing-song voice.

Elizabeth was the first one to recognize him. "Denzel from the Palace Theater."

He must have felt all eyes on him because he turned toward them. Reese smiled and nodded. He returned her greeting and kept it moving.

"Nah, ah" Liana said, as Reese got up and grabbed her bags. "Where are you going?"

"To get my man." Reese took off without bothering to say bye.

"Sit your hot ass down and—" Elizabeth started, but Reese had already widened her stride to catch up with her prey.

"I don't know about that girl sometimes," Jenna said shaking her head.

"She's a slave to men," Elizabeth said, as her cell phone rang. "Hey, baby," she said into her phone. "I'm at Crossgates with my friends… what am I doing at six? I'm doing whatever you want me to do."

Jenna stuck her finger in her mouth and pretended to throw up. Elizabeth threw a French fry at her.

"Yes, baby. I'll be home, dressed, and waiting. Just make sure you're on time… yes, I have a rent-a-car. You know I stay with one. I love you, too, bye." Elizabeth continued eating her fries with a smug look on her face. She looked up at Jenna and Liana, who were staring at her the whole time.

"What?" She said oblivious to why they were staring at her.

"Since when does a man have you jumping through hoops and balancing a beach ball on your nose?" Liana asked.

Elizabeth waved her off. "Girl, please. It's the other way around."

"Clearly," Jenna said with a chuckle.

"Fuck you, Fu Manchu," Elizabeth said, putting her hand in Jenna's face.

"You know what?" Jenna threw her burger down on her tray. "One day I'm not going to be in the mood, and you're going to come out the side of your face with one of your racist remarks, and I'm going to Fu Manchu you right in your face."

Elizabeth started laughing. "You never punched anyone in the face."

"Well, you can be the first." Jenna started to stand up.

"That's it. I'm out of here." Liana grabbed her bags. "Why can't we ever go anywhere without you two or Reese having to start some shit? I'll meet you in the car."

"Can't take you nowhere," Jenna said out the side of her mouth to Elizabeth as they both watched Liana walk off.

"You really wanted to punch me in the face?" Elizabeth said, avoiding eye contact.

Jenna sighed. "You know I was just talking shit."

"So was I. You know I didn't mean anything by it."

For the both of them, that was the closest they were going to come to an apology. They picked up their bags and headed to the car.

"Shouldn't we call Reese and let her know we're leaving?" Jenna asked.

"Humph, she's probably in Denzel's car, on her way to his place," Elizabeth said.

"She's not as fast as you think," Jenna said, trying to defend Reeses's reputation.

"You're right... she's faster."

***

Liana closed her bedroom door and flopped down on her bed. Nana told her that BJ's called and left a message. They were more than happy to give Liana her old job back. Nana was pleased to hear the news, but Liana wasn't. *I'm always going backwards. I went from a cashier at BJ's to a mini mansion in California, back to being a cashier at BJ's and moving back in with my grandmother.*

Liana looked at the three thousand dollar engagement ring on her finger. *So what if he fucks his baby moms every now and then. I'm going to be the one with his last name. I'm going be the one he comes home to every night. No man's perfect.*

Liana gathered her thoughts and looked at the 5x7 picture of her mother on the dresser. She struggled to remember her mother's touch, her voice, her smell; but losing her mother at two years old didn't give her a lot of memories to work with.

Her mother was the epitome of island beauty: Honey-gold complexion, long wavy hair. She could have had any man she wanted, but she chose Lee, Liana's father. Lee was a player from as far back as '83. Liana remembered Nana telling her that he moved to Albany from Brooklyn. He wore the slickest clothes and had the tongue to match. It was only a matter of time before he had Anna, Liana's mother, under his spell. Anna was four months pregnant when she found out that Lee was an undercover crackhead.

Liana turned away from the photo and stared at the ceiling. She blinked back to reality when her cell phone rang. She looked at the caller ID, and sighed. "What's up, Wayne?"

"Just called to see how you were doing."

"How'd you get my number?"

"Nana gave it to me. I told her I had to call and apologize."

"Apologize for what?"

"For upsetting you last Saturday."

"You didn't upset me."

"Yes I did."

"No you didn't."

"Yes I did."

"You're upsetting me now," Liana snapped.

Wayne remained quiet for a moment. "What are you doing tonight?"

"Eating a gallon of chocolate ice cream."

"Have dinner with me."

"I don't think so," Liana said in a depressed tone.

"Why not?"

"Because I don't want to."

"You scared you'll have a good time and forget about Rob?" Wayne poked.

"Ron."

"What?"

"His name is Ron; and no, I can never forget about my fiancé."

"He's not one of those insecure brothers, is he?"

"Where do you want to go?" Liana asked, not in the mood to play games.

"To my favorite restaurant."

"The Golden Corral isn't a restaurant, it's a buffet."

"I say tomato, you say tomahto. It's still a vegetable."

"Actually, it's a fruit."

"The Golden Corral?"

"No, silly. I was talking about the—"

"I know what you were talking about. Back to what I was talking about."

Liana closed her eyes. "What time are you coming to pick me up?"

"I'm already out front, hurry up."

Liana looked out her bedroom window. "I can't hurry up. I have to get ready."

"Get ready? This isn't a date. We're just going to grab something to eat."

Liana closed her eyes. "You know what? I think I'll pass."

"All right… you win. I'll splurge and take you to the Olive Garden."

"Save your money, Wayne. I don't have much of an appetite."

"You just said you were about to eat a gallon of ice cream."

"Trust me, I'm not going to be very good company."

"Whatever, Liana."

Liana heard the frustration in his voice. "Don't try to make me feel guilty."

Wayne hung up on her.

"Hello? No he didn't." Liana looked out the window just in time to see him pull off. She got his number off her caller ID and dialed the first three digits. *What the hell am I doing?* She slipped on her rabbit slippers and headed to the kitchen for her ice cream.

"You can't eat your problems away," Nana said, as she entered the kitchen and looked into the refrigerator.

"No, but maybe I can eat myself into a coma. That way I won't have to deal with them." Liana grabbed a spoon and headed back to her room. She picked up her pace when she heard her phone ringing.

"If you ever fucking hang up on me again—"

"Slow down, baby, I didn't hang up on you."

"Oh, Ron, it's you."

"You don't sound too happy to hear from me."

"What would ever give you that idea?" Liana dug into her ice cream.

"Liana, you need to come back home, so we can straighten things out. I fucked up. I know that now. I don't know what I was thinking. I didn't set out to purposely hurt you. Let me make this up to you."

"How can you make this up, Ron? You were in our home, in our bed, fucking Bridgette. How are you supposed to make that up? Please, tell me."

"I'm not seeing her anymore. I broke it off with her as soon as you packed your bags and left. This might sound crazy, but it took this situation for me to realize that I can't live without you. I'm hurting, Liana. I'm losing weight, I'm losing my hair, I'm losing sleep, I'm losing my mind. C'mon home, so we can make this right."

Liana opened her mouth to tell him to go fuck himself, but the words wouldn't come out.

"Baby are you there?"

"No, I mean yes, but I can't do this right now. I need time to think."

"I'll call you tomorrow night just to check up on you, okay?"

"Yeah, whatever." Liana hung up and tore into her ice cream.

Reese's gold digging words ran through her head, but that wasn't Liana's style. Jenna's words of rational entered her mind, but rational wasn't making much sense to her right now. Then Rasheem, Indio's cousin, the "perfect gentleman" Elizabeth introduced her to last week popped into her head. Rasheem was sweet and said all the right things. For Liana, that was a bad sign. *Men are the perfect companions until you get intimate with them. As soon as you let them into the most delicate areas of your life, they just kick off their shoes and show their asses.*

Liana thought back to the four men she'd been intimate with. There was Wayne, her first. Then there was Guy and

Steve, the two she dated when she went away to college. And then there was Ron. They all did her dirty, especially Wayne.

There's got to be one special man out there for me who will treat me the way I deserve to be treated. Her mind drifted back to Rasheem and how comfortable he made her feel. He knew the situation with Ron, and he knew she was vulnerable; but he didn't take advantage of her, even when Liana blatantly told him she wanted to sleep with him just to spite Ron. *He might be the one. Or maybe he'll be just like every other man I let into my life.* She put the box of ice cream down and rubbed her belly. She could feel a stomachache coming on. Good. She would welcome a stomachache over a heartache any day.

CHAPTER 3

Wayne was up before the sun and was on his third house by one o'clock. Tuesdays and Fridays were his father's days off so he had to work twice as hard. He stabbed at the dirt around Miss Levinson's house like an inmate shanking a CO. He always threw himself into his work whenever he didn't want to deal with unpleasant feelings. He made a fool of himself when he asked Liana out to dinner. When he pulled away from her house, he pulled a scab off of his heart as well. And now, he was trying to stop the bleeding by working himself 'til exhaustion. He headed to his pickup to grab the bag of fertilizer, and wasn't at all surprised to see Taz sitting in the passenger seat, bopping his head to his Sean Paul CD.

"And girl I, wanna be the papa, you can be the mom, ho-ho" Taz sang out loud, as he saw Wayne walking toward the back of the truck. He stuck his head out the window. "There's the hardest working man in Albany."

"How long have you been sitting in there?" Wayne asked, as he wiped the sweat from his brow.

"About half an hour."

"You've been watching me bust my ass all this time, and it didn't dawn on you to get off your lazy ass and give me a hand?"

"I was, but you were wielding that spade like a madman, and when I saw you arguing with yourself, I thought it be best for me to sit tight until you finished your argument."

Wayne grabbed the bag of fertilizer and hoisted it onto his shoulder. "I'm not going to be done here until around one-forty-five."

Taz got out. "I'll keep you company." He followed Wayne to the side of the house. "Aye, yo, you should've stayed at the hotel that night with me, Caroline and Peaches. I popped in that R. Kelly CD, and man... oooh weee!"

"I'm glad you got your shit off," Wayne said, getting on his knees and busting open the bag of fertilizer.

"Man... let me tell you. First I—"

"All right, I don't need all the details. Pass me that spade."

"Damn, you trying to work me like a Hebrew slave?"

"Stop playing and make yourself useful."

Miss Levinson slipped out the side door with a glass of lemonade in one hand and a plate of food in the other.

Taz arched his eyebrow. Miss Levinson was a fifty-year-old history teacher at Albany High. The students called her Grandma Dynamite because she had the banging body. She wore a pair of jeans and a button-up white shirt. As she got closer, Taz could see the imprint of her nipples straining against the fabric.

"Oh, hi Jamal," she said, calling Taz by his real name. "I didn't know you were out here working with Wayne. Can I get you anything?"

"Would you, please?" Taz said, wiping his forehead with the back of his hand and picking up the spade with the other. "Wayne got me working like I just snuck across the border last night."

Miss Levinson walked past him and held out the glass and plate to Wayne. "Take a break and put something in your stomach."

"Thank you, Miss Levinson."

She playfully punched him on the shoulder. "How many times do I have to tell you to call me Carol?"

Wayne smiled and took the glass and plate from her. She watched him walk to the picnic table and sit down. Wayne had on a pair of Levi's jeans, construction Timbs, and a blue tank top.

Taz could see Miss Levinson's nipples stiffening against her shirt. He cleared his throat.

"Oh, I'm sorry, Jamal. I'll go get you that drink." She folded her arms, trying to cover her chest as she walked by him.

Taz stared at her butt, and clinched his fists. "Umm, now that's some old pussy I wouldn't mind tapping. You should've seen the way she was staring at you. She looked like she wanted to put you on that plate and eat you for lunch. You saw how her nipples were poking out at you?"

Wayne took a couple of swallows of his iced tea. "You should've been here last week when I was installing a ceiling fan in her den. She was walking around damn near naked."

"She's got to be putting in mad hours at the gym because her shit is tight." Taz lowered his voice. "You hitting that, ain't you?"

"Nope."

"Get the fuck out of here. She's practically begging for the Mandingo."

Wayne looked at him like he was crazy. "She's a school teacher, and she's old enough to be my moms."

"You's about the corniest dude I know," Taz said, sticking the spade in the dirt and walking off.

"Where are you going?"

"To go see if I can make Grandma Dynamite go kaboom!"

Wayne finished the plate of food, and was getting back to work when his cell phone rang. A number appeared on the caller ID that he never saw before.

"Hello?"

"Hey, it's me," Liana said.

"I almost didn't pick up. I didn't recognize the number."

"I'm at Jenna's. Besides, I knew if I would've called you from my cell or Nana's phone, you probably wouldn't have picked up."

Wayne didn't say a word.

"Anyway, I just called to say I'm sorry about Saturday night."

"There's nothing to be sorry about. I asked you if you wanted to go for a bite to eat, and you said no."

Liana sighed. "I didn't say no, at first. It's just... well, I got a lot going on in my life, right now. I'm just trying to figure some things out. Nevertheless, forget about all that. I called to apologize and ask if you wanted to grab a bite to eat tonight, my treat."

"Hmm, I wish I could, but I got two more jobs to do before I call it a day, and I probably won't be done until about seven."

"We can make it a late dinner."

"The only thing I'm going to want to do after work is fall into my bed. I appreciate the offer, though. Maybe some other time."

"Yeah, maybe some other time," Liana mumbled.

"I have to get back to work." Wayne hung up and then clasped his hands behind his head. *I'm too old to be playing cat and mouse.* He pulled on his work gloves and got back to work.

Taz exploded out of the side door ten minutes later, screw faced. Wayne looked up at him, recognizing the expression all too well. "Damn, that was quick. Grandma Dynamite didn't have a heart attack riding you, did she?"

"Fuck that crusty, bitch," Taz said, spitting on the side of the house. "That bitch had the nerve to excuse herself and go put on a bra. Can you believe that shit?"

"She probably wanted to slip into something a little more concealing for you." Wayne chuckled.

"You got jokes? A real standup comedian, huh? Well, don't quit your day job."

Wayne stood up. "Either you're going to help me, or you're going to wait in the truck. I'm not going to get anything done with you grumbling about getting turned down by a woman twice your age."

"Yo, fuck all that. My main reason for hunting you down is to ask you for a favor."

"How much you need?" Wayne asked, knowing the drill.

"Damn, why I got to need money?"

"Your favors always involve me loaning you money."

"Well, I don't need money. I got plenty of that. I got so much that I bought a car."

Wayne's head rocked back. "You? Bought a car? Finally, you spent money on something other than jewelry and chicks."

"Yeah, and all I need you to do is put me on your insurance."

"What? You don't even got a driver's license. And even if you did, I wouldn't add you on my insurance." Wayne opened the bag of fertilizer. "I liked it better when your favors involved me loaning you money."

"C'mon. Don't even act like that. I'm tired of riding shotgun in your ride. Like you said, I finally spent my money on something else besides jewelry and bitches." Taz dug into his pocket. "Look, I passed my permit test, and I'm signing up for the five hour course or however many hours it is. I'll have my license by June."

"I'm happy for you, really I am, but I'm not putting you on my insurance. I didn't even put my pops on my insurance. What makes you think I'm going to put you on?"

"I'm your boy."

"Ain't happening."

Taz switched gears on the conversation. "So, when are you quitting this hobby of yours and getting a real job?"

"A real job like yours?" Wayne said, putting the bag of fertilizer down. "Yeah, I can see myself now scrambling on the block hollering 'two for five', 'two for five', barely making sneaker money."

"I remember when we started this mowing lawn bullshit together as a way to make some quick money during summer vacations," Taz said. "We were like fourteen. Here we are, twelve years later, and you're doing the same shit. It hasn't gotten you anywhere."

"And where has your drug dealing gotten you, Al Capone? Eighteen months in Detention for Youth, two state bids, and over ten arrests. My money may not come as fast as yours, but I have a bank account, credit cards, a house, a car, and I don't have to ask anyone to add me to their insurance."

"You already said no. You don't have to rub it in my face. I'll be waiting in the truck," Taz said, kicking a rock as he walked off.

Wayne's head was pounding. He just wanted to pack up his tools and call it a day. He caught a subtle movement coming from the window above him. Miss Levinson was watching him with a lustful eye.

I should go in there and give her the business. I can take all my frustration out on that old pussy. Wayne felt his heart starting to beat faster. *I can't believe I'm getting hard thinking about Grandma Dynamite. I'm losing my fucking mind.* He turned around when he heard a car pulling into the driveway. His heart started beating even faster when he noticed it was an unmarked car. He knew he hadn't done anything wrong, but he must have inherited his fear of police from his father.

Detective Harris got out and walked up the driveway. "How's it going?"

"Good," Wayne responded.

"Wayne, right?"

"Yes."

Detective Harris looked him up and down. "I heard you do an excellent job. You take jobs in other neighborhoods?"

"It depends on the neighborhood."

"Guilderland."

Wayne paused for a moment before answering. "Yeah, I got a couple properties I do out there."

Detective Harris nodded. "You have a business card or a way for me to contact you?"

I knew it. I knew this pig wanted something from me. He's probably going to run a check on the business to see if it's legit. Some people just can't stand seeing a young black man doing his thing.

Wayne dug out his wallet and pulled out his business card. "My home number's on the bottom."

"Marcus!" Wayne and Harris both looked up as Miss Levinson walked toward them. "Let Wayne finish up here. He's a busy man."

"I was just taking one of his business cards. I'm thinking about having him do some work on my yard, Ma."

Ma? Wayne tried to conceal his shock.

"Wayne, this is my son, Marcus, and he knows how I hate it when he shows up unannounced."

A thought flashed through Wayne's mind. Him having Grandma Dynamite bent over the dining room table and her son, the detective, showing up unannounced. *I can see the police report now. I walked into my mother's house, and I saw a nig... I mean an unidentified man on top of her. I drew my gun and that's all I remember. The next thing I know, Mr. Wayne Dupree was shot seventeen times.*

Miss Levinson grabbed her son by the hand. "Let's go inside and get you something to eat."

"I'll be giving you a call," Detective Harris said over his shoulder to Wayne.

"I'll be waiting." When they disappeared into the house, Wayne's head was pounding harder than a speaker at a block party. He finished his work and gathered his stuff as fast as he could. He wanted to be out of there before Harris came back outside.

When he got to his truck, Taz was sitting in it with the music and seat belt on. Wayne looked at him and frowned.

"What's up with you?"

"What Harris want?" Taz asked suspiciously.

"Nothing, he was just visiting."

"Visiting? Hell Nah. Not Harris. He's a scheming motherfucker. He asked you about me?"

"He's not thinking about you. Like I said, he was just visiting... his mother."

Taz's jaw dropped. "Grandma Dynamite? She's... oh shit! You mean to tell me I almost fucked Harris's moms? That's crazy, yo."

"Almost?" Wayne said confused. "I thought you said she put on a bra and gave you the cold shoulder."

"Yeah, but I could've hit that if I really wanted to. She was feeling me. I just didn't want to have her head banging on the headboard with you out here."

Wayne started his truck and pulled off.

"I'm going to hit that before the week is out, watch," Taz said, scratching the peach fuzz on his chin.

"You're going to fuck around and get an ass full of lead."

"And it will be worth every slug to be able to tell the hood that I fucked Harris's moms."

Wayne shook his head. "I'm willing to bet that your mother can collect disability for your crazy ass."

***

When Liana got off the phone with Wayne, Jenna was standing in her bedroom doorway, pointing at her. "You're trying to get back with Wayne on the low. I knew it."

"Don't start," Liana said with a huff. "We were friends before we started dating, and we were friends after we broke up."

"Broke up? You mean after you called off the wedding. After all those stupid rehearsals you made us go through, and you just up and called everybody and told us the wedding was off. I'm still waiting to know what happened. Why would you break up with your childhood sweetheart and hook up with a dude you barely knew and move all the way to California?" Jenna walked to the bed and sat down next to her.

"We're not going to talk about this today," Liana said, rubbing her temples. "We're not going to talk about this period. I have a right to live my life the way I want, and go out with who I want, and move to wherever the hell I want."

Jenna looked at her like she just lost her mind. "I'd expect a response like that from Elizabeth or Reese. They're air heads, but you?"

Liana kicked back on Jenna's bed and let her feet hang off the side. "Why is life so damn complicated for me? I see the way Efran makes you happy. I see how happy Elizabeth is with Indio. I even see how happy Reese is with her variety of men. Is it me? Am I creating my own misery? Am I looking for a man who doesn't exist?"

"Girl, you got to follow your heart to wherever or to whomever it may take you to. Efran is my heart. So what I'm Chinese and he's African American. So what if my parents can't see past the color of his skin. Efrin and I are in love, and I'm not going to let anyone come in between that."

"I have to go." Liana sat up and slipped on her shoes. "I don't want to be late for my first day back to work."

"Okay, BJ girl. Go and do your thing."

Liana walked out of Jenna's room flipping her the Finger.

"Tell Reese I said hi," Jenna said.

CHAPTER 4

Liana's first day back at BJ's felt as if she never left. She worked non-stop. Reese working alongside her made the afternoon go by quickly. Reese looked at her watch and then ran her fingers through her bouncy curls, making sure her 'do was right. Then she smoothed out her pants, and began touching up her makeup.

Liana stared at her the whole time out the corner of her eye. "What's all that for?"

"It's almost quitting time."

"I know that, but you're fixing yourself up like you're going out on a date."

"Can't I look good for my man?" Reese said innocently.

"Which one?"

"Dexter," Reese said like a high school girl in love.

"Who?"

"The one from the Palace theatre that looks like Denzel."

"Damn, Reese, you just met him in the mall a couple days ago, and he's already your man? You don't even know him."

"He packs a nine millimeter, he's working with nine inches, and he's not afraid to go the whole nine yards. What else is there to know?"

Liana swatted Reese on the shoulder. "Girl, you better slow you hot ass down. What kind of morals are you modeling for little Keysha by bringing all kinds of men around her?"

"Baby girl understands that mommy got to have her fun, too."

"She's three, Reese."

"What's your point?"

Liana threw up her hands in defeat. Dexter entered the store and headed straight for them. Liana knew no matter what she said to Reese at this point, nothing was going to change the way she allowed herself to be passed around like a blunt. Liana figured Reese had about a year left before dudes in the neighborhood labeled her "BDP" (Beat down pussy). Dexter grabbed Reese by the waist and stuck his tongue down her throat. He pulled back and shot Liana a you-know-you-want-me smirk.

"Liana, this is Dexter, and Dexter this is my home girl, Liana," Reese said, introducing them to one another.

Dexter put his finger to his temple, as if he was turning on his brain. "Liana? That's Spanish, right? No, Dutch. As a matter of fact, that's French."

"My father's name is Lee and my mother's was Anna. Thus, we have Liana."

"Hmm," Dexter said, nodding. "That's deep. I would've never thought of that."

"Most people don't," Liana said with a hint of sarcasm.

"Dexter and Reese," he said thoughtfully. "Dereese. Now, that's fly. What do you think about that name for a daughter, Reese?"

"You must be having a daughter by someone else named Reese, 'cause ain't no more babies coming out this coochie."

"I'll be waiting for you in the jeep," Dexter said, walking off with a smile.

"Einstein ain't got nothing on him," Liana said when Dexter got out of hearing range.

"You damn right. All that smarts Einstein had, and he couldn't even tie his shoelaces. If he had trouble with shoe-strings, I can imagine the trouble he must've had with his string-a-ling."

"It's time for you to go," Liana said laughing.

"I'm going, I'm going. But before I go. I heard you and Wayne are getting back together."

Liana almost dropped the stapler she was holding.

"Yes, Jenna couldn't wait to tell me all about your conversation on the phone with him."

"It's not even like that."

Reese shrugged. "You don't have to explain anything to me, girl. I'm not here to judge or be judged. Do your thang."

"I'm going to wring her neck when I see her for putting my business in the street."

"In the street? Jenna only has three people she can tell, and we can't count you, because it's about you. So, that narrows it down to me and Elizabeth. She's not going to tell Elizabeth, because Elizabeth will smack Wayne out of your mind. So, the only person she could share the juicy information with was me."

"Well, for your information, Wayne and I aren't getting back together. Not now, not ever. We're friends and we're cool with that."

"Whatever," Reese said, rolling her eyes.

Liana turned to tend the customer who just walked up to her register when someone called her from behind.

"Liana Thompson?"

Liana spun around at the mention of her name like a child caught doing something wrong. A man in a FTD uniform was holding a box of long stemmed roses in his right arm, and a clipboard in the other. Reese was smiling from ear to ear.

"Yes, I'm Liana Thompson," she said, blushing at the drawing attention.

"Sign here, please."

She signed and accepted the box of roses and the card.

"Wayne stepped his game up, huh?" Reese said with a tinge of jealousy.

Liana opened the card and looked at the bottom for the signature. She tried to hide her disappointment as she read the card.

"That's so beautiful," a customer at Liana's register said. "I wish my husband did something like that for me."

Tears of happiness and hurt welled in her eyes. She looked at the Internet address Ron had scribbled at the bottom of the card. www.ronandliana.com. She closed the card, put it back in the box of roses, and put the lid back on. Her face turned red when she looked up and realized everybody was staring at her.

"They're from Ron," she said to Reese.

"Even better."

***

When Liana got home, she sat in front of her computer and stared at the screen. *Fuck it.* She keyed in the website address. The site opened with a slideshow of photographs that they had taken during their three-year relationship. The site's layout astounded her. The pictures ranged from their three-week vacation in St. Thomas to their trip to Disney World.

There were seventy-eight pictures in all. Liana tried to imagine how many hours it must have taken him to put the slideshow together.

Liana's cell phone rang. The caller ID told her it was Ron. She sat there and let it ring in her hand. Her heart told her to answer it, but her soul said let it ring. She closed her eyes as her heart and soul argued back and forth. The phone stopped ringing and started to ring again. She quickly answered it before she changed her mind. "What do you want?"

"You got clothes on?"

Liana's heart fluttered as a huge smile appeared on her face. "Yeah, I have clothes on. "What's up?"

"Come outside."

She went to her window and saw Wayne's hunter green Range Rover parked out front. "Are you stalking me?"

"Just come outside," he said again, and then hung up.

She shut down her computer and slid her shoes back on. When she stepped outside, she expected to see him on the porch. He always met her on the porch. Instead, he sat in his truck, looking straight ahead. She approached the passenger side of the truck and looked in.

"Get in," Wayne said.

Liana hesitantly opened the door and climbed in. "It's kind of late, don't you think?"

"I know what time it is, shut the door."

She shut the door and leaned back against it.

"You don't have to say anything, just listen," Wayne started. "I'm a grown ass man; I don't have time to play games. Now, I still got feelings for you, the whole world knows that, and those feelings are never going to change. But that's something I have to deal with. Nana told me the real deal with you and Ron. I'm not here to get into your business or nothing, I just want you to know that no matter what I'm still your friend. I was a good listener back then, and I'm a good listener now. So if you need someone to talk to—"

"Thanks, but no thanks. I got my girlfriends to talk to."

"Reese is probably telling you to get back with Ron and milk him for his money. Elizabeth and her stuck up ass is probably telling you to stay far away from me. And the three of you are probably getting on Jenna, because she's probably talking the most sense."

Liana folded her arms and stared out the window. "You done?"

"Yeah, get out," Wayne said, starting his truck.

Liana got out and left the door wide open as she headed back to the house. Wayne stepped on the gas, jerking the truck forward, which jerked the door shut.

***

Friday night, Liana sat in her bedroom sulking. Tuesday, Wednesday, and Thursday all went by in a blur. Ron continued to send flowers and gifts, Elizabeth, Jenna, and Reese tried their damnest to pull her out of the funk she was in, and all she could think about was the conversation she had with Wayne.

Moving back to Albany was a big mistake, was the only coherent sentence she could put together in the past three days. There were too many bad memories to deal with. Albany, for her, held the memories of both her parents strung out on crack. Albany was the crime scene of her mother's murder. Albany was the county that sentenced her father to fifteen years to life. And Albany was the cemetery where she buried her love for Wayne. When her spoon hit the bottom of the ice cream box, she sucked her teeth and threw it in the garbage can.

A little after ten p.m., Liana forced herself out of bed and threw on some sweatpants and a tee shirt. She grabbed her car keys and a baseball cap on the way out. She pulled up to the grocery store on the corner of Second and Grandview and ran in to purchase a gallon of chocolate ice cream. On the way out, a dark-skinned brother was leaning against her Lexus SUV. He smiled at her as she walked toward him. She smiled back, preparing herself to politely tell home boy to go fuck himself.

"This your ride, shorty?" the guy asked, as he eased off her hood.

Liana nodded as she walked toward him.

He rubbed his chin while nodding his head. "Don't I know you from somewhere?"

Liana shook her head. *That has to be the weakest pickup line I've heard in a long time.*

"I know where I know you from," he said, snapping his fingers.

"Oh, yeah?" she said, genuinely interested this time. "Where?"

"You're the chick I jacked this Lexus from."

Before Liana had a chance to get scared, the brother punched her in the face. She stumbled back, and the brother cold-cocked her two more times, as she fell to the ground.

Liana felt her car keys and jewelry wretched from her. The sound of her Lexus peeling off reminded her of what was happening. Her legs felt like Silly Putty when she tried to stand. She fell and blacked out.

"Oh shit!" one of the scramblers on the block yelled. "Shorty got her ass whupped." The other dudes started laughing. Taz passed the blunt to his man and looked to see what the commotion was all about. He instantly recognized Liana laid out on the curb.

He ran across the street, fumbling with his cell phone. "Yo, Liana… Yo Liana" he kept screaming repeatedly as he hit the speed dial on his phone. "Yo. Wayne…"

Wayne pulled up to the scene a few minutes after the ambulance and police. He frantically looked through the sea of faces that gathered around, but didn't see Taz among them. He tried to rush to Liana, but a police officer held him back.

"I know her," Wayne pleaded with the officer who prevented him from going any farther.

"Let the paramedics do their job."

"Is she going to be all right?" Wayne asked, trying to inch closer for a better look. He shoved the officer and ran to her. A lump started forming in his throat when he saw Liana's bloodied face. "Oh, God," he managed to whisper before two cops yanked him away.

CHAPTER 5

Liana woke up in the hospital. Nana and Wayne were sound asleep in chairs next to the hospital bed. Liana looked down at the hospital gown she had on and started to panic.

"Nana?"

Her grandmother perked up at the hoarse sound of Liana's voice. She jumped out of her chair, awaking Wayne in the process, and squeezed her granddaughter's hand. "You had us scared half to death, baby."

Liana looked at Wayne and knew him well enough to know his eyes weren't swollen from a lack of sleep.

"Hey you," Wayne said with a smile.

"Hey," Liana responded weakly. Her face felt tender as she tried opening her mouth a little wider. "Ow, ow, ow."

"Easy, baby," Nana said. "You need to relax. Do you remember anything?"

"A black motherfucker knocked me on my ass last night and stole my car."

Nana and Wayne looked at each other.

"What?" Liana asked, getting scared all over again. *Oh God, please don't let them tell me no crazy shit like the motherfucker raped me.*

"He did steal your car, but it wasn't last night," Wayne said. "It was two nights ago."

"What?" Liana tried to process what Wayne just said. "What's today?"

"It's Sunday," Nana whispered.

"You mean to tell me I was unconscious for a whole day and a half?"

They didn't answer.

Liana closed and opened her eyes, as if she was dreaming. "I can't believe I've been in the hospital for two days."

"Don't worry, hon," Nana said. "Now that you're up, you'll be coming home real soon."

"You were here the whole time?" Liana asked Wayne.

"No, not really."

"You's a lie," Nana said. "This boy's been here since Friday night. He didn't leave that seat, but to use the bathroom, and he didn't eat anything, talking 'bout he'll eat when you wake up."

"Oh, that's so sweet," Liana said, smiling faintly.

"Damn, Nana, why you give me up like that?" Wayne said embarrassed.

"Oh, hush up."

A few minutes later, two detectives walked into the room and took a statement from Liana of what she remembered of the incident. They showed her a mug shot of Taz and asked her if she recognized him. When she asked why, they said when they arrived on the scene, he took off like a runway jet. Liana, Nana, and Wayne couldn't help but laugh. The two detectives looked at them like they had lost their minds.

"Jamal's paranoid like you wouldn't believe," Liana told the two detectives. "I wouldn't be surprised if he talked himself into believing that you would've arrested him for doing this to me if he would've hung around."

"He's the one who called me," Wayne said, cutting in. "And then I hung up with him and called the police."

With that said, they showed Liana mug shots of suspects. None of them was the motherfucker she wanted to beat the black off.

The next day, after some tests, and Nana raising hell, the doctors allowed Liana to leave. They rode home in Wayne's Range. When he parked in front of Nana's, he got out and walked Liana into the house and up to her room.

He pulled back the blanket on her bed. "C'mon, you remember what the doctor said."

"I laid up in that hospital for two days; that's more than enough rest."

"Don't make me body slam you into this bed. Let's go." Wayne pointed at the bed.

Liana pouted as she reluctantly kicked off her shoes. "If you don't mind, I'm not getting into bed fully dressed." There was an awkward moment of silence between them.

"Well," Wayne said, fidgeting with the zipper on his jacket. "I have to go, anyway. Besides, I know you have to handle your hygiene. You haven't brushed your teeth or washed up in two days."

"Get out!" Liana said, cracking a smile.

"I'll be by to check on you tomorrow."

She nodded as he walked out of her room and closed the door behind himself.

***

Wayne took out his cell phone and dialed Taz's number faster than speed dial. "Where you at?"

"Where I'm always at."

"I'll be there in five minutes." On his way to Second Avenue, all Wayne could think about was the pain he was going to inflict on the grimy motherfucker that put his hands on Liana.

Taz had called him Saturday night with the carjacker's name and history. He was a kid out of Schenectady named Boon; and from what Taz dug up about him, Boon jacked cars just to go back around the way and style for the chicken heads and wannabee gangsters.

Wayne turned off Second Avenue and onto Grandview Terrace. He spotted Taz sitting on a girl's stoop getting his hair braided. The girl was on the last cornrow. Wayne shut off the truck and leaned his head back on the headrest. It was the first peaceful moment he had since he pulled up to the carjacking scene Friday night. It was in that moment, that doubt of what he was about to do filled his mind. The butterflies in his stomach were in a fluttering frenzy. *What the fuck am I doing? Riding to Schenectady with Taz to talk to this dude is a big mistake. Riding with Taz to talk to anyone is a big mistake. I should go by myself. It shouldn't be hard to find a black, crispy motherfucker named Boon.*

Wayne opened his eyes when Taz tugged opened the door and jumped in.

"What up? What up? What up?" Taz said, as he slapped Wayne five. He was hyped, and was trying to transfer some of his energy to Wayne. Taz pulled his doo rag out of his back pocket, and was tying it on his head when Wayne saw the butt of a gun peeking from under Taz's shirt.

"Fuck is wrong with you?" Wayne snatched the nine out of Taz's waistband. "We're just going to go get the truck and the jewels. He knows we're coming, right?"

"Yeah, my people called him and put him on point. Motherfucker was copping a plea talking 'bout if he would've known Liana was family, he wouldn't have touched her. He wants to give the ride and jewels back to show he didn't mean any disrespect."

"So how come he just didn't come by and drop the stuff off with you and bounce? Why we got to ride all the way to Schenectady?"

"You know how that is. He's shook. He knows he violated, so he's not going show his black ass around here for a minute."

Wayne opened the glove compartment and tossed the gun in it. "With no gun, you won't act a fool."

"Nah, fuck that. We're going to Hamilton Hill, yo. I'm going strapped or I'm not going at all."

Wayne unlocked the doors. "Then get the fuck out."

"What?"

"I said get the fuck out. This ain't Boys In The Hood. I'm not with that street war bullshit. The kid doesn't want any problems.

He's trying to right a wrong. So, I don't need you and your itchy trigger finger turning his block into a shooting gallery."

"All right, all right," Taz said, shaking his head. "You know I'm not letting you go by yourself, but I'm telling you right now. If we get there and we come to find out that it's a set up, and we get our asses whipped, I'm going to say I told you so."

***

Wayne turned onto Craig Street and cruised down the block. Taz spotted Boon sitting on the stoop of a burgundy and white house talking to a group of girls.

"That's him pull over." Taz reached for the door handle.

"Hold on," Wayne said, as he checked out the area. "I'm going to park down the block, and we'll walk back up."

Wayne parked behind a Toyota. Without a word, they both got out and walked back toward the burgundy and white house.

"We're here to pick up what we came for and bounce, that's it, Taz," Wayne said sternly.

"I know, you don't have to keep telling me like I'm retarded or something."

"Just making sure we're on the same page."

Boon instantly recognized Taz and stood up. "What up, fam?" he said, as he jumped off the stoop and came down to greet them.

Wayne's facial expression turned sour. Boon was six-foot-two and thin as a street lamp. He imagined the wiry figure towering over Liana, beating her to a pulp before robbing her and taking off in her SUV.

"Yo, Taz, that's my word. I didn't know she was family. I would've never violated like that."

"Putting your hands on any woman is a violation," Wayne said through thin lips.

Boon looked at Wayne and could tell by the bulging vein throbbing on his forehead that he must have been the brother or boyfriend of the female he jacked. "No doubt, fam, you a hundred percent right."

"Yo, fuck all this, where the shit at?" Taz asked becoming inpatient.

Boon dug into his pockets and pulled out the jewelry he'd taken off Liana. He put them in Taz's hands who in turn handed them to Wayne.

"Where's the truck?" Wayne asked, pocketing the jewelry.

"I dumped it in the wooded area by Rotterdam Square Mall," Boon said nervously.

"What!" Wayne said so loud that Boon Jumped. "You beat a female unconscious, and steal her car just to dump it in the woods?"

Boon stared at him with the jackass look while Wayne stared him down with the killer ice grill.

"Let's go," Wayne said to Boon. "You're going to show us exactly where you left it."

"I ain't going nowhere, fam. I told you where it is, so now you can—"

Taz was only five-foot-six, so instead of having to jump in the air to reach Boon's chin with a jab, he put all of his power into the body blow he delivered to Boon's solar plexus. Boon doubled over and tried backing up at the same time, but he tripped over his size thirteen feet and fell to the ground into the fetal position.

"You don't tell us what you're not going to do," Taz shouted as he pulled out the thirty-two automatic from his jacket pocket.

Wayne saw his life flash before his eyes. *Oh God, we're going to jail.*

"Chill, fam," Boon said, holding his hands up in surrender.

"Get your punk ass up," Taz said, kicking him.

Wayne high beamed Taz with the whites of his eyes.

Taz kept the gun on Boon as he cut his eyes at Wayne. "I told you I wasn't coming without a burner."

Wayne shook his head, realizing that the nine he pulled out of Taz's waist was the decoy. Wayne headed back to the truck with Boon on his heels and with Taz keeping his gun pressed against Boon's spine.

Boon pointed in the wooded area as they pulled up to the mall. "Right there."

Wayne could see the silver color of Liana's SUV. They got out and walked toward it. The closer they got, the angrier Wayne became. He could see dents alongside the driver's door. "What happened to the driver's side window?" he asked Boon.

"I locked myself out. I had to bust the window to get back in."

Wayne looked inside the truck and understood why Boon didn't want to accompany them. Papers that had been in the glove compartment were scattered all over the front floor of the vehicle, as well as in the back. Food wrappers, beer bottles, and cans of Red Bull were also scattered throughout the vehicle. Looking closer at the backseat, Wayne felt nauseated as he spotted pink stains on the upholstery. On the floor amidst the trash, he saw used condoms. He turned to Boon, who was smiling nervously.

"Where are the keys?" Wayne asked, trying not to lose his cool.

"I left them in there."

Wayne looked inside one more time. "I don't see them."

Taz shoved Boon toward the truck. "Find them."

Boon climbed inside and shifted through the wet garbage on the floor. Ten seconds into the search, he climbed out holding the keys.

Wayne grabbed the keys and nodded at Taz.

"We straight, right?" Boon asked Wayne in a trembling voice.

Wayne answered him with two straight punches to the face. Taz's mouth dropped open as he watched Wayne jumped on Boon's chest and beat him silly. Taz got scared when Boon stopped moving and Wayne kept punching his face into the dirt. Taz grabbed Wayne from behind and screamed when Wayne flipped him over.

"Chill, yo!" Taz yelled, covering his face.

Wayne blinked hard as if he just snapped out of a trance. He got up and walked toward Liana's truck. He jumped in and brushed the trash off the driver's seat before climbing in. "Get off the ground and follow me home," he said to Taz.

Taz dusted himself off and kicked the side of the SUV. "That's hood nigga! Yeah, that's what I'm talking about! I knew you had it in you!"

Wayne pulled off without a word. Taz jumped into Wayne's truck and followed him back to Albany. Wayne parked in front of Nana's. Taz pulled up right behind him.

Wayne got out of Liana's truck and jumped into his to drive Taz back to Second Ave. "Thanks for the help."

Taz hopped out on Second Ave. "You don't have to thank me. You know how we do."

"Nah, Taz, really. I couldn't have gotten Liana's truck and jewelry back without your help."

"C'mon, bro. You don't have to thank me, but if you really want to show your appreciation, you can put me on your car insurance and we can call it even and—"

Wayne pulled off. He smiled when his cell phone started ringing. "What do you want?"

"That's how you treat your boy?"

"Talk to you tomorrow, Taz."

"Aye, yo, you know once Liana sees her ride outside, and you give her her jewels back, she's going to give you some pussy, right? Not only did I help you get her shit back, but I also helped you get some pussy. And what do I get?"

"Later, Taz."

"Yo, Wayne, that's messed up how you just—"

CLICK!

CHAPTER 6

Wayne pulled up to Nana's and dialed Liana's cell. Liana was lying in bed; listening to the CD Ron had sent her. It was a compilation of all her favorite songs. She answered her phone without bothering to look at the caller ID. "Hello."

"It's me."

Liana slowly sat up. "Where are you?"

"Meet me on the porch."

She grabbed her robe and caught a glimpse of herself in the mirror before heading down stairs. She looked like shit, but said fuck it. It was only Wayne.

When she opened the front door, she gasped. "Oh my God, I can't believe you got it back."

"That's not all I got back." Wayne pulled her jewelry out of his pocket and handed it over to her one by one. When he got to the engagement ring, he studied it real hard before handing it to her.

"How did you... how were you able to get everything back?"

Wayne shrugged. "I know a guy who knows a guy."

"Thank you so much. I don't know what to say."

"Don't worry about it. I called Cee at the garage. He's coming by tomorrow morning to pick up your ride. He's got to bang out a couple dents and replace the driver's side window and really clean it out."

"I don't have that kind of money," Liana said, calculating what a job like that would cost.

"I said don't worry about it. I'm taking care of it."

Liana stared at him for a moment.

"You know you freak me out when you do that."

"Do what?" Liana asked innocently.

"Stare at me without saying anything."

The only noises they heard for the next five seconds were rustling leaves, the soft whine of the night breeze, and Wayne's growling stomach.

"Come in, so I can fix you something to eat," Liana finally said.

"Nah," Wayne stretched. "I'm going to head home and call it a night."

"It won't take but five minutes for me to warm up something. It's the least I can do."

"I am kind of hungry." Wayne rubbed his stomach. He walked past her through the dining room and into the kitchen where he sat and watched her pull leftovers out of the refrigerator.

Liana didn't have on any makeup, her hair was uncombed, and her face had traces of black and blue marks from the assault. Nevertheless, in spite of her hideous appearance, Wayne couldn't take his eyes off her.

"Wayne!"

He jumped.

"I said what do you want to drink?"

He blinked away his erotic thoughts. "It doesn't matter, whatever you got is fine."

Liana turned around, and grabbed the orange juice out the fridge. Seeing the lustful look in Wayne's eyes made her self-conscious about her appearance. She subtly ran her hand through her hair as she poured the orange juice in the glass. She then put the plate of food in the microwave, and looked at her reflection in the microwave door. She cringed at what stared back at her.

"You really didn't have to go after the guy who did this to me," she said, trying to take her mind off how terrible she looked.

"Yes, I did. No man should get away with putting his hands on a female, especially one that I know."

"You actually saw him? I mean, you confronted him?"

"No doubt."

Liana was shocked. "When you said you knew a guy who knew a guy, the first thought that came to my mind was Taz found out who did it and went after the dude himself. You know how he is."

"Taz did find out who did it. And being that *I do* know how he is, I had to go with him to make sure he didn't do anything stupid."

The microwave beeped. Liana placed the plate of food in front of Wayne and watched him wolf it down.

"I wish I was there."

Wayne stopped chewing. "What do you mean you wish you were there?"

"You know what I mean."

"You mean to tell me that if me and Taz would've held him down, you would've beaten him down?"

"Fucking right. I would've beaten him like he stole something." Liana smirked at her joke, but Wayne didn't.

"That shit ain't funny, Liana. What dude did was wrong, but two wrongs don't make a right."

"So, what are you saying? He gave you my shit back and you just let him walk?"

Wayne didn't say anything, so she took that as a yes.

"This motherfucker knocks me the fuck out, robs me, and all you do is get my shit back? What about the shit you can't get back, like my pride or me feeling safe going to the store at night?" She snatched the half-eaten plate from in front of him and tossed it in the sink. "Did you at least call the police?"

Again, Wayne didn't respond.

Liana got up in his face. "You used to make me feel safe. Now, you make me sick. Get out!"

"You need to listen to me and stop yelling before you wake Nana."

"Nana's at church, like she is every Monday night, so she's not here to save you. Shut the door behind you." Liana headed upstairs.

Liana sat on the edge of her bed, twirling her engagement ring, somewhat relieved that she had gotten it back. When she officially broke up with Ron and he asked for it back, she didn't want him thinking she was running game on him to keep it by telling him that the ring was one of the items she was robbed of when she was carjacked. Liana sighed when she saw Wayne leaning against her doorframe.

"You really need to go," she said, looking away from him. She looked up at him when she felt his hand on her shoulder. "Wayne, please, you need to go."

When she looked into his eyes, she felt like she was transported to a plane where nothing or no one existed but them; and the only thing from reality that followed them to this vacuum of time was the words from Floetry flowing out of the CD player.

It's getting late...why you got to be here, beside me...watching, needing, and wanting me...

Wayne leaned in to kiss her. *No.* Liana eyes fluttered. *I'm not going to let this happen. I can't let this happen. I refuse to let this happen.* It took every ounce of her willpower to turn her face one degree to the left. Wayne's lips grazed the corner of her mouth, and kept going until they touched down on her neck.

Wayne's kiss jump-started feelings in her that she'd buried long ago. She tilted her head back, as if in a trance and gave Wayne the most sensitive part of her neck. She wrapped her arms around his waist, and drew herself to him, fitting into his embrace like the last piece of a jigsaw puzzle.

Wayne nibbled his way up her neck, all the way up to her earlobe. He reached up and held her face in his hands, and gently kissed the bruise on her cheek and then the one on her jaw, while she rubbed the backs of his hands. She stopped short when she felt his swollen knuckles and looked at them. She smiled. "You *did* put the beats on him."

Wayne winked. "Like he stole something."

"What happened to two wrongs don't make a right?"

"They don't, but I believe in an eye for an eye, tooth for a tooth."

Liana stood on her tiptoes, and ran her lips across his before sliding her tongue into his mouth. She desperately needed to taste him. Wayne's hands slipped down her sides to her hips and then around her butt. He pulled her body against his so she could feel his hardness. Liana gently pressed against it, letting him know she felt it, and wanted to feel more of it. Wayne slid the robe off her shoulders and unsnapped her bra so quick that Liana's breath got caught in her throat.

"Too fast," she said, breathless. "Way, too fast."

Wayne looked her in the eyes. "You've been back in town for a month. I say we've been moving too slow." He slid her bra straps off her shoulders and smiled when she let the robe and bra fall to the floor. He looked at her erect nipples, and goose bumps appearing all over her body. "So beautiful," he whispered, as he bent down and ran his tongue over her left nipple.

Liana grabbed him by the back of the head and pulled him to the bed. She lay back as he continued to suck on her breasts.

Wayne worked his way down her stomach, then to her belly button. As he ventured lower, Liana's legs began to shake with anticipation. Wayne moved her panties to the side and stared at her glistening pearl. The heat of his breath moistened the most sensitive part of Liana's body, causing her to arch her pelvis to his mouth. When he grazed her pink pearl with his tongue, Liana's soul damn near leaped out of her body. Wayne's second graze made her cry out. She clinched her teeth and grabbed a fistful of sheets while Wayne licked and sucked on her ravenously. He got energized off her juices as if he was swallowing pure adrenaline. When Wayne stood to take off his shirt, Liana sat up and started unbuttoning his pants. She pulled down his pants and underwear in one swoop, and gasped when Wayne's manhood jumped out at her. She had forgotten how long and thick he was.

Wayne pushed her back onto the bed and climbed between her legs. He rubbed his shaft up and down her opening, lubricating himself with her juices.

Liana could feel her walls stretching to the limit as Wayne sunk into her. She tried to relax as he sank deeper and deeper until he hit rock bottom.

She winced as she nibbled on his ear. "God, Wayne, I can feel you in my stomach." She opened her legs wider as their bodies harmonized like R&B. They took turns sucking on each other's tongues as the tempo picked up. Then the unimaginable happened. Liana felt Wayne getting bigger. She wrapped her legs around his waist and matched his thrusts. With a deep sigh, Wayne released inside of her. His spasms sent jolts of ecstasy through Liana causing her to come, and come, and come.

They lay motionless, listening to each other's heartbeat.

Liana gasped as Wayne stirred inside her. "You need to pull out of me, you too damn big to be lying up in there."

"You used to let me lay up in you."

"It's been a while since I had you inside me."

"You mean it's been a while since you had something like *this* inside you."

"Get off me," she said, blushing at his true statement.

Wayne lay on his back and allowed her to lie on his chest and close her eyes.

"What just happened?" she asked, rubbing his stomach.

"Something that should've never stopped happening."

"I can still feel you inside me." She lifted her head off his chest, looked into his eyes, and then put her head back down.

"What?" he asked. "You know I can't stand when you do that."

"I was going to tell you something, but I changed my mind."

"Liana!"

She smiled. "Promise me your head won't swell up."

"I promise."

"You're the only man I've ever been able to come with back to back." Liana sucked her teeth. "I should've never told you that."

"Remember our first time together?" Wayne whispered.

"Yeah, it was right in this room, on my pink Barbie sheets. We were fourteen, and we had no idea what we were doing."

"Remember the promise we made to one another?"

Liana didn't answer.

"Do you?"

"We promised that we would be each other's first... and last."

Wayne took a deep breath. "I never broke that promise."

Liana looked up at him in disbelief. "So, you mean to tell me you had sex with other women, fucked other women, but you just never made love to other women?"

"What I'm telling you is the only woman I ever had sex with, fucked or made love to was you."

"I don't believe you."

"Yes, you do."

Liana got quiet for a moment. "I wanted you to be my first and my last, but—"

"Don't even say it, Liana."

"You don't even know what I'm going to say."

"Let's not go through this, not after the trip we just took."

"If you would just put yourself in my shoes, just for a minute, and try to understand what I was going through."

"Here we go," Wayne said with a groan. "Let's blame it on me, once again."

"How can you be so cold?" Liana pushed away from him. "You didn't have a child growing inside you."

"Liana—"

"And your father wasn't up for parole."

"You were only two years old when your father went to prison."

"He killed my mother, Wayne! Why can't you understand how that affected me? Why can't you see that the stress of him coming home, and you pressuring me to get an abortion caused me to have a miscarriage?"

"Liana—"

"Don't touch me." She turned her back toward him. "You were glad I had a miscarriage."

"Now, that was cold."

"But it's the truth. When you found out I was pregnant, you tried to convince me to get an abortion, but when you realized I wasn't going to kill my baby you had no choice but to go along with it."

They lay in silence. Wayne knew there was nothing he could say that would change her mind about the events that happened years ago. So, he just lay there, stroking her hair and reminiscing on the events that led to their break up.

When Liana told him she was pregnant, Wayne was elated initially. But reality slowly set in. They were sixteen and didn't know the first thing about raising a child. He tried to get Liana to see that, but all she heard was abortion. Then, as if Liana's situation wasn't stressful enough, Nana had sat her down and for the first time told her the full story behind her mother's death and how her father was responsible.

Liana's father was hooked on crack and then got her mother hooked. Then he started pimping her out to support their habit. One night, two men were having their way with her while Lee sat in the next room blasted out of his mind. The next morning when he woke up to use the bathroom, he discovered Anna sprawled out on the floor, dead. He called the police and then sat there on the bathroom floor hugging her and crying until the police arrived.

Liana wondered why Nana had decided to tell her the full details of what happened. Her question was answered when Nana dropped the bomb. Liana's father was going to the parole board, and there was a strong possibility that he was going to be released. Between the stress of being pregnant at sixteen, Wayne riding her to have an abortion, and the possibility of her father being released, she had a miscarriage. Mad at the world, Liana broke up with Wayne and went away to college for two years. As fate would have it, her father didn't make the parole board. Liana believed it had something to do with the letter she wrote to them.

Liana moved back to Albany two years later, after obtaining an associate degree and got a job at BJs until she could find something more rewarding. In the process, she hooked back up with Wayne, and they got engaged.

Liana's life couldn't get any better. But then one day she received a letter from her father. She immediately dropped it and backed away. Wayne, not knowing what was going on, picked it up and read it. Her father was trying his best to express how sorry he was for what he did and how he was confident that he was going to make the upcoming parole board and couldn't wait to see her face to face so he could apologize for all the hurt and pain he knew he caused her. When Wayne tried reading the letter to Liana, she cut him off, ran to the bedroom, and slammed the door.

Wayne remembered standing there in the middle of the living room stuck on stupid, wishing he could kick himself in the butt. Unbeknown to Liana, Wayne's father was doing a bid for selling cocaine to an undercover. He just so happened to meet up with Liana's father in Clinton Correctional Facility. Wayne thought it would be a good idea to have Liana's father write her a letter. His idea was the worst he ever had. Three days later, Liana had a nervous breakdown.

In the hospital, when Liana finally had a chance to talk to Wayne alone, she explained to him that she couldn't be in Albany when her father was released. Wayne didn't understand what she was getting at until she just came out and asked him to move away with her. Wayne remembered telling her that he was born and raised in Albany, and that he couldn't just up and leave his family. He tried to convince Liana that she was overreacting but she was adamant about leaving Albany, with or without him.

As fate would have it, Ron, a guy who had been trying to get with Liana, called the hospital to see how she was doing. Liana broke down and explained her situation to him. He told her that he was moving to California in three weeks; and quickly added that she was more than welcome to come.

Liana called everybody, except Wayne, and told them the wedding was off. She packed her stuff and moved to California with Ron, and left Nana to do the dirty work of telling Wayne that the wedding was off and that she had moved away.

Liana's father didn't make the board, once again, but Liana couldn't bring herself to come back to Albany and face the only man she ever loved. So, she got engaged to Ron and tried to make their relationship work, only Ron failed to mention that he was still sleeping with his baby mama.

Meanwhile, Wayne was left to mend his shattered heart for the second time. This time around, he realized that the more something is broken and put back together, the more fragile it becomes. Wayne swore he was done with Liana. That was until he saw her at the Palace Theatre. He knew from the moment he spotted her that he couldn't help himself. He would always welcome her back into his life with open arms.

Liana turned over and put her head back on his chest, bringing Wayne back from his trip down memory lane. "I'm so sorry."

"For what?"

"For what I said. It was kind of cold."

Wayne grabbed her right hand, and twirled the engagement ring on her finger. "So, where do we go from here?"

Liana took it off and tossed it on the nightstand. "Wherever our souls take us."

CHAPTER 7

The next morning Liana and Wayne were jarred awake when the bedroom door banged open against the wall.

"Oh... my... God," Elizabeth gasped as she stopped short. Jenna and Reese pushed past her to see what stumped her in her tracks.

"Here we are, bawling with tears and busting our asses to get over here to check up on you, and you're laid up with... him," Elizabeth said, almost retching.

"C'mon," Jenna said, tugging Elizabeth and Reese by the crook of their arms. "We'll be back when you two are decent."

As Jenna pulled them out of the room, Elizabeth looked at Wayne as if he was vermin. Reese's eyes stayed glued to the crumpled part of the sheets that were doing a poor job of concealing Wayne's morning erection.

"Your friends are out of control," Wayne said to Liana when the girls left the room. "They just walk into your room without knocking or warning?"

"That's how they are. Nana probably let them in, not knowing you were here." Liana got out of bed and started picking his clothes off the floor, and tossing them at him. "You have to go."

"Wow! Use me, abuse me, and then kick me out like I'm some man whore."

She leaned over and kissed him. "You're not some man whore. You're *my* man whore, and don't you forget it."

Wayne got dressed, and then turned on his phone. He didn't even have time to clip it onto his belt before it began sounding off like an angry housewife. "Dad, what up?"

"What up? Today's my day off, that's what's up. And because you were nowhere to be found, I'm working my ass off on my day off. That's what's up. Where are you?"

"I'm on my way."

"That's not what I asked you."

"I'm at Nana's."

"Nana's? Oh... Nana's. So the reason why I'm busting my ass on my day off is because you were in some pussy all night?"

"Muslims don't talk like that, Dad."

"Don't tell me how I'm supposed to talk. I'm at the Bookman's. Hurry up and get your ass over here so I can go back home."

Wayne hung up and called Cee at the garage to find out what time he could come by and pick up Liana's truck so he could start working on it. Cee told him that he'd already come by and was working on the truck as they spoke.

"You don't play no games, huh?" Wayne said impressed.

"I aims to please Massa," Cee said, impersonating one of his ancestors back on the plantation.

Wayne pecked Liana on the cheek and got on his way to the Bookman's. When he got to the corner, his cell phone rang.

"You didn't get enough of me?" he said when he answered it.

"Well, seeing how I don't have any transportation, I was wondering if you could come by later and give me a ride to work."

"Work? You're supposed to be on bed rest."

"I was supposed to be on bed rest last night, but that didn't stop you from riding me like a race horse."

"I'm calling your boss and telling him you're not coming in."

"No, Wayne. I want to go to work. I'm not trying to stay cooped up in this house with Nana."

"I don't know, Liana."

"Please, daddy."

Wayne shook his head. Liana knew calling him daddy would get him to do anything she wanted.

Wayne broke down "What time do you have to be there?"

"Three o'clock."

"I'll be there at two-thirty. Make sure you're ready."

"Thank you, daddy."

Wayne could hear her cheesy grin. "What are you doing?"

"I'm soaking in the bathtub, getting ready for tonight."

"Tonight?" Wayne asked, thinking he missed something.

"Round two, boo."

Wayne's grasp on his phone tightened. *We're moving way too fast.*

"You there?" Liana asked when he didn't respond.

"Yeah, I'm here. Round two. Make sure you're prepared. I'm not going to take it easy on you like I did last night."

"Correct me if I'm wrong, but didn't you have to stop twice to catch your breath?"

"I thought I heard Nana coming in from church."

"You're so full of it."

Wayne chuckled. "See you at two-thirty."

"I'll be waiting."

***

Reese couldn't wait to get all the details when Liana showed up for work; everything from the carjacking to the butt-slapping romp with Wayne. She hung on to every word as Liana related the events as they unfolded. Liana even told her how Wayne found the raisin head sucker that did it, and how he put the beats on him, and got all of her stuff back.

"Wayne actually beat him up?" Reese had to say the words aloud to actually believe it.

"Whipped his scarecrow ass."

"Wayne has got to love you, because he doesn't put himself out there for nobody. I can't even remember the last time he had a fight."

"Well, he fought for me," Liana said, gleaming.

"Flowers for Miss Thompson," the FTD courier said standing behind Liana.

God, Ron is really starting to tick me off with his tired flower routine. Liana turned around to sign for them, and almost fainted. The FTD impersonator was Ron.

***

"When Elizabeth called and told me what happened, I got here as fast as I could," Ron said, as he reached out to touch the fading bruise on Liana's cheek. She quickly pulled away.

"You didn't have to come all this way, I'm okay." She looked around before whispering. "You shouldn't even be here."

"I had to come. *No one* was going to keep me from seeing you."

The no one he was referring to was Fat Sha. Ron and Fat Sha were like two sharks trying to co-exist in a fish bowl. As far as Ron was concerned, he had more than enough money invested in stocks and bonds, courtesy of his little brother Derrick, to live off for the rest of his life so he no longer needed Sha's drug money or business savvy. He sold the club/gambling spot, which Fat Sha was a silent partner in, and moved to California where he opened a legit sports bar. When he made that move, Fat Sha sent word, demanding five-hundred thousand, for breeching their verbal agreement. When Fat Sha's brother went to California to collect, he came back to Albany with a black eye and a message from Ron: The next person you send better have his life insurance paid in full. Ron knew he could never show his face in Albany again. Yet, here he stood in front of Liana. His presence in Albany told her the extent he was willing to go to get her back.

"I came here for two reasons," he started off, "I had to make sure you were okay, and I'm bringing you back home. This would've never happened in Cali."

"Nah, ah," Reese mumbled, as she eavesdropped on their conversation.

Liana put her closed sign on top of her register just as a customer walked up. "She'll take care of you," she said, pointing toward Reese. The woman gave her a sour look, to which Liana had no problem matching.

She grabbed Ron, and led him to an aisle with hardly any customers in it. "Number one, you know you shouldn't even be in New York State. And two, what makes you think I would go anywhere with you?"

"Baby, I know I fucked up. I can't go back in time and make it right. The only thing I can do is make our future right. Did you go to the website?"

"Yes."

"And what did you think?"

"I think we had a beautiful life together before I found out that you and Bridgette were still sleeping together."

"Liana, would you just look at everything I did before this one incident and everything afterwards. Don't end our relationship because of one accident."

"Accident?" Liana repeated, not believing Ron's choice of words.

"What part of fucking Bridgette was an accident? Fucking her in our house? Fucking her on our bed? Or was it accidentally thinking that you could get away with it?"

Ron didn't answer.

"Just go, Ron," Liana looked away. "And stop sending me flowers and gifts."

"What do I have to do, Liana? Just tell me."

"You need to move on, like I'm doing."

Ron bit back his anger and tears, and took a deep breath. He stared at her for a second that seemed like forever, and then he walked out without bothering to look back.

Liana walked back behind her register and removed the closed sign.

"I know you're not going to just stand there and act like I don't want to know what just happened," Reese said.

"Nothing happened."

"It must've been a whole lot of nothing, 'cause you were gone for ten minutes."

"I told him it was over."

Reese blinked. "You serious?"

"You saw who I was in bed with this morning. What do you think?"

"I thought that was just a booty call or one for old time's sake. You're really getting back with Wayne?"

"I don't know," Liana said with a huff. "What?" she asked Reese when she caught her staring at her.

"I'm just saying, you left Wayne at the altar. You don't think he'll hold that against you, like, forever? Besides, Ron has more going for himself."

"You mean he has more money."

"That's another way of putting it."

Liana shook her head. "It's not just about money. There's more to a relationship than just what a man can do for you."

"Such as?"

Liana threw her hands up in frustration. "I'm not going through this with you."

"No, tell me what a relationship is based on besides what a man can do for you? Isn't that why you broke up with Wayne in the first place? He didn't want to move out of Albany, for you, so you called off the wedding?"

"This conversation is over."

"Why, because I hit a nerve?"

Liana clasped her hands behind her head and closed her eyes. Reese knew how far to take a delicate conversation with Liana. She knew Liana didn't have a problem making a scene and getting both of them fired. She couldn't afford to lose her job.

***

When Wayne picked Liana up from work, he noticed her hard demeanor. He watched Reese as she walked out and jumped into Dexter's car.

"Reese is messing with Dexter?" he asked, keeping his eyes glued to the car.

"Who isn't Reese messing with?" Liana responded.

"Dexter and her daughter's father, Green Eyes, are like gasoline and fire. She's playing a dangerous game."

"You know Reese's middle name is drama."

Wayne drove off. Instead of turning onto Nana's block, he kept driving down Central Avenue.

"Where are we going?" Liana asked.

"I have to pick something up."

Liana reclined the seat and closed her eyes. She opened her eyes when she felt herself falling into a deep sleep. She didn't know how long she was sleep, but when she looked up, they were in Arbor Hill. "What are we doing here?"

Wayne pointed with his chin down the block toward Cee's house. Cee drove Liana's truck to his house for Wayne to pick up, because he knew Wayne wasn't going to make it to the garage by closing time.

Liana didn't wait for Wayne to shut off his engine. She jumped out and quickly walked to her ride. She could see the love Cee put into it. Her truck looked better than when Ron first bought it.

Cee looked up from the group of guys he was talking with and started walking toward her. Liana met him half way and hugged him.

"How you feeling, ma? When Wayne told me what happened—"

"I was a little shaken up at first, but you know me. It's gonna take a lot more than a carjacking to mess me up. Did you hear what Wayne did to him?"

"I couldn't shut Taz up. He came by the garage and couldn't stop talking about it. He was bragging about how he and Wayne were strapped—"

"Strapped?"

"Yeah, and then he went into graphic detail about how every time Wayne knocked dude out, he would pistol whip him awake, and how that went on for about an hour."

"Wayne didn't tell me all that." Liana continued looking at her vehicle. "New rims, Cee? And new tires? Damn, this doesn't even look like my truck."

"Wayne was paying, and you know how hard it is to get him to part with money. So, I said fuck it. I'm going to go all out and hook you up."

"I don't have a problem parting with money," Wayne said, walking up on their conversation. "So long as I'm getting what I paid for."

"Cee did an excellent job," Liana said, climbing into her ride. "A twelve disc CD charger, Cee?" Liana said, sticking her head out the window.

"Twelve, Cee?" Wayne said, feeling his bank account sinking like the Titanic.

"You told me to hook it up, so, I hooked it up."

"How much?" Wayne said, cutting to the chase.

Cee dug into his pocket and pulled out a folded up piece of paper, itemizing everything he did.

Wayne read the total and sighed. "I'll come by the garage tomorrow and take care of you." He gave Cee a pound as he inspected Liana's truck. He had to admit Cee had done a damn good job.

Liana followed Wayne to his house. When she pulled into his driveway, she saw his father sitting on his porch across the street reading the newspaper.

"Pop Pop," she called out to him as she got out of her truck.

Nevel waved her over. "How are you feeling? Wayne told me what happened."

"I'm okay, as you can see. And I got my truck back."

"I'm glad to see that."

"What up, Pop Pop?" Wayne said as he hopped out of his Range. Growing up, Liana considered Nevel to be her father and took to calling him Pop Pop. Nevel only allowed Liana to call him that and Wayne knew that.

"Don't be here on time tomorrow morning and I'll Pop Pop you right upside your head."

Wayne winked at him. "See you in the a.m. Tell mom I said I love her."

"Umm hmm," his father grumbled, as he went back to reading his newspaper.

Liana walked into Wayne's house, kicked off her shoes, and stripped down to her underwear. She couldn't stand wearing street clothes in the house. She walked into the bathroom, picked up his toothbrush, toothpaste, and walked into the bedroom while brushing her teeth and started unpacking her overnight bag.

Wayne laughed when she pulled out the top dresser drawer and pushed his underwear to the side to make room for hers.

"What?" she mumbled, while still brushing her teeth.

"You're unbelievable. You just walk up in my spot and make yourself at home as if you got it like that. Who do you think you are?"

Ignoring him, she put her three pairs of underwear in the drawer and went back into the bathroom to finish brushing her teeth. She came back a minute later, and started unbuttoning his shirt.

"What are you doing?" he asked, grabbing her hands.

"I have your bath running. Once I get you soaped up, I'm going to go cook dinner."

Wayne arched his eyebrow.

"What's that look for? I can't take care of you?"

Wayne released her hands and let her finish undressing him. While she waited for the tub to fill, she made him sit on the edge of the bed as she massaged his shoulders. She could hear a faint moan escape his lips as she increased the pressure.

She gripped and rubbed his muscles, feeling a slight quiver between her legs. She walked from behind him and straddled him. She sucked on his bottom lip, and moaned when she felt him swelling against the crotch of her panties.

Wayne's breathing became faster and hotter. He grabbed a handful of her panties and moved them to the side.

"Not yet," she said, grabbing his hand.

He held her by the butt, and slid her clit down his pole. She shivered when her clit stopped at the bottom. He positioned her back on top for another ride, but she hopped off him.

"Bathtub. Now," she said, breathing hard.

***

Wayne came downstairs in a robe. Liana was hard at work cooking dinner.

"When was the last time you cooked in this kitchen?" she asked.

Wayne walked up behind her and kissed her on the side of her neck. "Why are you cooking, anyway, it's almost twelve o'clock?"

"You act like we never had a midnight dinner before."

"I just figured you may have wanted to lie down and rest up."

"For what?"

"We got three years of love making to catch up on."

"You stupid." She walked away from him to check the rice. She took the rice off the stove, and the chicken out the oven. "Dish out the food. I'm going to go upstairs and take a quick shower."

"Hurry up."

"Shut up and dish out the food."

Wayne was in the midst of serving their food when Liana's cell phone rang. He would have ignored it, but the person hung up and called right back. He picked it up and looked at the caller ID to see if it may have been Nana or a number he may have recognized. When he didn't recognize the number, he put the phone down and let it ring. The person hung up and called right back again. Thinking that it had to be an emergency, he answered it.

"Hello?"

"Wayne?"

"What's up, Ron?"

"You tell me, seeing how you're answering, Liana's phone."

"It's too early to tell. We're just kicking it, you know?"

"Put her on the phone," Ron demanded.

"Hold on," Wayne said, raising his voice. "I'm not one of your flunkies who you can bark orders at. I don't see why you're getting upset, anyway. You're the one who got caught cheating."

"Listen, Wayne," Ron said in a calmer tone. "Can you put Liana on the phone?"

Wayne thought about it for a second. "Hold on." He took the phone to the bathroom and knocked on the shower pane.

"What's up?" Liana asked.

"Ron's on the phone."

Liana shut off the shower and slid the glass panel back. Wayne handed her the phone and left.

"What do you want?" Liana said into the phone.

"That's how it is? We haven't even been apart a full two months, and you're already fucking your ex?"

"At least I waited for us to be apart. It wasn't like you came into our house and caught me fucking him on our bed."

"I'm just calling to let you know that I put a stop on your credit cards."

"Whatever."

"And at your convenience, I would like my ring back."

"Anything else you want to take back while we're on the subject?"

"Now that you mentioned it, I want to take back all the words of endearment I expressed to you in all those cards over the past couple of weeks. I'm glad I found out about your hoish ways before we got married. I don't know how I let Elizabeth talk me into flying up here to see you."

"Hold the fuck up—" Liana started to light into Ron's ass, but he hung up. She called him right back, but his phone rolled right into voice mail.

"You straighten that out?" Wayne asked her later on, as they sat at the dining room table.

Liana dug into her food without saying a word.

"You're just going to sit there in silence?"

Liana got up from the table and went up stairs.

Wayne closed his eyes and took a deep breath. One of them had to keep a level head. Tonight, he had to think for the both of them.

No matter what happens, I'm not going to lose my cool. He cleared the table and headed upstairs. When he got to the bedroom, Liana was packing her stuff.

"What the fuck are you doing?"

Liana ignored him and zipped up her bag.

He grabbed her by the arm as she tried to walk past him. "What the fuck is wrong with you?"

"Get off of me." She broke free and tried to push past him, but Wayne had enough. He grabbed her by the elbow and flung her onto the bed; so much for not losing his cool.

Liana sprang off the bed, kicking and punching any part of his body she came in contact with. He spun her around and bear hugged her. He fell with her on the bed, immobilizing her with his body weight. She struggled until she had no other recourse but to stop struggling. Wayne let her go and let her curl up into a ball and cry. Wayne calmed down and allowed her to curl up on him.

"I see you're still the same crazy-ass female I fell in love with back in the day," he said, catching his breath.

She pinched his stomach. "I'm about to have a nervous breakdown, and you want to joke?"

"What did Ron say to get you all worked up?"

"It has nothing to do with him. I'm mad at myself. I don't know what I want. I wanted us to be together forever, but I fucked that up, and now, I fucked up my relationship with Ron."

"Whoa, hold up. He cheated on you, remember?"

"But he's a man, that's to be expected."

"What's that supposed to mean?"

"I made him cheat on me."

"I think *I'm* about to have a nervous breakdown." Wayne tried to keep his head from spinning.

"When you and I broke up, I promised myself that I wasn't going to do certain things with another man. He tried talking me into going down on him, but I told him to suck his own dick. When I walked in on him and Bridgette, she was doing what I refused to do."

"So, you're blaming yourself? If you would've sucked his dick, he wouldn't have cheated on you? That is the craziest shit I've ever heard."

"I shouldn't have refused him."

"Are you listening to yourself? Do you hear what you're saying?"

"I don't know what I'm saying, I don't even know why I'm here, or why I even came back to Albany in the first place."

Liana got off the bed and picked up her bag to leave. This time, Wayne didn't try to stop her. He began to realize that his dream of them getting back together was just that: a dream.

***

Early the next morning, Liana was parked across the street from Hertz rent-a-car, waiting for Elizabeth to show up for work. When she got home last night, she tossed and turned until she finally figured out what was bothering her. Before Ron hung up on her, he said he should've never let Elizabeth convince him to fly up and try to patch things up. Now, she felt like she was on a stake out, waiting for her suspect to pull into her place of work.

Elizabeth pulled up at seven-forty-five sharp, as she always did, to allow herself at least fifteen minutes to get herself ready.

Liana got out of her truck, and walked to the back of Elizabeth's car. She tapped on the window, startling her.

"You scared the shit out of me," Elizabeth said, stepping out of her car.

"I saw Ron yesterday." Liana decided to play it cool.

"Really? He came all the way from California to see you? That was sweet of him."

"It would've been sweet of him if he came up with the idea himself, but seeing how he had to be convinced, it wasn't that sweet at all."

"C'mon, Liana. You just expected me to sit back and do nothing? I couldn't watch you mess up a good thing."

"I can't believe you! Of all the people, you would be the last person who I thought would want to poke their nose into somebody else's business." Liana was referring to last summer when she, Jenna, and Reese tried telling her that although Indio opened a clothing store, he was still heavy into the drug game. Elizabeth had spazzed out on them, and told them to stay out of her personal life.

"Now the shoe's on the other foot, and instead of you minding your business like you told us to do, you call Ron and convince him to come up here, knowing the history between him and Sha."

Elizabeth adjusted the strap on her shoulder bag. "I did it for you, Liana."

"Stop deciding what's right for me, and who's right for me. I'm a grown woman. I can make my own decisions."

"Well, what decision did you make with Ron?"

"It's over between me and Ron."

Elizabeth squeezed her keys, as if they were Wayne's neck. "Wayne is fucking with your head, Liana. You have to dump him once and for all."

"Dumping him the first time, and the second time were the two worst decisions of my life."

"You mean to tell me that you're going to leave a million dollar man for a lawn mowing boy?"

Liana started walking away.

"Where are you going? Elizabeth asked.

"To get my man."

***

Liana called Wayne's cell and house phone, and kept getting his voice mail and answering machine. She decided to drop by his house to see if he stayed home from work, which she knew was highly improbable. When she didn't see the lawn truck, she walked across the street to his parents's house. Wayne's mother answered the door. After they chit chatted for a couple of minutes, Julie retrieved her husband's daily planner, and gave her an address in East Greenbush where they were supposed to be working.

When Liana pulled up to the address, her heart pounded with excitement when she saw the green and white pickup. She parked behind it and walked to the backyard where she heard the lawn mower. When she got back there, Wayne's father was back there by himself. She smiled and waved at him. He nodded to her and cut off the lawn mower.

"Hey, Pop Pop. Have you seen Wayne?"

"He's not with you?" Nevel asked surprised.

"No, I haven't seen him since last night."

"Motherfucker," his father yelled, pulling out his cell phone and dialing Wayne's number. "Ain't this a bitch? When he didn't answer his phone this morning, I assumed he was with you, but now you're telling me you weren't with him."

"You don't think anything happened to him, do you?" Liana asked, becoming a little worried. "We had an argument last night."

"Umm," Nevel said, as if she had filled in the missing piece of the puzzle.

"Umm, what?" Liana said.

"Nothing. Listen, I would love to chat with you, but as you can see, I'm short-handed. So, I got to get back to work. If he shows up later on, I'll tell him to give you a call."

"Thanks, Pop Pop."

Liana climbed into her truck and headed to Second Ave. As she neared the store where she was carjacked, her hands started to shake. At every stoplight, she tried convincing herself to turn around and head back home, but she kept going until she arrived at the corner store on Grandview.

Two houses down, she spotted Taz on the stoop, talking with some young kids. She honked her horn, and waved him over.

"What up?" Taz shouted, as he walked up to her window.

"Have you seen Wayne?"

"He just left."

"Did he say where he was going?"

"Said he was heading home. He's not looking too well." Taz backed up and got a good look at her truck. "Damn, girl, look at your ride."

Liana smiled with pride. "Cee hooked it up, but he couldn't have done it if it wasn't for you and Wayne getting it back for me. I'm going to go back over to Wayne's and see if he needs anything."

Taz scratched his head. "I think he needs to be alone."

"Why do you say that?"

"He just looked kind of distant this morning. Didn't say much. Just dropped by, gave me some money to take to Cee, and then he bounced."

"I'm going to go check on him, anyway."

"Suit yourself."

Liana saw Wayne's hunter green Range Rover in his driveway. As she walked toward the front door, she noticed the long scratch alongside his truck. She rang the doorbell. When he didn't answer, she knocked hard enough for the whole block to hear.

"You trying to break my door down?" Wayne asked, as he swung it open.

"You weren't answering. I thought maybe you were in the shower and couldn't hear me."

"What do you want?"

"I need to talk to you."

"I'm not in the talking mood."

"Well, just listen."

"I'm not too much in the listening mood, either," Wayne responded.

"What happened to your face?" Liana noticed a scratch going all the way down to his neck. "And what's up with that scratch on your truck?"

"Scratched myself a little too hard last night in my sleep. As for my truck, I was at Price Chopper this morning, and when I came out, I saw a shopping cart up against it."

"A shopping cart did that?"

"Can you believe it? I just spent a fortune getting your truck fixed; now I have to put mine in the shop."

"Listen, Wayne, about last night—"

"Not now, Liana. I got a splitting headache, and all I want to do is lay down. I'll catch up with you at a later time." He closed the door in her face.

Liana stood there for a minute, debating on what she should do. Her cell phone rang. It was Reese. Liana wasn't really in a talkative mood, but she decided to answer it, so she could tell her to tell their manager that she wasn't coming in to work today.

"Hey Reese—" Was all she got out before Reese blurted out three words that made her grab onto Wayne's handrail, and sit on the steps before her legs gave out.

"Did you hear me, Liana?" Reese shouted into the phone. "Ron is dead!"

CHAPTER 8

Elizabeth, Jenna, and Reese sat with Liana trying to comfort her. She couldn't accept the fact that Ron was dead.

"He came to Albany because of me," she sobbed. "I'm the reason he's dead."

"Don't say that," Jenna said, holding her hand.

According to an eyewitness, Wednesday night at approximately eleven o'clock, while Ron was at a traffic light, a man ran up to his car, and yanked him out the window. They tussled for a minute before Ron managed to pull away from the assailant, and started running. On wobbly legs, he stumbled onto oncoming traffic and was hit by a car. The assailant took off, as well as the motorist, which led the police to believe that the assailant and motorist were working together. Everybody in Albany knew that Fat Sha was behind the whole scheme. The police even brought him in for questioning, but had to let him go, due to a lack of evidence.

Liana, along with Ron's brother, Derrick, took care of the funeral arrangements. Derrick informed her that Ron had added her to his will. At first, she refused to accept anything, because as far as she was concerned, they had broken up on their last phone call. After explaining to Derrick what had recently happened between her and Ron, Derrick was still adamant in executing the will as Ron had stipulated.

"Regardless of what happened between you two," Derrick said, "I know that he loved you, and he would want you to have what he left you."

"But Derrick—"

He held his hand up. "I expect to see you at the house for the reading of the will. You're going to get what you're entitled to. What you do with it afterwards, is up to you."

All Liana could do was nod.

Wayne didn't attend the wake or the funeral. Liana needed him more than ever, and he was nowhere to be found. Elizabeth used his absence to bolster her argument of why Liana needed to be done with him completely.

As soon as everyone cleared out of Nana's, Liana took off her dress and slipped into a pair of jeans and a sweater. She drove to Wayne's and pounded on his front door until he swung it open, and stared at her.

"You're not going to say anything?" she shouted at him.

"What do you want me to say?"

"Anything!"

"I'm sorry about Ron. I wish I could've been there for you and—"

"Bullshit! If you really wanted to be there, you would've made it your business to be there. There was nothing stopping you."

Wayne shoved his hands in his pants pockets and shrugged. "What do you want from me, Liana? I've been racking my brain trying to define what we're doing. Are we rekindling our relationship, or are we just reliving our past? Or are we just living for the moment? Tell me what keeps bringing you back to me."

"Back to you?" she repeated sourly.

"You buried Ron yesterday, and here you are today at my front door."

"What makes you keep accepting me back?" Liana asked, flipping the question.

"I've never accepted you back," Wayne yelled. "How can I accept you back if I never let you go?"

Liana wagged her finger at him. "You're not going to flip this on me."

"I'm not flipping anything on you. I'm just stating the facts. You moved on with your life. I didn't. In my mind, I always knew you would come back. I refused to accept it was over between us."

Liana looked him in the eye, hanging onto every word, but she didn't respond.

"I will do anything for you. You know that. I've always put you before me. All these years, I've shown you just how deep my love runs for you."

"And how deep is that?"

Wayne stared into her eyes. "Do I really have to answer that?"

"I see you got that scratch off your truck," she said, quickly changing the subject.

"No matter how things may seem, Liana, I am here for you, and you know that." Wayne grabbed her hand. "You hear me?"

She nodded.

"How you holding up?"

"As cold as it may sound, I'm not taking it as hard as I thought I would."

"If there's anything I can do—"

Liana walked off, leaving Wayne to finish his sentence to himself. She got into her truck and peeled off without looking back.

She drove around Albany, trying to clear her head, and prepare for what awaited her in California on Saturday. She could deal with Ron's family, but Bridgette was a completely different story. She knew Bridgette was going to be at the house, acting a fool.

When Saturday came, the drama for Liana started at the airport. One of her suitcases was missing. It just so happened to be the one with her outfits. Luckily, she brought enough money with her to buy a couple outfits. One for each day she was staying.

Ron's family, especially Derrick, treated her well. Bridgette shot venomous stares at the family members who were trying to make Liana feel at home. Liana came to find out that Ron left the house and the Sports bar in care of Bridgette for his daughter. Liana was even more surprised to find out that Ron had left her a portfolio of stocks worth two-hundred thousand dollars. She convinced Derrick to manage the portfolio for her until she could find a broker of her own.

On her flight back to New York, Liana remembered bits and pieces of the last conversation she had with Wayne. *Are we rekindling our relationship, or are we just reliving our past? Or are we just living for the moment?*

"What *are* we doing?" Liana whispered to herself as she fell asleep.

***

Elizabeth, Jenna, and Reese met her at the airport. Liana got into the front seat of the Ford Taurus.

"When are you going to stop being so damn cheap, and buy your own car?" Liana asked Elizabeth.

"Girl, please. As long as I'm working at Hertz, and I can drive any car off the lot when I want, I don't need to buy a car."

"So, how was your trip?" Jenna asked Liana from the backseat.

"I didn't have to smack the shit out of Bridgette, so, I guess it went well."

"Well?" Reese said. "You've been in this car for a whole forty-five seconds, and you haven't mentioned what Ron left you."

"Nah, ah," Jenna said, elbowing Reese in the side. "You ain't right."

"Well?" Reese asked, ignoring Jenna.

"He left the house and Sports bar in Bridgette's care until his daughter turns twenty-one."

"Oooo, that sheisty motherfucker," Reese seethed. "How come he didn't just leave it in your name or his mama's name until his daughter turned twenty-one? What kind of shit is that? That's why motherfuckers got his ass."

"What the fuck is wrong with you?" Jenna asked, visibly upset. "How are you going talk about Ron like that?"

"It's okay, Jenna, Liana said. "I've heard crazier shit fly out of her mouth."

"Yeah," Elizabeth chimed in. "We all know Reese done got beat down many a nights by females, because she can't control what comes out her mouth, or what cums in it."

Elizabeth, Jenna, and Liana started cracking up, giving each other high fives.

"Ha, ha, very funny," Reese said, cutting her eyes at all of them. "You don't have to tell us what he left you. He probably didn't leave you nothing, but bills."

"For your information, he left me a whole lot of money."

"What's a whole lot?" Reese asked with a tinge of excitement.

"None of your business."

"Forget you, then," Reese said, kicking the back of the car seat.

"You need to calm down," Jenna said.

"You need to stop riding me. You've been acting like a real bitch ever since Efran put that seed up in you."

Liana's whole body whipped around in the seat. "You're pregnant, Jenna?"

Jenna cut her eyes at Reese. "Yes, but I wanted to tell you myself when you were a little happier."

"This is the kind of news I need to hear in order to be a little happier, girl." She grabbed her hand and squeezed it. "I can't believe it."

"Neither can her mother and father," Reese said.

Liana's mouth hung open. "What are they saying?"

"They told her to pack her shit, and get the fuck out," Reese said, answering for her again.

"Will you shut up? Damn," Liana said.

Jenna placed her hand on her stomach. "They're bugging right now, but they'll come around. They just need some time."

"And who are you staying with meanwhile?"

"Nana," Reese said, budding in again. "You know she was livid when she heard what Jenna's parents did. She told Jenna she was staying with her, and that was that."

"What's Efran saying?" Liana asked.

"He's so excited," Jenna said, perking up. "He can't wait to drive up this weekend. Nana's putting together a cookout this weekend to celebrate."

"I'm so happy for you," Liana said, cheesing. "Is Efran going to transfer to a college up here or are you moving down south to be closer to him?"

"No, we're going to stick with the plan. He's going to complete his degree in December, move back up here, and then we're going to look for an apartment."

"I'm so jealous," Liana said.

"I can't wait to wear my sky blue satin dress to the cookout," Reese said, envisioning herself being the center of attention. "Everybody who's anybody is going to be there. What about you, Elizabeth? What are you wearing?"

"I don't know yet, but it's nothing hanging in my closet, that's for sure. Indio's coming up from the city, and I haven't seen him all week. So, you know I have to look tantalizing."

They laughed and chitchatted the rest of the way home. Although Liana was deep into the conversation, she was deep in thought. Her girlfriends all had their different reasons for wanting to look their best. Efran was flying up from Virginia, Indio was driving up from Brooklyn, and Reese wanted to look good for anyone who may be checking her out. And Liana, even though she would never admit it, was hoping Wayne would show up.

***

Someone once told Nana a long time ago that if she ever ran for any government office in Albany, she would win by a landslide. Everyone, young and old respected and loved her. She was eighty-two years old, but moved with the pep of someone half her age. Nana was everybody's surrogate mother, whether they liked it or not. For as long as anyone could remember, Nana had been raising kids from her teenage days as a baby sitter, to her days as a social worker, to now as a highly respected elder of the community.

Whenever Nana had a cookout, all she had to do was tell one person, and it would spread like wild fire. So many people would show up that her cookouts looked like block parties. This one was no different. Crowds of people showed up with food and gifts for Jenna. Nana's basement looked like a warehouse for Kids R Us. Jenna received cases of diapers, toys, and cards filled with cash.

Jenna leaped out of her lawn chair when she saw Efran pulling up. Everybody who knew him congratulated him and shook his hand. Jenna ran into his arms and gave him a big, long kiss.

Reese was sitting on Dexter's lap on the back porch, talking to Elizabeth, while Dexter was telling Indio that he was interested in starting a business of his own. He asked Indio if he could give him an outline on what he had to do to get started.

Elizabeth beamed with pride as her man broke down the dynamics of getting started, and the intricacies that people didn't speak about.

Liana chose to help serve the food. Yesterday, she went to Crossgates mall with her crew, but she didn't' buy anything. She didn't want them to think she was trying to look good for Wayne. She decided to keep it simple and just throw on a pair of jeans and a button up shirt.

When she saw Taz gorilla-walking up the driveway, slapping everybody five, she casually looked around for Wayne. When she didn't see him, she was pissed at herself for looking around.

"Liana, what up?" Taz asked, walking up to her with a plate in his hand.

"I'm fine, what's up with you?"

"You know my story's the same. A black man trying to survive in white America the best way he knows how."

"Umm, hmm," Liana mumbled, putting two pieces of chicken on his plate.

"Where's the mother-to-be? I got something for her." Taz reached into his pocket, and pulled out a wad of cash. He peeled off five twenties.

"That's so tacky, Taz. You could've at least put it in a card."

"I was going to stop at the store and pick one up, but Wayne wouldn't pull over."

Liana came alive when she heard Wayne's name. "I see you got a plate for yourself, but what about your boy?"

"He's not crippled. He can get his own."

He is here. Finally, Liana saw him. He was talking to Efran and Jenna. She looked away when she saw Jenna pointing in her direction.

"What else do you want?" she asked Taz, trying to sound casual.

"Hit me with some of that macaroni salad, and give me another piece of chicken. I works hard, girl."

"If you got a legit job, you wouldn't have to work as hard."

"And I wouldn't be making as much money," Taz rebutted.

Liana smiled a little wider when she peeped Wayne walking toward them. She wanted him to think she was really into what Taz was talking about.

Wayne walked up and grabbed a plate. "What do I have to do to get something to eat around here?" he asked Taz.

"Liana will hook you up, but she's stingy with the chicken, though."

"Get out of here," Liana said, raising the thongs at Taz. She looked at Wayne, and waited for him to speak.

"How you doing?" he finally said.

"Been better."

Wayne nodded, but he didn't say anything else.

"You got a plate in your hand, so I take it you want something on it."

"Yeah, a piece of chicken, and some of that potato salad."

"That's macaroni salad," Liana said, giving him a nasty look.

Wayne did a double take. "Who made that?"

"I did."

"Well... just give me a little bit."

Liana rolled her eyes and piled the macaroni salad on his plate. Movement over Wayne's shoulder caught her attention. She put the spoon down and brushed past him.

Wayne turned around and saw Dexter and Green Eyes squaring off. *Aw, shit, here we go with this uptown, downtown bullshit.* Reese was in the middle, trying to calm them down, but they were only part of the problem. Wayne could see guys from both posses milling around, instigating. Innuendoes were thrown in the air about certain people being pussy. Those who were there just to have a good time quickly separated themselves from the escalating drama.

Wayne put his plate down and followed Liana to the ruckus. Before they could get there, Nana was there, pointing her finger in Green Eye's face. Then she turned to Dexter and shared a few choice words with him as well. She went back and forth between them. They were both huffing and puffing, and bearing their teeth, but neither of them was going to be the first one to throw a punch with Nana in the way.

Green Eyes turned to Reese and made one last attempt to save face. "Make sure your ass is home tonight. I'm coming over to see my daughter." He bopped off, acting like he didn't hear Dexter say that she would be home, but she would be too busy to answer the door.

"That's enough out of you," Nana said to Dexter. "It's time for you and your friends to leave."

Without a word, Dexter and his crew left.

"Not you," Nana said to Reese, calling her back. "Go help Liana serve the food."

"I can't serve food in this dress, Nana."

"That's what aprons are for, and there's plenty of them in the kitchen. Get going! Don't let me have to tell you again!"

When Reese stormed off, Nana spoke to Liana. "You better talk to that girl, she's playing a dangerous game with those two."

"I'm going to talk to her, Nana."

"Nana, what's up, Ol' school?" Taz stuck his fist out to give her a pound.

"Get your weed smelling behind out of my face, Jamal," Nana said, as she walked off.

"I smell like weed?" he asked Liana and Wayne. "I only took a couple pulls."

"Behave yourself, Taz," Wayne said. "I don't want to have to pull Nana off you."

Taz locked onto a shorty wearing a red dress. "You're going to have to pull somebody off me, but it's not going be Nana." He walked over to shorty, and eased into the conversation she was having with her girlfriends.

"So, I heard Jenna's staying with you and Nana," Wayne said to Liana.

"Yes, she is."

"That's foul the way her parents are treating her."

"It's their culture. So I guess certain things are ingrained in them."

"Then why even come to this country if they cared so much about tradition?" Wayne said rhetorically. "I'll tell you why. They want the best of both worlds. They want to enjoy the freedom of America, yet not be a part of America. How do they expect Jenna to—"

"I want to come back," Liana said cutting him off in mid-sentence.

"Come back?" Wayne repeated, not knowing if he heard her correctly.

"I want to move back in with you."

"I... I don't know what to say."

Liana took a step closer to him. "Just say yes."

"Yes... definitely yes."

***

That Saturday, Liana and Wayne moved all of her stuff into his house. The weekend was awkward for them. They slept in the same bed, but they didn't have sex that whole weekend nor the week that followed.

For Wayne, it felt good to come home after a hard day's work and have dinner waiting, as opposed to having to stop at the Chinese restaurant for takeout. And for Liana, it felt good to be appreciated.

On a Saturday afternoon, just as Liana was deciding what she was going to cook for dinner, Wayne called and told her they were going to the Standard for dinner.

When he got home, he took a quick shower and then stood in front of the full-length mirror to lotion up. Liana stood by the doorway watching him.

Wayne looked up at her through the mirror. "Don't you have something to do?"

Liana continued to stare at his naked body. "I'm doing it right now."

Wayne put on a linen suit, and then pulled his diamond ring and Rolex watch out of his jewelry box. He walked up to Liana, taking the time to notice how her cream-colored dress was fitting snug in all the right places. Liana tilted her head back and welcomed his tongue in her mouth. When their tongues met, they both felt the sparks flying. Wayne smacked her on the butt and pulled back from her.

"Time to go, hot mama."

Liana brought her hand up to his crotch, and felt him stiffening. "That's not what he's saying."

"I'm listening to the big head tonight."

They arrived at the Standard at eight o'clock. Wayne talked about his day while they ate. Later on that night as they ate their desert, Liana noticed that Wayne looked lost in thought.

"What are you thinking about?"

He seemed to be debating if he should tell her or not. "I really can't put my finger on it. From the night I saw you at the R. Kelly concert, I've been having mixed feelings." He put his spoon down and took her hand in his. "Are we really together this time, Liana?"

"Of course we are. Isn't this what you wanted?"

"Yes, and this is what I wanted the last two times." Wayne took a deep breath and released it slow. "I'm trying to give you my all, Liana, but something inside me is preventing me from doing that."

Liana caressed his cheek with her free hand, and stared at him for a moment. "I'm never leaving you again Wayne Dupree."

Wayne was so lost in the sincerity of her eyes and words that he didn't feel her foot snaking up his leg. He jumped when her big toe landed on his crotch. He cut his eyes around the room to see if anyone peeped what she was doing.

"You trying to get us kicked out of here?" he said, barely moving his lips.

"You want me to stop?" she said, licking her lips.

"No"

Liana couldn't help but laugh at his sharp reply. She continued running the heel of her foot up and down the stiffening bulge in his pants.

"It's time for us to go," Wayne said, panting out his words. He waved the server over for the bill, as Liana slipped her foot back into her shoe.

"We have to sit here for a moment," Wayne said.

"And why is that?"

"You know why. You don't want me to stand up like this do you?" He looked down at the bulge in his pants.

"Hurry up, and get yourself together so we can get out of here."

Wayne could hear the lust in her voice, which made it even harder for him to go soft.

As soon as they got in the truck, Liana popped in the Anthony Hamilton CD. *Can't let go* flowed through the Alpine speakers as they drove down Washington Ave.

Wayne moved his hand from the armrest to Liana's thigh. She took his hand in hers, and guided it to her chest. Her heart was beating a message in Morse code only he could decipher. She raised his hand to her lips and seductively licked his fingers one, by one. When she got to his thumb, she gave him a sample of what was in store for him when they got home.

They stumbled through the front door, lips locked, groping one another. Wayne scooped her off her feet without missing a beat, and carried her upstairs to their bedroom. He put her down and started unbuttoning his shirt and kicking off his shoes when she stopped him.

"Slow down, baby. We got the rest of our lives together."

"You're right," he said, taking a deep breath. "Besides, I don't want you thinking I'm thirsty."

"A little too late for that," she said, lighting the candles, and turning on the CD player. She walked up to him and put her hands on his chest, and made him sit down on the edge of the bed.

She stepped back slowly, and swayed her hips to the rhythm of Floetry's *Imagination*. She slipped out of her shoes, and seductively slid the straps of her dress off her shoulders. Wayne bit his bottom lip to make sure he wasn't dreaming.

Liana, pleased with his reaction, turned her back to him and wiggled out of her dress like a snake shedding its skin. She looked over her shoulder at him as she bent at the waist, giving him a better view of her crotch less panties. Wayne had been to strip clubs before, and saw some pretty impressive routines, but none of the females moved as fluid and as entrancing as Liana. From when they were kids, she wanted to be a choreographer. Every curve and every dip on her body communicated with him. Her eyes, her mouth, her facial expressions brought forth an animalistic growl from within his being.

Liana inched closer and closer to him swaying her hips like a belly dancer. She pushed him back on the bed and climbed on top of him as she sucked on his tongue. She tugged at his shirt, popping each button, as she hungrily sucked on his neck and chest. She climbed off him and pulled his pants and briefs down. Wayne closed his eyes when he felt her hot breath on his manhood. He moaned when she licked it and then sucked it like a lollipop. She climbed back on top of him and pressed her dripping hot box along the length of his penis.

Wayne flipped her over onto her back and tugged at the hook on her bra. She stopped him.

"Rip it off," she whispered in his ear.

With one swipe, he ripped the flimsy lace bra off and sucked on her ripe nipples. He reached down between her legs, ripped off her panties, and threw them.

Liana lifted her legs and placed them on his shoulders. That was her way of telling him she didn't want him to make love to her tonight. Tonight, it was going to be straight beasting. She dug her nails into his back as he entered her. His rhythm was steady, yet calm. Wayne didn't want to explode yet, and she knew it.

"Let me get on my hands and knees so you can hit it from the back," Liana said, talking dirty.

Wayne's eyes rolled to the back of his head as he exploded inside of her. When he opened his eyes, she was grinning innocently.

"You dead wrong," he said to her. "You know I can't hold out when you talk to me like that."

"You had me in another world." She felt him going soft inside her. She started rotating her hips.

Wayne shook his head. "I need a few minutes."

"You sure?" Liana moaned. "I need you to spank me from behind. I've been a bad girl." She smiled when she felt him growing inside her.

"You sure know how to get me going, don't you?" Wayne said, still catching his breath.

She put her finger to his lips. "Shut up, and punish me."

CHAPTER 9

The next morning, Liana woke up feeling the soreness of last night's total body workout. She raised her head from Wayne's chest and kissed him on the corner of his mouth, then looked down at his morning erection and stroked him until he stirred.

"Good morning to you, too," he said running his hand across her back.

Liana grabbed his other hand and placed it between her legs to show him how moist she had gotten from stroking him. Wayne had the delicate fingers of a pianist, who at the moment, was striking all the right cords.

Liana clamped her thighs down on his hand as she began to shiver. One, two, three orgasms later, she knocked his hand away. "Get away from me."

"You got a lot of shit with you," Wayne said, smiling. "You wake me up, jam my hand between your legs, and swat it away when you're done."

Liana lay on her back, grinning with her eyes closed, basking in the warmth of her juices.

"What are you thinking about?" Wayne murmured.

"My soul's dancing," she moaned with a smile.

"Your soul's dancing?"

"Yeah," she said, "but that's too deep for you to understand."

Wayne chuckled and started to recite. "You are the best thing life has ever given me. If I were to die today, know that I would leave this world with no regrets, because with you my life has been completely fulfilled in more ways than you can ever imagine..."

Liana's eyes popped open as Wayne finished reciting the words he memorized over ten years ago. "You read my diary!" Liana pinched his arm. "I can't believe you read my diary!"

"I read it by accident."

"Accident?"

"One day I came over and you were in the shower, and Nana told me to wait in the kitchen. Your book bag was hanging off the chair, so I figured I should search it, just to make sure you weren't stashing guys phone numbers. When I unzipped your book bag, your diary popped open."

"There was a zipper and a Velcro strap on it. How could it just pop open?"

"After I unzipped it and ripped off the Velcro strap, it just popped open."

"Oooo, I can't believe you. And you just read my inner most secrets and memorized them?"

"That's your fault. If you would've hurried up, like I told you, I wouldn't have had all that time to read all that I read."

"I'm so embarrassed," Liana said, thinking back to some of the perverted things she had written in her diary back in the days.

"C'mon, baby. There was nothing to be embarrassed about. No, wait, there was that hemorrhoid incident—"

Liana hit him in the face with a pillow and jumped off the bed. "Wayne Dupree, know that we have eternal beef. From now on, the word privacy no longer exists between us."

"I have nothing to hide," he said, as he stroked his manhood.

Liana caught herself being mesmerized by his actions. "I hate you right now," she said walking off to the bathroom. Wayne looked up at the clock on the wall when the house phone rang. *Who the hell would be calling at eight in the morning?*

"Hello?"

Elizabeth's words came out in spurts as she struggled to put a coherent sentence together.

Wayne jumped off the bed and ran to the bathroom where Liana was just about to step into the shower. "We have to get to the hospital."

The word hospital, and the alarm in Wayne's voice turned Liana's stomach inside out. "What happened?"

"It's Reese. She's been shot, and she's not going to make it."

***

When Liana and Wayne walked into Albany Medical Center, Jenna rushed to them to tell them how last night's events unfolded. Reese and Dexter were at Noche Lounge when Green Eyes and his crew walked in. They started beefing back and forth. It got so hectic that the bouncers kicked Green Eyes and his crew out. When Reese and Dexter walked out of the club two hours later, two men in ski masks opened fire on them. Dexter, being the snake that he is, pulled Reese in front of him. Two bullets hit her in the chest before he tossed her and ran. The gunmen gave chase, but Dexter's fight or flight response kicked in, and he took off like a turbo jet.

Reese was in critical condition. The doctors were able to remove one bullet, but the other one was dangerously close to her heart, and was going to be difficult to remove. The doctors gave her a fifty-fifty chance of surviving the surgery.

Liana tried her best to console her friends and Reese's family, but she kept breaking down like the rest of them. Wayne, not knowing what to do, jumped in his truck and brought Nana to the hospital so she could bring some easiness to the situation. Nana gathered everyone and told them what Reese needed right now was prayer, so they had to pull themselves together and pray for her.

Wayne caught Liana's attention and waved her over. He whispered so he wouldn't interrupt Nana. "Baby, I have to go to work."

"What?" Everybody looked up at her and Wayne. "Reese is lying in there dying, and you want to go to work?"

"Don't do this, Liana, not now," Wayne said in a low, but angry tone.

"You know what?" she said, regaining her composure. "Go!"

Wayne reached out to her. "Liana."

"Just go," she said recoiling from him, and walking away. Elizabeth hit her with the I-told-you-he's-a-waste-of-time look.

***

A few hours later, Indio came to the hospital, along with his cousin Rasheem. Elizabeth ran into Indio's arms and cried on his chest. Rasheem looked around, not sure of what to do until he saw Liana. Her back was to him as she soothed Reese's daughter, Keysha.

Rasheem walked up on her hesitantly. "How you doing?"

Liana turned around, surprised to see him. "What are you doing here?"

"Elizabeth called Indio, said she really needed him right now. He didn't want to travel up here by himself, so he asked me to tag along."

Liana nodded.

"So, you didn't answer my question. How you doing?"

"Not good," Liana said, tears welling in her eyes. "Not good at all."

"I'm sorry to hear about your friend. Indio told me what happened. What homie did was foul."

Keysha, seeing the tears falling from Liana's eyes, started to cry all over again.

"Shh, Key-Key," Liana rubbed her back and kissed her on the cheek.

Keysha cried even louder.

"Hey, Key-Key," Rasheem said, kneeling down to her. "That's your mommy in there right?"

Keysha nodded.

"We got to be strong for her, okay? They're going to let you in to see her real soon. And when they do, you make sure you give her a big hug, okay?" Rasheem wiped her tears away as she nodded. "You don't want her to see you crying. You don't want her to worry about you, right?"

"Nah, uh," Keysha finally spoke.

"Okay, then," he said, opening his arms. "Show me how you're going to hug mommy."

Keysha stepped forward and hugged him.

"That's good." Rasheem hugged her back. "No crying now. Be strong for mommy. And what's the first thing you're going to do when you walk in there?"

"Give mommy a hug."

"That's a good girl." Rasheem dug into his pocket, and pulled out a dollar bill. "You want something to drink?"

Keysha looked at Liana. When Liana nodded, she nodded.

"Okay, let's go get you and Liana something to drink."

"Auntie Liana," Keysha said, correcting him.

"My bad. Auntie Liana," he said, smiling at Liana.

Rasheem bought a Pepsi for each of them. When Keysha got hers, she ran to Nana and showed her the bottle of soda, and told her that she got it from Auntie Liana's friend.

"Tall, dark, handsome, and good with kids? You're the perfect man," Liana said, teasing him.

"I got two of my own, so you can say I have some experience."

"Two?" Liana asked surprised.

"Yeah, two boys. Donelle's three and Lionel's four."

"Two by the same woman?"

"Yes, by the same woman, but we've been separated for the past six months."

"Why's that?"

Rasheem's eyebrows shot up.

"Oh, I'm sorry," Liana said. "It's none of my business. I'm just trying to take my mind off this whole situation."

"No, it's okay. I don't have a problem talking to you about it. My son's mother and I are from two different worlds."

"How did y'all meet up then?"

"Well, we were from the same world, once. Club hopping, pill popping, living-for-the-moment. One day, I had a moment of clarity, and I realized we had two children that we weren't raising. We were shuffling them between her mother and mine. I decided it was time for me to be a father. I got a job and stopped clubbing. Marissa, on the other hand, kept doing her thing. Needless to say, I got custody of my two boys six months ago."

"Got a job? You were twenty-eight years old, and you didn't have a job?"

"I was getting plenty of money, but I didn't have a job." He allowed her to read in between the lines. "But then Indio hooked me up with a manager position."

"In his store?"

"Yes, in his store." Rasheem caught on to what she was implying. "I don't know what you heard or what you once knew about Indio, but he's one hundred percent legit, now."

"I didn't say he wasn't."

"Sometimes we say what we really mean by not saying anything at all."

"Um hmm," Liana mumbled, as she looked away.

"You want to grab some coffee or something? I think we can all use a cup"

"Coffee sounds good right about now."

In Starbucks, Rasheem, Liana, Indio, and Elizabeth sat around the small table talking about anything other than what happened last night.

"Did you tell Liana that you got your own store, Rasheem?" Elizabeth asked him, but it was more for Liana's information.

"No, because I don't have my own store."

"Sure you do, cuz," Indio said, cutting in. "I'm opening it, but you're running it."

"That doesn't make it mine, though," Rasheem said.

"We're family. What's mine is yours," Indio said with a wink.

Liana sipped her coffee. "So, you went from store manager to store owner. That's great. I'm happy for you."

Rasheem focused on stirring his coffee to keep from blushing.

In the five seconds of silence, Liana got a whiff of his cologne. *Fahrenheit,* she thought, as she inhaled him again to make sure. *Umm, it is Fahrenheit.* Smelling her favorite men's cologne on him made her see him in a different light. The "tall, dark, and handsome" comment she made at the hospital started ringing true in her mind. He was definitely tall, six-foot-three, dark like her coffee, and handsome, like "Damn! Who dat?" handsome.

Her cell phone vibrated in her pocket, breaking her out of her trance. It was Nana calling to let her know that Reese was on her way back into surgery. They gathered their things and rushed back to the hospital.

Two hours later, the surgeon came into the waiting room and informed everyone that Reese successfully made it through surgery, and she would be able to receive visitors in the morning. There was a collective sigh, and murmurs of family praising God.

As they left the hospital, Liana let Rasheem put his cell phone number into her phone, and promised to call him to keep him informed on Reese's recovery.

***

Wayne walked in the house exhausted and hungry. Anger was quickly added to the list when he noticed Liana hadn't cooked anything. He knew this was her passive-aggressive way of showing her anger. He opened the freezer and pulled out a pack of hot pockets, and threw them in the microwave, then walked into the bedroom and found her lying in bed reading.

"How's Reese doing?" he asked, sitting on the chair, unlacing his boots.

"You care now?"

Wayne sat up in the chair and stared at her for a moment. "You're not going to upset me tonight."

"Whatever," she said, getting back to her book.

"So, you're not going to tell me how she's doing?"

"The doctors were able to get to the second bullet. She's going to be fine."

"I'm glad to hear that."

Liana didn't respond. She felt his eyes on her, but continued reading as if he wasn't there.

Wayne sucked his teeth and headed to the bathroom to take a shower. *You want me to spaz on you. I'm not feeding into your bullshit, not tonight. I'm too fucking tired. You want to catch an attitude because I didn't sit at the hospital with you? Fuck out of here. And the next time I see Elizabeth, I'm going to give her a piece of my mind.*

Wayne had to stop talking to himself, because he was winding himself into a rage. Liana walked into the bathroom, pulled down her pajama pants and sat on the toilet.

Wayne shook his head. *You know damn well when she's done, she's going to flush the toilet. The water's going to get hot for a quick second, but you can handle a little heat.* Wayne braced himself.

After taking her sweet time wiping herself, Liana pulled her pajama pants up and walked out the bathroom. Wayne listened intently. He was surprised she didn't jump at the chance to be passive-aggressive. He closed his eyes and slid back under the shower. His finger grazed the scratch along his face and neck. It triggered a memory that made him oblivious to the faint sound of a toilet flushing. He jumped out of the scalding shower, screaming like a girl. "What the fuck is the matter with you?" he shouted, standing in front of her butt naked, dripping wet.

She looked up at him innocently. "I forgot to flush the toilet."

He glared at her as she calmly crawled back into bed and picked up her book. He yanked his dresser drawer open and grabbed some underwear, then got dressed and swiped his keys off the dresser.

"Where are you going?" she asked.

"None of your fucking business."

"Excuse me? Did you just curse at me?" She jumped out of the bed and followed him to the staircase.

"Yeah, I just cursed at you, because you're acting like a bitch."

Liana's head snapped back as his words smacked her in the face. She ran down the steps after him. "Who the fuck you calling a bitch?"

Wayne ignored her as he got closer to the front door.

"You want to see a bitch?" Liana yelled from behind him, as she pushed him. "I got your bitch for you." She ran back to the bottom of the stairs and grabbed the baseball bat that Wayne kept concealed there.

Wayne stopped walking and started to turn around to give her a few choice words. Lucky for him he did, otherwise he would have never seen it coming. Liana swung the bat at his head like she was Barry Bonds. Wayne dove to the ground as the bat went sailing over his head.

"What the f—"

Liana swung the bat again, determined to hit a home run. She grazed him on the left side of his head. Wayne screamed as he snatched the bat and shoved her to the ground. He threw the bat down, grabbed her by the throat, and pinned her to the wall.

"This is it! It's over between us. Pack your shit and get the fuck out of my house!" He threw her to the floor and walked out the front door.

Liana stood up, rubbing her neck. She tried calling his name, but nothing came out. "Wayne," she finally managed to whisper, but he was already in his truck, pulling off.

She walked halfway off the porch then stopped when she realized he was long gone. She sat on the porch steps and began to cry. When she touched her neck and felt the scratches on it, she cried louder. From the corner of her eye, she saw a shiny metal glistening in the moonlight in the bushes. She wiped her tears and looked at it more closely. It looked like a key.

She reached into the bushes and picked it up. It was a key, and it had hunter green paint on it. Her whole body grew cold. It wasn't because it was the key that put the big scratch on the side of Wayne's truck. It was because the key was Ron's.

***

She ran inside, threw on a coat and snatched her keys off the table. She dialed Jenna's number through teary eyes. "Meet me out front," she said to Jenna when she picked up.

Jenna got out of bed and tiptoed downstairs, past Nana's room, and slowly opened the front door. It was all in vain, because Liana screeched to a halt in front of Nana's. She jumped out and ran up the steps, clutching Jenna's hand as she pulled her inside.

Both of them jumped when they saw Nana standing by her bedroom door.

"What's going on?" she asked, putting on her glasses.

"Nothing," Liana said out of breath. Nana looked down at Liana's pajama pants and slippers. "Nana, I'm all right. I just need to talk to Jenna."

Nana huffed as she went back into her room and closed the door.

"What's going on?" Jenna whispered in a shaky voice.

Liana kept shaking her head. "I don't know. I mean I don't know what to think." She pulled out the key and showed it to her.

Jenna looked at it and shrugged. "It's a key."

Liana took a deep breath. "Two weeks ago, Ron called my cell phone when I was at Wayne's house. Wayne answered it. Ron was livid. He cursed me out and hung up on me. Later that night, Wayne and I had an argument, and I left. The next day, when I went to his house, he had a couple of scratches on his face. He told me some story about scratching himself in his sleep. Then I noticed the long scratch alongside his truck. It looked like somebody had keyed it. Tonight, I found this in the bushes in front of his house." Liana showed her the chips of paint still embedded in the grooves of the key.

Jenna blinked, still not seeing where Liana was going with this.

"This is Ron's house key, Jenna."

Jenna's mouth hung open. "Holy shit!" She covered her mouth with both hands and stared at Liana.

"Ron must've come over that night looking for me, and when Wayne told him I wasn't there, he probably started keying his car. Wayne must've run outside, and that's how he got that scratch on his face and neck."

Jenna dropped her hands to her sides and whispered. "Please tell me that you're not thinking Wayne had something to do with Ron's murder."

Liana looked away from her.

Jenna grabbed her by the shoulders. "You need to get that thought out of your mind, right now. There's no way Wayne would ever do something like that. As a matter of fact, ask him."

"How am I supposed to ask him something like that? Uh, hey Wayne did you murder Ron?"

"Ask him if Ron came by that night."

"He's going to say no. He already lied to me about how the scratch on his truck got there."

"Well then, you go to plan B. Confront him. Let him know that you know he's lying and show him the key."

Liana shook her head. "I can't, Jenna. I'm shaking right now just thinking about it."

"So, you're not going to say anything?"

"I don't know what I'm going to do." Liana sat down on the couch.

Jenna sat down with her, and held her hands. "Let's go back to what we know. The police said that an unidentified man ran up on Ron's car and pulled him out of the window. Can you picture Wayne pulling anybody out of a car window? And according to the eye witness, they said the assailant had a gun, and that's why Ron was stumbling away from him. Now, we both know Wayne doesn't have a gun. He never even fired a gun." Jenna watched Liana's eyes narrow. "What? What's that look about?"

"Cee said that Taz couldn't stop talking about how he and Wayne beat that kid up who stole my truck. He said Taz and Wayne had guns."

"That's impossible. Taz probably had a gun, but Wayne? Besides, everybody knows that Fat Sha was behind the whole thing with Ron."

"Everybody is assuming Fat Sha was behind it."

"You sound like you really believe Wayne did it."

"No, Jenna." Liana took a deep breath. "I'm just a little shaken up. As crazy as it may sound, when I found Ron's key, it was then that it really dawned on me that he's dead. He's really gone, Jenna."

Jenna hugged Liana as she cried on her shoulder.

Liana quickly pulled away from her with a nervous smile. "I'm so used to disconnecting myself from pain for so long that I didn't even realize that's what I did in order to cope with Ron's death. How else would I be able to bury him and then move in with another man all in one month? What's wrong with me?" Liana pulled away from her. "I have to go,"

"Slow down, you don't have to go now."

"Yes, I do." Liana wiped the tears from her eyes. "I have to go back and pack my stuff."

"Liana, wait."

"No. It's really over between us this time." Liana laughed. "And can you believe, he actually broke up with me this time?" Liana watched Jenna go to the closet and grab her jacket. "Where you going?"

"I'm going to go help you pack and bring your stuff back here."

Liana shook her head. "No, Jenna, this is it. I'm tired of moving backwards."

"Backwards. You're talking real crazy now."

"Nah, I was crazy for coming back to Albany. I'm packing my things, and I'm heading to the city."

"City? Who do you know in the city?"

"I'm going to be all right."

"What are you going to do for money?"

"I got a nice piece of change that Ron left me, remember? And I know it won't take me long to get a job."

Jenna started wringing her hands. "I don't know, Liana. I think you should talk to Nana first."

"Nana? I'm grown, Jenna. I don't have to consult with Nana."

"I didn't mean it like that—"

"I'll give you a call when I get to the city." Liana headed toward the front door.

"Liana," Jenna whispered as loud as she could. "This is a big mistake."

"Tell Reese I'll be up in a few days to check on her," Liana said, as she walked out the front door.

***

Monday morning started like any other for Wayne and his father. When they pulled off from McDonalds, his father decided to ask him about the new client they had in Guilderland.

"So, what's up with this guy, and how did he hear about us?" he asked with a piece of egg McMuffin flying out his mouth.

"He's Miss Levinson's son."

"Grandma Dynamite? I didn't know she had a son."

"Neither did I. He showed up one day while I was doing her yard. Said he liked what he saw. So, I gave him a business card, and lo and behold, he called."

"Guilderland, huh? A lot of *police* live around there," Nevel said, placing emphasis on police.

"You don't have anything to worry about, Dad."

"You damn right. I'm not doing anything for them to put me back in jail. I learned my lesson. It took about twenty years, so I guess that makes me a slow learner, huh?"

Wayne shrugged.

"So, this guy's a cop, huh?" Nevel said, tired of beating around the bush.

"Yeah," Wayne nodded. "A detective, actually."

"And you just happen to forget to tell me that."

"I didn't think it would make a difference. Like you said, you're on the straight and narrow."

Nevel finished the rest of his coffee. "Well, don't expect me to be all friendly 'n shit. I'm not too far removed from the criminal lifestyle. I still got some issues I'm working on."

***

When they pulled up to the house, Nevel didn't bother getting out.

"What up?" Wayne asked his father, as he started heading up to the front door.

"Nothing, go on ahead and let them know we're here."

"You hanging back to see if you know this guy?"

"Not at all, just go knock on the door," Nevel said, sinking deep into the seat.

Wayne walked up to the front door and rang the bell. A white woman in her early thirties answered.

"You must be Wayne," she said, extending her hand.

"Yes, and you must be Mrs. Harris."

"Yes, Frank told me you already know what to do, correct?"

"Yes, we discussed what he wanted done over the phone. He's not here? He told me he would be."

"He was, but he stepped out for a moment. He'll be back shortly."

"Okay, my partner and I—" Wayne looked toward his truck, and noticed his father had put his cap on, and had sunk even deeper into the seat. "Uh… like I was saying, we should be done in about three hours."

"Uh, okay," Mrs. Harris said to Wayne, while she kept her eyes glued to Nevel's suspicious behavior. "If you need anything, I'll be right inside."

"Thank you, Ma'am. Wayne walked back toward the truck and started unloading bags of mulch and grass seeds. "The coast is clear Mr. America's Most Wanted," he said to his father who was still sitting in the truck.

"I'm just waiting on you to hurry up and unload the stuff, so we can get started."

"A little help would be nice."

"No, no. I'm not trying to throw my back out again. The last time, I was out of commission for two months. Besides, your mother and me got plans tonight. I need to be in optimal condition when—"

"Dad! Dad! Way too much detail. I get the picture, unfortunately."

The stunt Liana pulled last night gave Wayne the energy to finish the job in a little under two hours. While he worked, he thought about how she had the nerve to pick up a bat and try to take his head off. He hoped and prayed that when he got home, she was long gone. He also hoped and prayed that she didn't get on no Waiting to Exhale bullshit and try to burn his house down.

When he pulled up to his house that night, her truck wasn't anywhere in sight, and his house wasn't burned to the ground. When he walked in, it was eerie quiet. He didn't have to go upstairs to know that she was gone for good. He opened the freezer, pulled out a box of Hot Pockets, and placed it in the microwave. No more home-cooked meals, and no more... He thought of how good it felt to release himself without having to wait for the far and in between wet dreams. His mind raced as he thought of all the women he'd brushed off, because of that stupid promise he made to Liana when they were teenagers.

I must have been out of my mind. "Tammy with the big whammy." He smiled as Taz's words echoed in his head. *She practically begged me to fuck her.* Wayne said to himself as he jumped up and grabbed his Hot Pocket out the microwave. "Tammy with the big whammy," he said out loud, nodding.

CHAPTER 10

"Go on home, Liana," Rasheem said to her as she rang up her last customer. "I'll close up tonight."

"You sure?"

"I'm positive. You have to wake up early tomorrow morning, and be on the road by five if you want to be in Albany by eight o'clock."

Liana nodded as she took off her vest and headed to the back. It had been seven months since she moved from Albany to Jamaica, Queens. Finding an apartment was harder than she thought, and landing a decent paying job was damn near impossible. She finally broke down, listened to Elizabeth, and called Rasheem. He showed up at her closet-sized apartment the next morning, and moved her into a spacious, two bedroom apartment in Springfield Gardens. The following week, she was working the register at Indio's new clothing store that Rasheem managed.

The day Rasheem showed up at her closet-sized apartment, she told him up front that she considered him a friend. And although he was as fine as he could be, and she'd already fantasized about making love to him every which way possible, a friend is what he will always be to her.

He couldn't help but laugh and let her know that he would respect that. She had to define their relationship up front to keep herself in check. After the final breakup with Wayne, she decided to be by herself for a while so she could get the feeling of having to be with a man out of her system.

She grabbed her purse and coat and headed back toward the front of the store. Jenna gave birth to a beautiful baby boy, and was released from the hospital today. Liana knew if she didn't show up to see her godson on time tomorrow, Jenna would never forgive her. Liana also knew she had to be there because Jenna's parents still weren't speaking to her. So, her, Elizabeth, and Reese were her family support.

"I'll definitely be back by Tuesday," she said to Rasheem.

"Don't rush back, we got this," he said referring to him and his assistant manager, JD.

For an instant, she thought about taking advantage of Rasheem's kindness and spending the whole week in Albany. She missed hanging with her girls. Although Elizabeth drove down to the city every other weekend, most of her time was occupied with getting her some of Indio.

"Nah, I'll definitely be back by Tuesday. I don't want you giving my job away to the next girl who walks up in here with a big booty."

Rasheem laughed. "I'm not JD."

"Hey," JD said. "I'm not that shallow. She's got to have big breasts to go with that big booty."

"Let me go before I find out just how shallow you really are," Liana said, waving him off as she walked out the store.

***

When Liana entered her apartment, the red light on her answering machine was blinking. She dropped her purse on the couch, and left a clothes trail to her bedroom. In just her bra and panties, she went to the bathroom and ran herself a hot bath. On her way to the fridge, she checked her messages.

"Liana," Nana's voice boomed. "I'm just calling to let you know that Mrs. Watkins stopped by again today, and told me to tell you, again, that it's urgent you contact her."

Liana's stomach jumped at the mention of the District Attorney's name. She reached inside her fridge for a Pepsi, but after hearing the message, she reached past the Pepsi, wrapped her hand around two Heinekens, and headed to the bathroom. She needed that hot bath more than ever. She stripped out of her bra and panties, and slowly stepped into the tub. The water was uncomfortably hot, but she welcomed the heat, hoping it would melt away the stress that had just avalanched on her.

Mrs. Watkins was the DA that built the case against her father and convinced the jury to hand down a guilty verdict. Mrs. Watkins first contacted her when her father was scheduled to appear before his first Parole Board. It didn't take much for her to convince Liana to write a letter to the Parole Board Commissioners begging them not to unleash her father on society. Every twenty-four months, for the past six years, Mrs. Watkins would contact her and have her update her letter to the Commissioners.

As Liana lay back in the tub, she closed her eyes and let the hot water and bath oil do their job. *I can't believe it's been two years, already.* Time was creeping up on her. She was twenty-seven, the same age as her mother when she was… murdered. She shook off the cold chill that ran down her spine and grabbed the half-empty Heineken bottle off the edge of the tub. She polished it off with a long sigh.

Twenty-minutes later, she caught herself falling into a deep sleep. She climbed out of the tub, nearly knocking over the two empty Heineken bottles. She walked into her bedroom, and caught a glimpse of the suitcase she packed during the week, and thanked God, because she was in no shape to pack tonight. She put on her nightclothes and curled up in her bed. As she drifted off to sleep, one question rolled around in her head. *What will you do if the Board released your father?*

***

Liana pulled up to the apartment on Theatre Row that Efran rented for Jenna. She got out and walked up a staircase she thought would never end. When she got to Jenna's apartment on the third floor, she was panting like she just ran a marathon. She fanned herself before knocking on the door.

Reese opened the door, pulled her in, and hugged her tight.

Liana hugged her back. "It's good to see you, too."

Reese pulled back from her. "Damn, girl. I haven't seen you in almost a year."

"It's only been seven months, Reese."

"It seems longer than that." Reese sized her up. "I see you're putting on some weight. Don't tell me Rasheem put a seed up in you already."

"It ain't even like that. We're just friends. I'm by myself for now."

"I feel you, girl." Reese slapped her five. After the shooting in front of the club seven months ago, Reese realized that it was only by the will of God that she was still alive. Dexter's actions that night shifted her perspective on life and men. Life was too precious to squander it on men, who weren't shit. Since then her life revolved around one thing: her daughter.

Reese guided her through the tiny apartment to the living room where Jenna was sitting on the couch with her feet propped up.

"Hey, girl," Jenna said, holding her arms open for a hug.

Liana gave her a hug and a big kiss on the cheek. "Congratulations, mama, where's my godson?"

"Oh God," Jenna said. "Elizabeth just put him in his crib. He was screaming and carrying on all night."

Liana's head turned toward the back room when she heard little Efran Jr. crying. She walked into the room, and saw Elizabeth trying to rock him to sleep.

"Oh my God!" Liana said. "He's so cute." She reached out for him. Elizabeth was more than happy to dump him in her arms. Liana followed Elizabeth out into the living room while Efran Jr. kept screaming until Liana handed him to Jenna.

"He's got a set of lungs on him," Liana said, sitting next to Jenna. She watched as little Efran snuggled against Jenna's breast and fell asleep.

"I'm so jealous right now," Liana said.

"That's because you haven't had one yet," Reese said.

"Humph, thank God I don't have any, and it's going to stay that way," Elizabeth said.

"Stop playing," Liana said. "You mean to tell me that we're not going to see any little Indio's running around?"

"Girl, please." Elizabeth rolled her eyes. "I'm not putting my body through nine months of torture, getting all fat and nasty. Then I have to go through hours of labor. Then after I have the thing, I have to worry about stretch marks, and losing all the weight I packed on. No thank you."

"Nah, ah," Reese said. "I know she didn't just refer to a baby as a thing."

Elizabeth continued. "And you know once their big head stretches your coochie out of place no man's going to want you."

"Nah, ah, I know you didn't take it there," Liana said.

"Yes, I did. I'm not trying to lose my man because my shit is stretched out like the I-95."

"So, what are you trying to say? Efran is going to leave me?" Jenna asked.

"I'm just speaking for me," Elizabeth said.

"But you're making it sound like after you have a baby, men will no longer be interested in you." Jenna's face was reddening.

Elizabeth looked at Reese.

"Why you looking at me?"

Elizabeth rolled her eyes.

"Hold the fuck up," Reese said, forgetting that she was a Born Again Christian. "What the fuck was that look about?"

"That's enough!" Liana cut in. "We're not going to let Elizabeth's insecurities ruin this moment for us. Jenna's a mother and we're Godmothers." She stroked little Efran's head. "I'm surprised he didn't wake up with all the hollering going on."

"I was just speaking for me." Elizabeth mumbled, having to get the last word in.

"Forget about you, for once," Liana said. "And let's focus on little man. We have the honor of spoiling him rotten. And I, for one, can't wait."

"Amen," Reese said.

Liana stood up and brought her suitcase into the living room. "You're not going to believe what I got Efran." She pulled out a pair of brown and beige baby Timbs with a matching outfit.

"That's so cute," Jenna said.

"That's creepy," Elizabeth countered.

Liana cocked her head.

Elizabeth got on the defensive. "I'm just saying. Wayne came over earlier and he brought by the same exact Timbs."

"That's not creepy," Liana said.

"And the same exact outfit."

"Well, that just shows that he has good taste," Liana said with an air of arrogance.

"Humph, hard to tell, with him hooking up with Tammy," Reese said.

"Tammy? Tomboy Tammy?" Liana said surprised.

"Them muscles done softened up and fell in all the right places," Reese said. "She's still knocking dudes out, though."

Liana shook her head. *Wayne, you fucking bastard.* Out of the blue, she started laughing. Her girls looked at her, waiting for her to share the joke, but she just kept laughing until Elizabeth and Reese starting laughing. They were laughing, because they thought Liana had lost her mind. Liana was laughing to camouflage her pain.

"Okay, I missed it. What's so funny?" Jenna said.

Liana started fanning herself. "I was just thinking how pathetic Wayne really is."

"Ain't he?" Elizabeth, Liana and Reese started laughing again.

Jenna looked at them and shook her head. Maybe they were sane and she was the crazy one. "I still don't get it." She said, genuinely lost. "What's wrong with Tammy?"

"What do you mean what's wrong with Tammy?" Reese snapped. "She's bald for one."

"She has a brush cut," Jenna said.

"Because she can't grow her hair," Liana said, giving Reese a high-five.

Jenna chuckled. "Why don't you just come out and say it, Liana? You're jealous."

"I know... you didn't just take it there," Liana said loud enough to cause little Efran to stir in his sleep.

"She's not jealous," Elizabeth spat. "She has nothing to be jealous about."

"Oh yeah?" Jenna blinked surprised. "How about Tammy's twenty-four and is co-owner of Step It Up women's gym? Or how about the fact that she has a cardio-kickboxing video that's selling faster than crack?"

"How you know about all that?" Liana asked.

"I watched her video."

Elizabeth, Liana, and Reese looked at her like she'd just committed treason, and they were deciding her fate.

"What?" Jenna said. "Somebody gave it to me as a gift at the baby shower."

"Just so you know," Liana said, looking her dead in her eyes. "I can get any man I choose. I can snatch Wayne from her in my sleep. Like I was telling Reese when I first walked in, I don't have a man right now, because I *choose* to be by myself."

Reese nodded in agreement.

"I'm living my life, and thank God, Wayne is living his."

They all glared at Jenna, daring her to challenge what Liana just said. Buckling under the pressure, Jenna nodded.

Liana wheeled her suitcase in the corner. "I'm going to leave this here until I get back."

"You just got here," Jenna said disappointedly.

"I have to go see Nana. Mrs. Watkins has been calling her off the hook trying to get in touch with me."

Hearing the DA's name, her friends knew what it was about and knew not to pry. They nodded.

"I'll be back later. Hopefully, little Efran will be awake, so I can take some pictures." Liana hugged Jenna. "Too bad we all can't go out. I know those stitches in you—"

Jenna stopped her. "Please don't mention it. You're going to mess around and talk up the pain."

"Be back later." As Liana walked down those long flights of steps, she couldn't believe how easy it was for Wayne to move on. *I can't believe I fell for that You-were-the-only-one-I've-been-with bullshit. What else did he lie to me about?* Her question triggered memories and feelings of the night she found Ron's house key in Wayne's bushes.

She climbed into her SUV and slammed the door. She gripped the steering wheel as she steadied her breathing. *I have to ask him. If I don't, it's going to eat away at me for the rest of my life.* Her grip on the steering wheel was so tight her forearms throbbed. She let her hands fall into her lap and leaned back. After a couple of minutes of deep breathing, she drove off.

***

When Liana turned onto Nana's block, her stomach did a back flip when she saw Wayne's utility truck parked in front, and his father mowing the front lawn.

I shouldn't even be surprised. This is how my luck works. She parked across the street and took her time getting out of her truck. She knew Wayne would probably be sitting with Nana in the kitchen, and she would want her to sit down with them as if nothing ever happened.

She slammed her truck door shut and made up her mind that if Wayne was talking to Nana, she would hightail it out of there before Nana got a chance to tell her to sit down.

Nevel glanced up at her as she approached. He did a double take when he realized it was her. He smiled and waved her over as he cut off the lawnmower. He approached her with open arms. "How you doing?" He hugged her and kissed her on the cheek. She hugged him back stiffly.

Nevel felt her cringe when his dirty work gloves landed on the back of her shirt. "I would have taken off my gloves, but I got a nasty cut on my hand. Don't want to get any blood on you."

"It's good to see you," Liana said, forcing back the urge to retch when he mentioned cut and blood.

"It's good to see you, too. I heard you doing real good for yourself down in the city."

"I'm barely making it."

"That's not what Nana's saying."

"You know how she is." Liana cut her eyes looking for Wayne. "She's always exaggerating when it comes to me and what I'm doing."

Nevel grabbed the lawnmower's handle to start it back up. "Wayne's in the backyard." Nevel smiled at her as he started the lawnmower. Liana smiled and headed to the side door of the house, wondering why he was being so nice to her. She could hear the clipping sound of hedge cutters coming from the backyard. She breathed a sigh of relief thinking she could stop in and see Nana and be out before Wayne even knew she was there.

Nana was in the kitchen deep into her television show, which was why she didn't hear or see Liana until she was right up on her.

Nana looked up surprised to see her. "Girl, how many times I have to tell you to make some noise when you walk up in here?"

"It's good to see you, too, Nana." Liana gave her a big hug.

Her grandmother hugged her back and scrunched up her face. "You need me to send you some money for food? I can damn near wrap my arms around you, twice."

"Nah ah, Nana." Liana pulled away from her. "Why would I need you to send me money when I'm doing real good for myself? Isn't that what you're telling everybody?"

Nana waved her hand. "You know how I exaggerate when it comes to you and what you're doing."

"Oh yeah, I do."

Nana cut her eyes at her.

"What, Nana? I'm agreeing with you," Liana said, smiling.

"Keep thinking you can pull fast ones on me. You hear?"

"Nanaaa," Liana whined.

"Nana! We're done, we're out of here," Wayne said, as he walked into the kitchen through the same door Liana just entered. Liana and Wayne stared at each other. Liana could feel her heart pounding in her head. She instinctively folded her arms across her chest and lowered her chin, guarding her throat, as the first memories that came to her mind were Ron's house key and the night Wayne had her pinned to the wall by her throat.

As if reading her mind and body language, Wayne immediately held his head down in shame. Liana, realizing her reaction had betrayed her, tried to clean it up by forcing a smile on her face.

"Liana, this is Wayne. And Wayne, this is Liana," Nana said sarcastically.

"Haven't seen you in a while," Wayne said, trying to clear the lump in his throat.

"Yeah," Liana said, exhaling hard, trying to expel her nervousness through her mouth, "It's been awhile."

Wayne turned his attention to Nana. "We got two more houses to go before we can call it a day." Wayne turned and left, but not without stealing a glance at Liana.

Liana watched him walk off and kept staring in the direction he left in, as if he was going to reappear and tell her that they needed to talk.

"Leave that man alone!" Nana said, jolting Liana out of her trance.

"What?"

"You heard what I said." Nana walked back to the stove to check on her dinner. "He found himself a good woman."

"What are you trying to say Nana?" Liana put her hands on her hips. "I wasn't a good woman?"

"You broke that man's heart so many times that he doesn't bother putting it back together."

"That's not fair, Nana. He broke up with me the last time."

"Only because you were trying to break a bat over his head. I would've broken up with you, too." Nana turned the oven down to one seventy-five, and lowered the fire on her collard greens. "He hooked up with a nice girl who lives on Pearl Street. What's her name again?"

"Tomboy Tammy."

Nana swatted her with the hand towel she had draped over her shoulder. "Don't be jealous of her because she got more meat on her bones than you."

"Nana, please. Ain't nobody trying to look like He-man."

"Well, just make sure you don't start no shit." The kitchen phone started ringing, interrupting their conversation. Nana answered it on the third ring.

"Hello?" Nana answered. "Yes… yes she is, finally." She looked at Liana.

"Who's that?" Liana mouthed.

"Hold on." Nana handed her the phone, and walked back to the stove. "You know who it is."

"Hello?"

"Liana, hi," DA Watkins started. "I've been trying to track you down for a couple weeks now. I'm glad I finally caught up with you… Liana? Are you there?"

"Yes, I'm here."

Uncertain on how to interpret the aloofness she picked up in Liana's voice, Mrs. Watkins decided to chitchat a little before getting into the real reason of why she called. "Your grandmother tells me that you're living in the city, now. Queens to be exact."

"Basically." Liana decided to get right to the point. "So, when do you need the letter?"

"Oh... well... the Parole Board will be meeting next month, actually in 27 days."

"Do I have enough time to get the letter in?"

"We're cutting it kind of close, but you would have to get started on it right away."

"I'll see what I can do."

Mrs. Watkins got quiet for a moment. "Liana, I don't want to seem cold, but your letters are the strongest argument we have against your father's release."

"You'll be hearing from me in a couple days."

"You might want to give me your phone number in case—"

Liana hung up on her. She had no love for her father, but speaking to the person directly responsible for convicting him and making sure he spent the rest of his life in prison curdled her blood. Liana watched her grandmother get on her tiptoes and reach into the cabinet for a glass pitcher A question buzzed around her in mind like pestering fly. A question she never had the courage to ask Nana. At the moment, she realized that it wasn't the question she was afraid to ask; it was the answer she may receive. She sat back down and took a deep breath.

"Nana, let me ask you something."

Nana busied herself with cutting lemons for her lemonade, but Liana knew she heard her.

"How come you never write a letter to the Parole Board?"

Liana's question was sharper than the knife Nana was holding in her hand. Liana knew she struck a nerve, because Nana stopped cutting halfway through one of the lemons. She wiped her hands on the hand towel and sat at the kitchen table. The expression in her eyes told Liana that she knew it would only be a matter of time before Liana worked up the nerve to ask her that question.

Nana folded her hands, placed them on top of Liana's, and punctuated each word by squeezing her hands on top of Liana's. "Judge not... lest... you be judged." Nana's eyes held so much pain in them that Liana was forced to look away. "Lee was a good man. I sensed it when Anna first brought him to the house. He had some slickness in him, but I knew from looking into his eyes that he truly loved my baby. But when he got addicted to that crack..." Nana closed her eyes as two decades of buried pain rose to the surface.

Liana shook her head, regretting that she asked the question. "Forget I even asked, Nana." She started to get up.

Nana kept her glued to her seat with a firm grip on her hand. "I was devastated that afternoon when the two detectives came here and told me Anna was dead. And when they told me the circumstances of how she died, I refused to accept it. My daughter in a crack house? with two men?" Nana's voice started to quiver. "Oooo, chil,' I was mad at the world. All the good I've done, and to have my daughter... snatched from me like that? I became bitter. And believe me when I tell you, if I was given the opportunity to flip the switch on the electric chair with Lee in it back then, I wouldn't have hesitated."

Tears welled in Liana's eyes as she felt Nana's heart along with her pain wrap around hers.

"Lee was arrested, tried, and found guilty. For me to write a letter every time he goes before the Parole Board would be me judging him again and again and again for the same crime. A crime that he turned to God and asked forgiveness for. A crime that he turned to me and asked forgiveness for."

"Did you forgive him, Nana?" Liana's words came out so low that her grandmother had to read her lips.

"I couldn't put my baby's soul to rest in my heart and move on with my life if I didn't."

"God, Nana," Liana's tears came down like a pouring rain. "I wish I was as strong as you. I wish that I could... forgive him, but I can't. I try, but when I look at what he took from me... he didn't just rob me of a mother, he robbed me of a father as well. How can I forgive him for that? I feel like if I forgive him, it's like I'm saying what he did wasn't that bad."

Nana let a thin smile stretch across her face. "Baby, when it comes to forgiving him, it's not about him. It's about you moving on."

Liana stared off in the distance. "I'm sorry, Nana, but I can't." She stood up and kissed her on the cheek. "I just stopped by to let you know I was in town. I didn't plan on coming here and dumping my issues on you."

"Chil' please. That's what I'm here for."

Liana kissed her on the cheek again. "I'll stop by tomorrow before I go back to the city."

"And make sure you give that DA lady your phone number, so she can stop ringing my phone off the hook."

Liana gave her two thumbs up before walking out the side door. As she sat in her truck replaying the kitchen scene in her head, she couldn't get over the fact that when Wayne was leaving, she had to literally grind her teeth together to stop from calling after him. A quivering sensation started rippling down her legs, along her arms, and up her chest. Liana calmed her breathing while she pulled out her cell phone, and dialed Jenna's number.

"Hey," she spoke into the phone when Jenna picked up. "I'm on my way back. You want me to pick you up something to eat?" She listened to Jenna as she rattled off what she wanted from Roy's Caribbean spot. "Hold up," Liana said, looking for a pen and a piece of paper. She wrote down Jenna's order. "Damn, girl. You sure you ain't pregnant again?"

"Don't even wish that on me," Jenna said. "If I never get pregnant again, that's too soon."

Liana started her truck. "I'll be there in a little while."

CHAPTER 11

"You sure we're getting in?" Liana asked Reese, as they drove by Sneaky Pete's and saw the line of people, waiting to get in.

"Don't worry. I told you I'll get us in," Reese said.

"You better," Elizabeth said, as she found a parking spot around the corner. "I'm not even trying to wait on nobody's line."

"I said I got this." Reese flipped her hand at Elizabeth.

As they walked up the block and past the people waiting to get inside, Liana got a good look at the behemoth working the door. He had his massive arms folded across his doublewide chest, as a red-boned cutie tried to work her magic on him to get in. He smiled as he politely removed her hand off his bowling ball-sized bicep.

Liana shook her head, mad at herself for allowing Reese to talk her into coming here on her last night in Albany. "We should've just spent the night with Jenna. After all, that was the main reason why I came up here," she said to Reese.

Reese discreetly unbuttoned the two top buttons on her blouse, and put a little more umph in her step.

"Didn't you just see how he dismissed home girl?" Elizabeth said to Reese.

"I'm not home girl," Reese said, as she locked eyes with the human wall and smiled from ear to ear. He cracked a smile and winked at her.

"How you doing, Jabbar?" Reese said, as she walked up to him with her arms wide open.

Jabbar unfolded his arms and allowed her to disappear into his embrace. "After seeing you, I'm doing just swell." The red-bone's face got even redder as she sized up Reese.

Jabbar stepped to the side and opened the door for her. She waved Elizabeth and Liana over as she stepped past Jabbar.

"These are my girlfriends Elizabeth and Liana. Y'all, this is Jabbar."

Jabber nodded. "Ladies, enjoy yourselves."

Elizabeth and Liana nodded back and smiled.

Red-bone put her hands on her hips. "I know you ain't just let them up in there, and I've been waiting for an hour to get in."

Jabbar smiled. "You'll be going in soon enough."

"Soon enough is right now." Red-bone tried to walk past him. Jabbar folded his arms across his chest and stood between her and the door. Red-bone had a better chance at passing through the eye of a needle than getting by him, but she tried pushing past him anyway. Before she had time to react, Jabbar grabbed her by the wrist. His grip sent volts of pain shooting up her arm, all the while, Jabbar smiled as he placed her back in line and told her to be patient. She massaged her wrist as she pouted. Too embarrassed to turn around to see if anyone saw what happened, she got off the line and walked away mumbling under her breath.

It had been so long since Liana had been to Sneaky Pete's. She felt out of place. Most of the females had on outfits that were so scarcely tailored that they looked like the women just snatched them right off the designer's mannequin while he was still in the process of making them. The fellas were the exact opposite. They were draped in denim, flannel, silk, and linen. They further covered themselves with platinum chains, iced-out bracelets, watches and rings. Liana felt like her ears were being assaulted by the thumping music pounding out of the speakers. Reese grabbed her by the hand pulling her out of her daze and toward the bar.

"Three Pineapple Cosmos," Reese shouted to the bartender, as she bopped her head to the music.

The bartender returned with their drinks, and held his hand up when Reese reached in her purse to pay. "The drinks are already paid for."

"Oh really? By who?" she asked with plenty of attitude.

The bartender pointed to a brother at the other end of the bar. He smiled at Reese when she locked eyes with him, and he winked at Liana when she finally looked his way.

"Tell him, thanks, but no thanks, we can pay for our own drinks," Reese said, reaching into her purse.

Elizabeth put her hand on top of hers. "Hold on Sister Scorned, we came out tonight to enjoy ourselves, and part of enjoying ourselves is not spending our money, right?"

Reese cut her eyes at her.

"Am I right?"

Reese mocked the smile the brother was flashing their way and mouthed thank you, before rolling her eyes and passing Elizabeth and Liana their drinks.

"Now, that wasn't hard, was it?" Elizabeth asked, as she sipped her drink.

"Humph, that was the easy part," Reese retorted. "The hard part is prying his paws off you."

"Oh, please," Liana said, sipping her drink.

"You know how these men are. They buy you a drink, and they think they own you." She looked at Liana. "You saw when he winked at you? Mark my words, he's gonna be sniffing your tail all night long."

"Did we come here to have fun or did we come here for a man bashing convention?" Elizabeth gave Liana and Reese a hard stare before heading to the dance floor. "You know where I'll be."

"There's an empty table over there," Reese said, pointing.

They weaved through the crowd, and sat down. Liana looked around and smiled at the men she made eye contact with.

"It's not the same without Jenna," she said to Reese, who was looking at Elizabeth shake her butt on the dance floor with a light-skinned brother.

"Yeah, I know what you mean. This may sound funny coming from me, but I'm not really feeling this."

Liana looked at her shocked. "You're right, that does sound funny coming from you. You practically lived in the clubs."

"Yes, but that was a long time ago."

"Eight months, Reese?"

"Eight months is a long time. Just ask them inmates in Albany County jail."

"You so stupid, Reese."

"How are you ladies doing tonight?" The brother from the bar asked them, as he stood in front of them in a Rockawear suit, and platinum chains.

"We were doing just fine," Reese fired back, taking him by surprise. Liana watched as he mentally staggered back, trying to recuperate. He was a deep brown, but his complexion couldn't hide the redness in his face.

"How are you doing? My name's Liana," she stuck out her hand.

"My name's Vincent, but people call me Vince," he said shaking Liana's hand. He turned to Reese. "I didn't mean to intrude. I'm just trying to have a good time like everybody else. If you want me to bounce—"

"As a matter of fact—" Reese started, but Liana cut her off.

"As a matter of fact, how about you and I go on down to the dance floor, and continue this conversation?"

Vince was shocked at Liana's forwardness. All he could do was nod as she grabbed him by the hand. She winked at Reese as she led Vince to the dance floor. When they got there, they blended right in. Liana turned her back to Vince, giving him a full view of her apple bottom, as she waved at some familiar faces she hadn't seen in seven months. She tensed up when she felt Vince's hands land on her hips. She looked over her shoulder at him, and smiled as she put her arms in the air and clapped to the music.

She caught Elizabeth's attention and smiled. When Elizabeth saw whom she was dancing with, she rubbed her left forefinger back and forth over her right one. Naughty, naughty, she mouthed as she turned away from her, and backed into her dancer's arms.

Liana turned around to face Vince, and couldn't wipe the devilish grin off her face when she realized he was still staring down at where her butt was just a second ago. He looked up at her, and smiled. She was surprised Vince could actually dance. He didn't just move from side to side nor was he doing that hold-your-nuts-and-bop-your-head thug dance. Not only was Vince a good dancer, but he could also hold a conversation, and most of all, he kept Liana laughing.

Two hours, and three drinks later, Liana was winding and grinding on him, not able to remember the last time she had this much fun. Reese even loosened up and was dancing with a kid she went to school with back in the days. The DJ slowed the music down, and Liana wrapped her arms around Vince as they slowed danced. Liana could see the lust in his eyes, and feel his lust poking her in the stomach. Vince twirled her around, and with her back facing him, he pulled her back into his arms. Vince's lips grazed her neck as his hardness rested on the crack of her butt. Liana closed her eyes and went with it. *Fuck it. I'm not going to see him after tonight.*

She arched her eyebrow when she felt Vince's tongue glide across her neck.

"I know you're not licking the sweat off my neck," she said, as she leaned back on him.

"Baby, I'll lick the sweat off your toes if you let me," Vince whispered in her ear.

"Only if you promise to lick everything in between," Liana said playfully.

"And then some," he said, as he nibbled on her ear.

Liana grabbed his wrists with both her hands, stepped out of his embrace, and fanned herself. "I need to go to the bathroom."

"I'll be here waiting for you," Vince said with a wink.

Liana took her time getting to the bathroom, but when she walked in, she rushed to the sink and splashed cold water on her face. *What am I doing? In a few more seconds, I would've been all over him.* She spruced herself up in the mirror, and walked into the stall. She peed for like twenty seconds nonstop. On her way back to the sink, she started thinking about Vince and felt herself heating up again. She shook her head and splashed cold water on her face again. When she looked up in the mirror, she spun around in shock. Vince jammed his tongue in her mouth.

Liana surprised herself when she didn't try to bite it off or knee him in the nuts. She was even more surprised when she moaned and kissed him back. Vince broke their tongue lock, sucked on her neck, and squeezed her breasts through her shirt. *What am I doing?* Liana heard herself repeat over and over in her head. Vince started guiding her to the stall she'd just come out of, and she wasn't stopping him. *Stop this right now. You don't even know this man, and you're just going to let him take you into a pissy bathroom stall and have his way with you?*

"Vince, wait," Liana finally said.

He stopped and looked at her.

"I can't... not like this."

"It won't take, but a minute."

Liana blinked. "I don't care how long it takes." Liana felt an icy sliver of fear run down her back when she saw Vince's face twist into a mask of anger. "I'm not saying it's not going to happen between us," Liana said, hoping that leading him to believe that there was a chance of him getting some would get her out of the bathroom unmolested. "All I'm saying is if you're really feeling me the way I'm feeling you, you would respect me, and you wouldn't treat me like some club ho."

Vince smiled. "You know what really amazes me? You dance like a club ho, you sucked down the drinks I bought you like a club ho, and you were slobbing me down just now like a club ho, but when it comes to putting out, all of a sudden you want me to respect you?"

Liana brushed his hands off her and attempted to get away from him. Vince grabbed her by the neck, and slammed her against the stall. Liana clawed at his hands as she struggled to scream for help.

"You think I'm some lame-ass trick you can rub your ass on and think I'll be satisfied?" He reached under her mini-dress and grabbed a handful of her panties. The more Liana struggled, the tighter he gripped her around her neck. She stopped struggling. Vince watched as she dropped her hand to his crotch and started massaging him through his pants.

"That's what I'm talking about," he said licking his lips, and releasing his grip.

"It's only going to take a minute, right?" Liana asked, seductively.

"Sixty seconds," Vince licked her cheek.

Liana focused all of her adrenaline and fear into the heel of her right palm and brought it up in a blur. She caught Vince smack-dab under the chin, causing him to bite his tongue. He bent over and put his hands over his mouth as he howled in pain. As Liana tried to run past him, he grabbed her by the waist and flung her against the stall.

"You fucking cock-teasing bitch," he slurred as his tongue swelled up. He groped at her panties while jamming his shoulder into her stomach, forcing her lungs to fight for every ounce of air. As she started losing consciousness, a disturbing vision came to her mind. The vision of her mother in a bathroom, struggling against two crack heads trying to rape her as her father was high, out of his mind, in the next room. Here she was, in a club with over a hundred people not even thirty feet away, and she was about to suffer the same fate as her mother. She could feel her body going numb and her mind taking her someplace else, preparing her for the inevitable.

Both their eyes popped open when the bathroom door crashed against the wall. Wayne was heaving, more from rage then from being out of breath. The look on his face went from rage to confusion. Seeing the horror on Liana's face, and the blood on the front of Vince's shirt, set him off.

"What the fuck is going on?" He locked onto Vince, like a bull seeing red, and charged. Vince let go of Liana and tried to defend himself against Wayne's attack, but Wayne had gained too much momentum. When their bodies collided, Vince's feet dangled in the air as his body sailed into the wall. Wayne hit him with sledgehammer blows to the side of the head. Vince made a feeble attempt to cover up. Liana nearly got hit with one as she stepped in front of Wayne to deliver two calculated kicks to Vince's groin. It was his body's instincts of knowing that death was imminent that compelled Vince to scramble to his hands and knees and scuttle out the door. Wayne ran to the door, but knew he wasn't going to catch him. He put his hands on his knees and took deep breaths. He looked up when he heard a girl scream. Taz, seeing Vince busting out of the bathroom with Wayne on his tail, grabbed a wine bottle off his table, and waited patiently as Vince ran toward him. Vince turned around to see if Wayne was chasing him. When he turned back around, the last thing he saw was a bottle connecting with the bridge of his nose. Taz got a few stomps in before the bouncers tackled him and pinned him to the floor.

Wayne turned his attention toward Liana, who was standing in the middle of the bathroom floor hugging herself and shivering. Unbeknown to Liana, Wayne was in the club that night. He spotted her as soon as she walked in with Elizabeth and Reese. He also spotted her on the dance floor doing everything short of having sex with the dude that had her pinned against the bathroom stall. When he saw her go to the bathroom, and Vince following behind her, he was furious.

"I can't believe she's going into the bathroom with that motherfucker." He remembered telling Taz.

"What are you going to do? Bust up in there on them?" Taz had said.

Wayne sat at the table, shaking his leg. He pictured Liana in the bathroom with Vince bending her over a sink or a toilet. He slammed his fist on the table and headed to the bathroom. He didn't care that she wasn't his woman anymore, he just wasn't going to allow her to disrespect herself. "You all right?" he asked her. When she didn't respond, he walked toward her. "Liana? You okay?" When he touched her, she flinched. "Liana?" Without warning, she hugged him around the waist and buried her face into his chest as she cried like a baby. Wayne, slowly put his arms around her, and rubbed her back. Women were piling up in front of the bathroom to see what was going on.

"We have to get out of here," Wayne said, but she refused to move.

"Wayne, what's going on?" Wayne's rigidity made Liana look up. Although she hadn't seen Tammy in years, she recognized her standing at the threshold of the bathroom. Reese was right. Her tomboy body did soften up, and her curves bore witness to her femininity.

Wayne looked at her and then back to Liana. Liana's eyes pleaded with him not to tell her about the humiliation she just suffered.

"Wayne!" Tammy said, starting to jump to conclusions.

"Nothing's going on," Wayne backed away from Liana. He brushed past Tammy. The police had Taz and Vince hand-cuffed, and were leading them out of the front door.

"Wayne, what's going on?" Reese asked him, as he walked towards her.

"Go to the bathroom, and check on Liana."

Elizabeth and Reese raced to the women's room.

"Yo, hold up," Wayne shouted to the officers. "Yo, yo, hold up," he said again, trying to get their attention as they escorted Taz and Vince to two separate police cars.

One of the officers following his partners turned around.

"I know that man," Wayne said, pointing to Taz. "He didn't do anything wrong."

"Witnesses say he bashed that guy in the face with a wine bottle. I call that something wrong."

"That's only because—"

"Fuck that, pig," Taz shouted, as the officers tried forcing him into the back of the police car. "Don't tell him a mother-fucking thing."

Wayne watched as they shoved Taz in and slammed the door.

"That's why we're arresting him," the officer said to Wayne. "He's got a feisty mouth."

"I'll be out by tomorrow morning, and I'm suing all you bitches for harassment," Taz screamed at the top of his lungs. "Yeah, you, you fat motherfucker," Taz said to the officer who just sat in the driver's seat.

Wayne waved his hands in the air to get Taz's attention. "Chill, yo," Wayne said to him.

Taz cut his eyes at him and quieted down.

Wayne locked eyes with Vince, and was shocked when Vince ice-grilled him like he was tough. Wayne nodded at him, letting him know that wherever he saw him, it was on.

"Wayne, what happened in there?" Tammy asked, as she walked outside toward him.

Wayne exhaled hard about to explain what he walked in on when Tammy stopped him and grabbed his hands.

"My God, what happened to your hands?"

Wayne looked at his hands, surprised that they had swollen up like balloons. He closed his eyes, thanking God that the officer he'd just talked to didn't see them. "Listen, Tammy. You got to promise me you won't say a word."

"I promise, what happened?"

"Dude was trying to rape Liana in the bathroom."

Tammy's eyes widened. "Are you serious?"

"I was on my way into the men's bathroom when I heard her screaming for her life." Wayne felt bad having to tell a small lie, but he couldn't tell Tammy what made him really bust up in the women's bathroom. "I opened the door, and I saw this dude... trying to rip her clothes off, and..."

"We have to tell the police what happened."

"No, Tammy," Wayne said, grabbing her.

"No?"

"I mean not right now. Liana's kind of shaken up, and I'm quite sure she doesn't want people knowing what happened to her."

Tammy looked back at the entrance, and then back to Wayne.

"We got to respect her privacy," Wayne said. "If she wants to come forth in a day or two, that's up to her."

"But you're okay, right?" Tammy caught him staring at the entrance. She turned around and saw Liana, flanked by two other women. Liana locked eyes with Wayne. Tammy noticed how Liana's initial reaction was to start toward him but she stopped and allowed her friends to lead her down the block.

"Ouch." Wayne winced when Tammy squeezed his hands, to remind him she was standing there.

"Let's go home." She was referring to his place. "We have to clean these cuts, and soak your hands so the swelling can go down."

"I'm all right, Tammy."

"What did I say?" she squeezed his hands.

"All right. Let's go."

CHAPTER 12

Wayne looked both ways before entering the precinct. He tossed and turned all night when Taz called him from the police station and told him that Vince had told the police some bullshit.

"Yo, man. This motherfucker is trying to say I approached him, drunk out of my mind, with an empty bottle in my hand. He said when I told him to buy me another drink, and he refused, I cracked him in the face with the bottle."

"That lying coward." Wayne explained to Taz what happened in the bathroom last night.

"That motherfucker. If I would've known that when he was running toward me last night, I would've broken the bottle first, and then stuck it in his neck."

"I'm going to keep it real with you, Taz. I don't think Liana's going to come forth, and press charges."

Taz got quiet for a minute. "Fuck it; I'm not mad at her. The newspapers would be all in her business, digging into her past, and all kinds of dumb shit. Then the courts will make her take the stand and re-live the whole shit, and after all that, they'll probably find that piece of shit not guilty."

"Well, we still have to do something. Right now, it's his word against yours. With your criminal record, street rep, and the fact that every policeman in Albany can't stand you, they're going to try and send you up north for this."

"Fuck it; at least I'm not going up for no bullshit."

"You're not going up, at all. I'm going to talk to Harris."

"Wayne, don't go running your mouth. It doesn't make sense for the both of us to be going up north. Who's going to send me packages and money for commissary?"

"You's a funny dude, Taz. I'll come and check on you in the morning."

The following morning as Wayne walked up to the officer's desk, it dawned on him that this was a bad idea, but it was too late to back out. The desk officer had looked up from what he was doing, and was now staring at him.

Wayne cleared his throat. "Can I speak to Detective Harris, please?"

"Maybe I can help you out. What do you need?"

"It's a private matter, and—"

"Say no more," the officer said, holding his hand up, and picking up the phone with the other. He dialed a number and then spoke. "Yeah, tell Harris one of his CIs is at the front desk."

CI? Wayne quickly deciphered the initials confidential informant, a.k.a. snitch and almost lost his cool. He held his head, hoping he wouldn't have to wait long. Before the cop had time to slap any more labels on him, Detective Harris stuck his head out of an office. He cocked his head at Wayne, and then waved him over.

When Wayne walked into the cramped office, he noticed that Harris was putting on his jacket, and reaching for a folder.

"You kind of caught me at a bad time," Harris said, grabbing his 9mm out of his desk draw, and shoving it in its holster. "What brings you down here, anyway?"

"I don't want to take up too much of your time. I just wanted to speak to you about a situation that happened last night at Sneaky Pete's."

Harris grabbed his mug off his desk and sipped his lukewarm coffee. "You got to fill me in. I have no idea what you're talking about."

"A friend of mine was arrested for supposedly picking a fight with someone there."

"Well, that's why I don't know what you're talking about. I strictly deal with homicide. Nobody died last night so it's none of my business." Harris tapped the folder against his leg, signaling Wayne that his time was up.

"Detective Harris I know you're busy and all, and it's true that no one died last night, but in my opinion, something far worst happened."

"Wayne… I really don't have time to—"

"Last night, I caught someone trying to rape my ex fiancée in the women's bathroom."

Detective Harris crossed his arms, and leaned on his desk.

"I walked in on it, and I stopped it."

"You stopped it?"

Wayne held up his bruised knuckles. "Yeah, I stopped it. He managed to get away from me, but he didn't get past my friend."

"So, what do you want me to do?"

"I was wondering if you could make a call, and somehow clear this up, because the guy's trying to say that my friend just beat him up for no reason."

"Did your ex fiancée tell the officers at the scene what happened?"

"I don't believe she's going to come forth."

"Don't take this the wrong way, Wayne, but how am I supposed to believe anything you're saying if she won't come forth?"

"I have no reason to lie to you. I came into your office, and implicated myself in an assault, and I'm willing to accept the consequences, but one thing I can't accept is allowing this guy to not only get away with what he tried to do to Liana, but then he's going to trap off a good friend of mine in some bullshit."

"Liana? Liana Thompson?" Harris asked, more so to jog his memory.

"Yeah," Wayne said suspiciously.

"Her fiancé was murdered at a stoplight last year... so how's she your ex fiancée?"

"We were engaged before she was engaged to Ron."

"Right, Ronald Banks," Harris said, remembering the case more clearly. "That poor girl lost her mother at an early age, and her father is still in jail, because of it. Then her husband-to-be is murdered at a stoplight, and now you're telling me she was almost raped last night?" Harris shook his head. "Give me your friend's name, and I'll make a couple of calls."

"Jamal Henderson," Wayne said, and then held his breath.

"Taz?" Harris raked his hand through his hair. "How in the world is Taz a friend of yours?"

"We grew up together."

"Grew up together, huh? So that means you two must be into the same things."

"Hardly, you know what I do for a living."

Harris stared at him for a second. "I'm going to tell you like it is. If the fella that you beat up last night doesn't confess that he, in fact, did try to rape Liana, or if he doesn't admit that Jamal didn't just assault him out of the blue, Jamal is going away for a long time."

"I know if you put pressure on that dude, he's going to crack, trust me."

"I'm not promising you anything."

"I appreciate whatever you can do. The next time I do your yard, it's on the house."

"Let's get something straight," Harris said, pushing himself off the desk. "The only reason why I'm going to look into this, and not lock you up for assault is because my mother likes you. She's always talking about you and how nice you are to her."

Wayne swallowed the lump in his throat. If Harris only knew how much his mother liked him.

"So, don't think I'm doing you a favor. You got that?"

Wayne, nodded.

"I have to go, so if you don't mind…" Wayne opened the door. "Thanks Harris."

"*Detective* Harris," Harris said, correcting him.

"Yes, Detective Harris." When Wayne climbed into his truck, he exhaled. Now, he can only pray that Vince fessed up or at least admitted that he lied about the reason why Taz attacked him.

***

Last night's scrap shook Liana up, but it didn't stop her from getting on the road, and speed balling it all the way back to Queens.

As she sat behind the register at work the next morning, her thoughts were a collage of images that had her bouncing between happiness, sadness, anger, fear, and confusion. Vince had seemed so... sweet. She replayed the night in her head, as painful as it was, but even in hindsight, she couldn't pick out any clues that should've told her that he was a piece of shit. She shuttered when thinking of all the women he must've had his way with. It was probably the only way he could get off. Liana always considered herself a strong woman, who could thump with the best of them, but last night showed her just how weak she was. Not only couldn't she fight Vince off her, but she had given up. She was going to let him have his way with her just to get it over with. She remembered turning her head and going to a place where she only knew love. She mentally walked into Wayne's arms. Vince would have her body, but he would never get her soul. When Wayne busted into the bathroom, she didn't know if he was really standing there, or if it was an image of her wishful thinking. When she blinked and he was still standing there, her heart almost flew out of her chest.

Then she saw the animalistic side of him. The fury he unleashed on Vince would've had most people backing away in fear, but it pulled her to him.

Liana spun around on her stool and looked out the store window. Last night, among the melee, she fell in love with Wayne all over again. She hugged herself and rubbed her arms. She knew from the feral glare that Tammy was shooting her with last night that there was no chance of her ever getting back with Wayne.

In the deepest recesses of her soul, she always knew that Wayne was her safety net. Whenever the world threw her for a loop, she knew he would always be there to break her fall, even if he got his heart broken in the process. Wayne had played the part of so many men in her life: Brother, boyfriend, best friend, lover, and fiancé. She realized that she truly didn't know how much she loved him, until she saw how much someone else did.

Liana flinched and knocked Rasheem's hand off her shoulder when he touched her from behind. "What's wrong with you?" she said, screwing her face up at him.

"Whoa," Rasheem said, backing up. "I didn't mean to scare you. I was calling you for about a minute, and you were in another world. You've been looking spaced out all afternoon. Everything okay?"

Liana allowed her shoulders to slump, and softened the lines in her face. "I'm fine. I just got a lot on my mind."

"Anything you want to talk about?"

"Not right now."

"Yo, JD!" Rasheem called out, waving him over. "Take the register."

"I'm okay," Liana said weakly.

"No, you're not. You look like you drove from Albany straight here and just started working. Go home, please, and get some rest."

"Home is the last place I need to be right now."

Rasheem looked at his watch, and then grabbed her by the hand. "Watch the store, JD; we'll be back in a few."

"Where are we going?" Liana asked, trailing behind him.

"I have to pick my sons up at the after school program, and bring them to my mother's."

"Rasheem I—"

"Shhh." Rasheem quieted her. "The fresh air will do you some good."

Five minutes into the ride, Rasheem glanced over at Liana, and watched her as she gazed out the window. "Hey!" he called out, startling her. "You've been in the same position for five minutes. You sure you're all right?"

"Maybe you should take me home."

"I thought you said home was the last place you needed to be."

Liana didn't respond; she just kept staring out the window.

"Take me to where you're at right now," Rasheem said, placing his hand on hers.

"Huh?"

Rasheem looked over at her. "I said take me to where you're at right now."

"You don't want to go there."

"Why? You already there with someone?"

Liana didn't respond.

"I got a question for you," Rasheem said. "If you had the chance to be anywhere in the world right now, besides the place you're at in your mind, where would it be?"

Liana actually gave the question some thought. "Bermuda."

Rasheem chuckled. "You serious?"

"Yes… I'm serious."

Rasheem nodded. "Why Bermuda?"

"I don't know. It was a place I always used to hear about. The white sands, clear water, breath-taking scenery—"

"The Triangle," Rasheem threw in.

"Oh, please. You don't believe that crap, do you?" Liana said, cutting her eyes at him.

"Ask the people who disappeared if they believe it."

"Those people disappeared because they wanted to. They just got fed up with life and wanted to be left alone."

Rasheem turned serious. "Is that why you want to go there?"

Again, Liana didn't respond.

Rasheem removed his hand from hers.

"What?" Liana looked at him challengingly.

"You are one complicated woman."

"Shut up," Liana said, punching him in the arm. "Don't be trying to dis me."

"Chill," Rasheem said, as they pulled up to the school. "I don't want my boys to see you hitting me like that. They may think I'm a sucker."

"You are a sucker." Liana punched him in the arm again.

"Only for you."

Liana made the mistake of gazing into Rasheem's eyes a second too long. She felt herself being pulled deeper and deeper into his ink-black pupils. She snapped out of it when the back doors opened and Rasheem's boys jumped in. She quickly drew back from Rasheem, not knowing how she had gotten into kissing distance.

"Who's that, Daddy?" Lionel, who was five, asked.

"This is Liana; she works at the store with me."

"Look at my drawing," Donelle said to Liana from the backseat, as he held it out for her to grab.

"This is beautiful," Liana said, turning half way around to look at it.

"That's me," he said, pointing to the shortest stick figure. "And that's Lionel, and that's daddy and mommy holding hands."

Liana noticed how Donelle drew a heart around all of them. "You guys are one, big, happy family." Liana could see Lionel, through her peripheral, shooting daggers at her. "And how was your day?" she asked him.

"Dad, can you take us to mom's house?" Lionel totally ignored Liana.

"You're going to your mother's on the weekend."

"Why we can't go today?"

"I want to go to mommy's house," Donelle chirped in.

"I'm going to drop you off at grandma's, and come pick you up after work."

"Aw, c'mon, Dad," Lionel whined.

"That's the end of it," Rasheem said, ending the conversation.

Lionel glared at Liana as if it was her fault.

Rasheem dropped them off and introduced Liana to his mother before pulling off.

"I don't think Lionel digs me much," Liana said, resting her head on the headrest.

"But Donelle spoke to you. He doesn't speak to anybody; and just like that." Rasheem snapped his fingers, "He just opened up to you."

"Well, I guess one out of two ain't bad."

"Well, if you want to get with me, it's going to have to be two out of two."

"I'm not trying to get with you, so I don't have to worry about winning anybody over."

"I love that about you. About us."

"What's that?" Liana asked.

"Our relationship. This may sound corny, but…"

"But what?" Liana asked pointedly.

"We're just friends. Nothing's ever going to happen between us, right?"

"Right."

"I just wanted to establish that before I put my cards on the table."

Liana shrugged. "Whatever."

"You're the only woman who's been able to resist me."

"It's not hard to do." Liana flashed back to thirty minutes ago when she was staring into his eyes and almost buckled.

"I'm serious. I don't want to come off as being conceited, but every woman I've ever gone out with gave me the booty."

"And you said you're not trying to sound conceited?"

"I'm just saying—"

Liana held her hand up. "Save it for the women giving up the booty."

"All you're doing is just making me want you more, you know that, right?" Rasheem locked eyes with her.

"Keep your eyes off of me and on the road."

***

The next morning, Wayne awoke to Tammy hustling between the bathroom and the bedroom, getting ready for work. Tammy was heavy-footed, so when she walked in any part of the house, it vibrated. Wayne wiped the sleep out of his eyes and looked at the clock. It was five-thirty. Tammy stood in front of the full-length mirror, staring at her stomach.

"Damn, baby, I've never seen a girl with washboard abs," Wayne said with a wink.

She rolled her eyes and walked back to the bathroom. Wayne rolled over and threw the pillow over his head, to get an hour and a half more worth of sleep before his father started ringing his phone off the hook.

"That whole situation with Liana in the club Saturday night still doesn't sit right with me," Tammy said, as she walked back into the room putting in her nose ring. She looked at Wayne's inert body and kicked the bed. "I know you hear me."

"Let it go, Tammy," Wayne whined from under the pillow.

"I can't let it go. There's a pervert out there raping women and getting away with it." She was referring to yesterday morning when Wayne told her that Vince had been released after he admitted that the story he told the cops wasn't entirely true. He admitted to having a little too much to drink, and coming on a little too strong to Liana, but that was it. He emphatically denied that he got violent with her. He said they exchanged heated words, and he walked away from her. And then that's when he said Taz hit him with the bottle. Of course, the story wasn't entirely true, but it was enough for the police to release him and Taz on their own recognizance.

"That's some bullshit," Tammy said. "That man should be in prison."

"The only way he's going to prison is if Liana steps up, and tells what really happened. I know her. She's not going to do that. The last thing she wants is to be in somebody's newspaper."

"Well, if it was me—" Tammy started to say.

"But it's not you. Not everyone is as strong-willed as you are. So, let's just stop talking about this situation once and for all."

Tammy stared at him for a moment. "I'm sorry."

When Wayne didn't respond, she sat on the bed next to him, and rubbed his neck. She removed the pillow off his head, and lay on top of him, allowing her nipples to brush across his back. Her lips hovered over his ear.

"What do I have to do to make you love me the way that you love her?"

Tammy's words and tears on his cheek took him by surprise. He lifted his head. "What are you talking about?"

"You know what I'm talking about. I saw the way both of you looked at each other that night when she came out of the club."

"I was just seeing if she was okay."

"You wanted to do more than just see."

"You bugging." Wayne tried to sound nonchalant.

"Am I?" Tammy got off him and started walking away.

Wayne sat up and grabbed her by the hand. He tapped his thigh for her to sit. "I would be lying to you if I told you that I didn't have feelings for her. I will always have feelings for her, but don't ever think I don't love you, or that I will ever put her before us."

Tammy put her arms around his neck and hugged him.

Wayne stood up and wrapped her legs around his waist. "You are so beautiful," he said, making her blush. "I know what I'm going to do."

"What?"

"I'm going to get you pregnant. That way you'll never leave me."

"Put me down," Tammy said, trying to wiggle out of his grip.

"As a matter of fact," Wayne said, falling on top of her on the bed, "I'm going to get you pregnant right now."

"Stop, Wayne," Tammy said, as she put her hands on his chest. "You didn't even brush your teeth, yet." She turned from side to side as he tried to kiss her.

"Okay, you got a choice. Let me kiss you or you're going to be late for work."

"C'mon, Wayne, stop playing."

"You know how those soccer moms be wanting to jump on you when you have them in that gym waiting for you to show up."

"Okay, okay," Tammy said. "A small kiss."

"That's all I want." Wayne kissed her and knew by Tammy's moan that she was going to be late for her kickboxing class.

***

Taz took a long pull on the blunt before offering it to Wayne. Wayne just stared at him.

"Damn, you don't have to look at me like that." Taz took another pull and held his breath for a minute. "Motherfucker," Taz said, as he exhaled. "I almost died in county lockup. I went a whole day without smoking. You know what that shit can do to a motherfucker?"

"No," Wayne said. "I don't."

"Of course you don't. The only weed you touch is the ones you pull up out of people's yards. You don't know how close I was to crushing up some apple seeds and rolling them in some bible paper."

Wayne frowned at him. "Isn't that some crazy shit you used to do in DFY?"

"No doubt."

"You're a grown ass man," Wayne said. "Weed isn't addictive. It's all in your head."

"Spoken like a true non-weed smoker." Taz took another pull and let it rush out his nose. "I'm like a vampire; and weed is my blood supply." Taz took another pull and closed his eyes as if the weed actually possessed some regenerative qualities. Taz's eyes were demon-red when he opened them. "So, what are we going to do about this rapo?"

"We ain't doing a motherfucking thing," Wayne said with authority.

"That piece of shit tried to rape your girl."

"Liana's not my girl."

"Man... who you think you talking to? She's always going to be your girl. No matter who she's with or who you're with."

"Tammy's my girl; and from what Elizabeth tells me, Liana's messing with some cat in the city named Rasheem."

"Indio's cousin, Rasheem?"

"How should I know?"

"It better not be the one I'm talking about." Taz said, finishing off the blunt.

"Why do you say that?"

"Why you want to know? Liana's not your girl. Tammy is," Taz said, mocking him.

"Fuck you, Taz."

"That's what I'm talking about. Get hyped and let's go castrate that fucking rapo."

"We can't go anywhere near him, Taz. Give me your word that you won't."

"What? Hell, nah. Why would I do that?"

"Because I gave Harris my word that you wouldn't go near him."

"You did what?" Taz's high crash-landed.

"How the fuck you think you got out of jail? You think Vince just had a change of heart, and told the police that he lied on you?"

"Uh… yeah."

"Uh… no. I went to the precinct like I told you I was, and I talked to Harris."

"So you mean to tell me that Harris is the reason why I'm not in jail right now?"

"Yep."

Taz twisted the cap off the Sprite bottle and took a swig of the Smirnoff he poured in it a couple hours ago. "You should've left me in jail."

"You talking out your ass, now," Wayne said.

"I'm dead serious. Every time I bump heads with this motherfucker now, he's going to give me this smug look like 'yeah it was because of me that you didn't go up north.'"

"Think what you want. If anything happens to that dude, we're the first ones they're coming after. So, do me a favor, and let that man be, for now."

Taz shook his head. "You're definitely a better man than me. I could never allow someone to do that to someone I cared about and get away with it."

"What goes around comes around. Vince is going to get his."

"Sure you right." Taz took another sip and offered the Sprite bottle to Wayne.

Wayne snatched it and took two gulping swallows, trying to deaden the bitter aftertaste of his words. *What goes around comes around.* Fuck that! He would deal with Vincent in his own way. "So, what's up with this Rasheem cat?" Wayne passed Taz back the Sprite bottle.

Taz turned it up and finished it off with a smack of his lips before he answered. "Think of the grimiest dude you can think of. Then multiply his griminess by a hundred. That's Rasheem."

CHAPTER 13

Liana leaned her head back against the rim of the bathtub as she inhaled the lavender scent of her bubble bath. Rasheem had given her the past two days off. She protested at first, but deep down, she knew she needed the time off to shut down and reboot. She raised her foot out of the water and looked down at her wrinkled toes. It was definitely time to get out. As she walked into her bedroom wrapping a towel around her head, the phone rang. A few seconds later, Rasheem's voice was coming through the answering machine.

Liana quickly answered the phone. "What's up, Rasheem?"

"Just calling to make sure you're still alive. You know how JD and I worry about you when we don't see you in a few days."

"You mean how you worry about me. Don't throw JD into it."

"I'm that obvious?"

"Yes... you are."

"Well, the real reason why I called is because Elizabeth has been trying to reach you, but you're not answering your phone. She figured that if I called, you would pick up. You don't answer your best friend's calls, but you answer mine. There's hope for me yet."

"Please, I only answered because I thought maybe you needed me to come in to work."

"JD and I are holding it down. I called you because Elizabeth is at Indio's, and she wants you to come over."

"I just got out the tub; I'm not going anywhere now."

"C'mon, it's Friday night; your friend drove all the way from Albany to hangout."

"To hangout with Indio."

"And you. Why do you think she's been ringing your phone off the hook?"

Liana sighed. "Fuck it. I've been cooped up in this apartment for two days already."

"I'll be by to pick you up in about thirty minutes."

"I know how to get to Indio's house."

"I have to pass by your place to get there, so we might as well carpool."

"Carpool?"

"I'm just fucking with you, but seriously, though. JD and I are closing up now. I can be there in about thirty minutes."

Liana was quiet for a moment before answering him. "I'll be waiting."

***

Liana came right out when Rasheem pulled up. She had on a pair of jeans and a blue cotton t-shirt. Even when dressed down, Liana's sensuousness made whatever she had on look high-fashioned. She hopped into Rasheem's H2, and allowed the seat belt to adjust itself to her body.

"Are those Apple Bottom jeans you're wearing?" Rasheem asked, mocking the Bugle Boy jeans commercial.

"Just drive," Liana said, placing her hands in her lap.

"So, how was your mini vacation?" Rasheem asked, referring to the last two days.

"Enlightening."

"How so?"

"With all the drama going on in my life, I realized that it's all a little bit more bearable when I take some time out to pamper myself."

"You know the best thing about pampering?" Rasheem asked as he stopped at a light.

"What's that?"

"Getting pampered."

"Umm hmm, let you tell it."

"I'm talking about a professional pampering. I'm talking about a manicure, pedicure, mud bath, full body massage… the works."

"If I had 'the whole works' money, I wouldn't have stayed in my apartment."

"Are you asking me for a raise?" Rasheem asked smiling.

"Maybe you need to treat your employees to a day at the spa every six months or so."

"That's an idea I can look into Ms. Thompson. Thanks for your input."

When they pulled up to Indio's house, Liana saw him rummaging around in the trunk of Elizabeth's rent-a-car. He slammed the trunk shut and spun around when Rasheem's headlights swept over him. The hairs on the back of Liana's neck stood up seeing Indio looking like he was up to no good.

Although Indio left the drug game a long time ago, it wasn't hard to tell from his lifestyle that he used to be deep in the mix. His expensive taste was the same, his desire for quick money intensified, and his shifty eyes, from having to always be on point, made him look guilty, even if he wasn't doing anything wrong.

"Damn, cuz, you trying to blind me with them bright ass lights?" Indio said, as Rasheem and Liana exited the H2.

Rasheem gave him a pound and a hug. "What are you doing out here, anyway?"

Liana's ears perked up to hear his response.

"Me and Elizabeth went shopping earlier. I took all the bags out except for one." Indio held up the bag, showing them the imprint of a shoebox. "How you doing, Liana?"

"I'm fine."

"Elizabeth's upstairs recuperating," Indio said with a devilish grin that made Liana want to vomit.

"So, what's the plan for tonight?" Rasheem asked, as they walked inside.

"We just chilling," Indio said. "My baby wants to spend a quiet evening with her home girl; so I got us a couple of movies. I was waiting on you guys to show up so I can order the pizza."

"Movies and pizza?" Rasheem said a little disappointed. "When you said hangout, I didn't think you meant we were going to hang in."

"I'm cool with it," Liana said, cutting in. "I didn't really feel like going anywhere, anyway."

"The women have spoken," Indio said. "My woman wants to stay in, and her best friend wants to stay in. So, we're staying in."

Rasheem shrugged. "So be it."

"Hey, girl," Elizabeth said, coming down the staircase.

Liana met her at the bottom of the stairs and hugged her.

"Are you okay?" Elizabeth asked. The look in her eyes told Liana that she wanted to know how she was holding up after the club incident.

"Yeah, I'm fine." Liana turned to Rasheem. "Thanks to my boss, here, I had a few days to get my head right."

"Jenna and Reese, as always, send their love. Jenna was talking about coming down to stay with you for a few days. Efran and Efran Jr. are driving her crazy."

"No problem. All she has to do is call me," Liana said.

"Duh, she's been trying to call, but somebody's not answering their phone."

"I'll call her tomorrow."

After the pizza came, they made themselves comfortable in the living room in front of the fifty-inch plasma, high definition screen. Elizabeth started the movie.

"If y'all want something a little stronger, I got some vodka in the kitchen cabinet." During the movie, Elizabeth and Indio sat in the loveseat, cuddled up together. Liana sat in the Lazy Boy while Rasheem sat on the floor, by her feet.

Liana would look down at him every now and then trying not to be so obvious. She didn't know if it was the liquor or her seven month dry spell, but her thoughts of Rasheem were becoming erotic. *He sure is fine. He's been nothing but the perfect gentleman. He's gotten me an apartment, a job, and he listens when I need someone to talk to.* She imagined herself grabbing him by the back of his head and guiding his mouth down onto her nipple as he made love to her. She quickly focused on the television screen and coughed, trying to camouflage the moan that escaped from her lips.

***

"That shit was all right," Indio said at the end of the movie. Rasheem agreed with him.

Elizabeth and Liana were in the kitchen putting the plates and cups into the dishwasher and having a conversation that they didn't want Indio and Rasheem listening to.

"You know that punk motherfucker Dexter is in jail, right?" Elizabeth said to Liana, as she turned on the dishwasher.

"No, I didn't know that," Liana responded.

"Yeah, he got caught with a kilo of coke in Texas."

"In Texas? He's fucked."

"Good for his stinking ass," Elizabeth said with lethal venom. "He's going to pull Reese in front of him as a shield. Fuck is wrong with him?"

"Does Reese know he's in jail?"

"Not yet. Indio told me today."

Liana yawned. "I have to get home. It's been fun, but I have to go."

"Go? Where are you going? Tomorrow's Saturday. You don't have to work," Elizabeth asked disappointedly.

"I have something to do."

"Like what?"

Like take a cold shower. Liana realized that it wasn't the liquor or the seven month dry spell that had her feeling like a cat-in-heat—it was both. Liana knew she had to get out of there before her scent got up in Rasheem's nostrils.

"You sure you don't want to hangout just a little while longer?"

"No, I really have to go."

Elizabeth snatched her car keys off the kitchen table.

"What's up?" Rasheem said when he saw Elizabeth with her keys in hand.

"I'm giving Liana a ride home."

"Home? This early?" Indio asked, surprised.

"She has things to do in the morning," Elizabeth said.

"Well, let Rasheem take her home."

Rasheem got up from the floor and stretched. "Yeah, no problem."

"Nah, I got it," Elizabeth said.

Indio walked up to her and whispered something in her ear to which Elizabeth's mouth dropped open. "Boy, you so nasty."

Oh God, Liana thought.

"I'm going to call you tomorrow, girl," Elizabeth said to Liana, as Indio looped his arm around her waist and guided her toward the bedroom.

"Kids," Rasheem said, shaking his head.

***

Liana didn't say a word the whole ride to her apartment. She sat as close as she could to the H2's door so Rasheem couldn't feel the heat radiating off her.

"Are you sure you're all right?" Rasheem asked, as he shut off his engine.

"I'm fine." Liana opened the door and stepped out. "See you Monday."

"Whoa, whoa." Rasheem got out and ran around to the passenger side. "No good-bye or I had a nice time?"

"Good-bye, I had a nice time." Liana saw the frustrated look in his eyes as he turned to leave. "You want to come in for a few minutes?" Liana knew it was a bad idea, but she couldn't just let him leave feeling some kind of way.

Rasheem shook his head. "I think I'm going to head home." He closed his eyes for a long time and then reopened them.

In that instant, Liana realized that he might have had a little too much to drink, which also explained why he didn't try to talk to her on the way home. He was too busy focusing on the road.

"If you don't mind, Rasheem, I would really appreciate it if you came in for awhile."

Rasheem looked around, and then walked back to the driver side of his truck and shut the door.

Liana stood at her front door. "Hurry up."

Rasheem jogged up the steps.

The last time Rasheem was in Liana's apartment was the day he helped her move in. He could see the love she'd put into it. The brown and beige border across the top of the living room walls matched her brown and beige furniture.

"You have to excuse the mess," Liana said, scooping clothes off the living room couch. "I wasn't expecting company."

"Nah, that's cool. Mine ain't no better."

"I have some soda in the fridge," Liana said, pointing to the kitchen.

"You don't have anything a little stronger?"

"I think you had enough to drink."

"I'm not drunk. I'm just a little saucy."

"Sit your saucy ass down before you pass out." Liana threw the clothes she was holding into her bedroom and shut the door. She walked to the fridge while Rasheem took her advice and sat down. He rubbed his eyes and focused on a scribbled-on pad on the table. He noticed the crumpled up pieces of paper on the coffee table. He looked back to the pad, squinting to read what Liana was trying to write.

"Why are you writing to the… Parole Board?" he shouted toward the kitchen.

Liana walked back into the living room with two bottles of Pepsi. She handed him one and then sat down on the couch, facing him. "It's a long story."

Rasheem looked at his watch. "I got time."

"And it's kind of personal."

"I thought we had a connection here, you and me."

Liana just stared at him.

Rasheem shifted in his seat. "Well, whatever this person did must've really scarred you, for you to be writing the Parole Board."

"Scarred is putting it lightly."

"Just answer me this question, and I swear I'll leave it alone. Did this guy... hurt you?"

"He didn't rape me, if that's what you're asking." Liana could see him exhale.

"Nah, I was just thinking back to this girl I used to mess with back in the days. She got raped, and she was never the same. She could never have a healthy relationship."

Liana looked up at him and hit him with a question out of left field. "You ever been in love?"

"It depends on your definition of love."

"If you were to break up with someone and hook up with someone else, and your ex was to come back, you would leave whoever you were with and get back with your ex."

Rasheem thought about it for a moment. "That's some heavy shit right there. You mean all this person has to do is just come back in the picture, and that's it? At anytime?"

"Anytime, anywhere."

"That's some scary shit."

"No, that's loving someone from the soul."

"Well, I guess I would have to say I've never been in love." Rasheem took a couple sips of his soda. "So, that's how your ex in Albany feels about you?"

"That's how he used to feel about me."

"Used to? The way you just described that type of love, it sounded like it would always be."

"It will, until you break that person's heart so many times that they no longer have anything to love you with."

Rasheem watched Liana as she stared off into space. He expected they were going to talk, but he didn't know it was going to get this deep. "So, what you're saying is you made him stop loving you?"

"That's fucked up, right? The only man I ever opened my soul to, the only one who accepted me and my family's history, and I drove him into another woman's arms." Liana pulled her knees up to her chest and rested her head on them.

Rasheem shot off the couch. "Get up!"

Liana looked at him, as he held his hand out to her.

"C'mon, get up. I know what you need."

"What's that?"

"Trust me." He grabbed her hand.

When Liana saw he was heading toward her bedroom, she stopped in her tracks.

"You remember what you told me a long time ago? You said there was never going to be anything between us. That we're just going to be friends, remember?" Rasheem asked as he looked her in the eyes.

"Yeah."

"Well, now I'm just being a friend." He tugged her by the hand. "Trust me. I didn't take advantage of you when Ron broke your heart, and I'm not going to take advantage of you now."

Liana trusted him, but she didn't trust herself. Her panties was moist, and her body was craving the sheltering embrace of a man. She took a deep breath, and squeezed his hand, giving him the okay to proceed.

Rasheem led her into the bedroom. He kicked off his shoes, lay down, and tapped the bed for her to lie next to him.

"Yeah, right," Liana said, crossing her arms.

"What happened to the trust?"

"Trust doesn't have anything to do with it."

"I know I'm not your ex. And from the look in your eyes, I know that right now you want to be in his arms. All I'm saying is lie down and pretend that he's holding you."

Liana busted out laughing. "This is the craziest shit I've ever heard in my life. You want me to call you by his name, too?"

Rasheem only responded by tapping the bed again. Liana would've kicked him out a long time ago, but her not wanting to be alone convinced her into seeing if Rasheem's arms would deaden her obsession with Wayne. She kicked off her shoes and lay next to him.

She turned on her side and rested her head on his chest as she felt his arm come down across her back.

"This is corny," she said, tensing up.

"Shh, relax." Rasheem started caressing her back.

Liana shook her head. *Fuck it. If I didn't want to see if this bullshit could work, I wouldn't have laid down in the first place.* She closed her eyes and inhaled. The scent of Fahrenheit intoxicated her more than the liquor did. She could feel the steady beat of Rasheem's heart. The warmth of his body began melting the tenseness out from her shoulders. Her eyes popped open as flashbacks of her lying in Wayne's arms raced through her mind. She smiled, not believing how real the flashbacks felt. She closed her eyes and pressed herself closer to Rasheem, determined to feed her need for love without having to have intercourse.

"Feeling better?" Rasheem asked, as he swept her hair from her neck.

Liana didn't respond, but for Rasheem, that's all he needed to hear.

Liana could feel his eyes staring down at her. She knew if she looked up, her eyes would tell him to forget everything she said about being friends, and handle your business. A question came to her mind that she had to know the answer to. She casually raised her knee and brushed it across his crotch. He was rock hard. *What the hell am I doing? Fuck you Wayne. You moved on with your life. I'm tired of torturing myself. I got a man in my bed that's ready to do whatever, and I'm saving myself for you?*

Liana could feel her breaths getting shorter as she worked her knee in tiny circles on his hardness. *Once you do this, there's no turning back, girl. I'm about moving forward, anyway, fuck turning back.* Liana lifted her head and stared into Rasheem's eyes. Only, his eyes were covered with his eyelids.

"Rasheem." She nudged him. "Rasheem." She nudged him again.

"Umm Hmm, yeah, a couple more minutes, and I'm gonna take y'all to school," He rolled over, giving Liana his back to stare at.

Liana shook her head. So much for the dry season being over.

***

Rasheem moaned as he rolled over onto his back. His head felt like it was under a church bell, and two construction workers with sledgehammers were swinging for broke. He sat up and looked down at his bare legs. *Where's my pants.* He whipped his head around and immediately regretted it. His head stopped spinning but the room didn't. When the room finally stopped, he pulled his briefs open and checked himself. He sighed a breath of relief when he didn't see any vaginal juices on his shaft. He would've cried if they had gotten it on, because he couldn't remember a damn thing after kicking off his shoes and telling her to lie next to him.

He grabbed his pants that was draped over the chair and pulled them on. Once he got his bearings, he shuffled out into the living room.

Liana was sitting with her legs tucked under her thighs, wearing pajama pants and a white tank top. Her hair was pinned up with a wisp of hair hanging down the side of her face. She had her glasses on, pad in hand, and pen cap in her mouth.

"You look like a sexy ass school teacher," Rasheem said, noticing for the first time that his chin was throbbing.

Liana looked up at him, and then dropped her head back to her letter.

"If you were my teacher, I would've failed your class on purpose just so I could take it over and over again."

When Liana still didn't respond, he looked at his watch. It was one o'clock. "Damn! I can't believe I slept so hard and for so long. That liquor really put me out. I'm so embarrassed. Speaking of which, I didn't do anything embarrassing last night, did I?"

"Aside from you scaring the shit out of me when you tried to jump in the shower with me? No, you didn't do anything embarrassing. How's your chin by the way?"

Rasheem held his head down in shame. "I can't believe I played myself like that. You can't hold that against me. You know if I was in my right state of mind—"

"You wouldn't have slipped and banged your chin on the bathroom sink when I screamed and pulled the shower curtain closed?"

"That's why my jaw's sore?"

"Nah, your jaw's sore, because when I was dragging your heavy ass to the bed, you pulled my towel off, and I popped you."

Rasheem desperately searched his mind for the naked moment. *Of all the times to black out.* "I'm never drinking like that again."

"There's some orange juice in the fridge." Liana pointed with her pen, as she focused back on her letter.

Rasheem walked to the fridge and poured himself a glass. He gulped it down and placed the glass in the sink. "I'm out. I know JD's cursing me out for having to hold the store down until I get there." Rasheem read the numerous text messages on his cell. Yeah, JD was cursing him out.

Liana nodded, as she seemed to be doing well with her letter. Rasheem looked down at her, dying to know that sliver of history that she refused to share with him.

"See you Monday," he said, as he headed for the door.

"Definitely."

"And Liana?"

She turned and looked at him.

"Please don't tell JD about this."

"About what?" she smiled.

"Exactly," Rasheem said, closing the door behind himself.

Liana looked at the pad, and was disgusted with her handwriting. That's why she always typed her letters. She thought back to the first letter she had submitted to the Parole Board. Mrs. Watkins said it was good, but asked if she could write it rather than type it. "A typed letter," she said, "is too impersonal." Liana sucked her teeth when she misspelled devastated. Oh how she needed the spell check on her computer right now. She tried to change the i to an a, but it only made things worst. She flung the pad across the room and pulled her glasses off.

Why am I even writing this fucking letter? They should have a copy of the last three I wrote. What are the chances of the Board letting him out, anyway? She thought back to Nana's words. Every time she wrote a letter to the Board, it was like convicting her father all over again, because she knew her letter was a guaranteed twenty-four month hit at the Board for him. Liana thought back to all the mistakes she made in life and how Nana had forgiven her. She thought of all the times she had broken Wayne's heart, and he had forgiven her and had taken her back. *Where would I be if the ones I loved didn't forgive me?*

"It's not even about him," Nana's words echoed in her head. "It's about you moving on." Moving on. Those two words reverberated in her head until something clicked. She finally understood what her grandmother meant by moving on.

She picked up the phone and dialed a number from memory.

"Hello?"

"It's me." She could hear the lawnmower rattling in the background.

"Hold on a minute," Wayne said, as he cut off the lawnmower. "I'm surprised to hear from you."

"I don't want to take up too much of your time, but we really need to talk."

"Okay… talk."

"Face to face." Liana could hear Wayne sigh.

"I don't know, Liana—"

"It's about my father… and Ron and what happened at Sneaky Petes."

"Liana, don't do this to me."

"Please, Wayne. If it wasn't important, I wouldn't be calling you." Liana noticed she was holding her breath, waiting for Wayne to respond.

"When's the next time you coming up to Albany?"

"Well… I was kind of hoping you would come down here."

CHAPTER 14

Wayne took the Hillside Avenue exit like Liana told him, and turned onto Francis Lewis Boulevard. He checked out the landscaping of the properties he drove past, cringing at the sight of uncut lawns, untrimmed hedges, and houses that were yelling "paint me." *I could make a killing out here.* He was so engrossed in the scenery that he almost missed Liana waving from the other side of the street. He pulled over and let her hop in.

"I thought you were going to keep going for a second," she said, breathing a little hard from the brisk walk to the Land Rover.

"I was checking out the neighborhood."

"Yeah, right, you were probably looking at all the un-kept lawns, and thinking about maybe coming down here on the weekends to make some extra money."

"I was not," Wayne said unconvincingly. "There's plenty of work in Albany for me to tend to."

Liana turned around in her seat and looked in the back.

"What are you looking for?" Wayne asked.

"Just making sure you didn't bring your lawnmower."

Wayne busted out laughing. On his way to her place, he decided he was going to keep it as frosty as possible because he knew how fast things could heat up between them, but she always had a way of melting him quicker than a snowflake.

"I'm not always about work, you know? Even though that's what Tammy thinks I'm doing now. If she knew I was down here in the city meeting with you, she would kick my ass, literally." Wayne eased his foot off the brake pedal. "So, where do I go from here?"

"Turn down here," Liana said, pointing.

When they pulled up, Wayne stared at her lawn.

"The owner usually comes by on the weekends to mow it," Liana said, reading his mind.

"Looks like he missed the last three."

"I didn't call you down here for your lawn expertise, Mr. Wayne 'the Lawn Lord' Dupree."

"What *did* you call me all the way down here for, Liana?"

"Can we at least get inside?"

Wayne looked up at her place, and then back to her. Without saying a word, he turned off the ignition and stepped out. He followed her up the steps and inside. He noticed how clean her apartment was. "You must really have something important to talk about, 'cause you straightened up."

"My place is always this clean."

Wayne gave her the remember-who-you-talking-to-look.

"It's almost always this clean," she said, walking toward the fridge. "You want soda or juice?"

"Juice is fine." Wayne sat on the living room couch. He noticed the typed letter to the Parole Board. He lifted his eyes from it when Liana brought the drinks and sat next to him on the couch, at arm's distance.

"Thanks." He grabbed the glass from her. "I see you decided to type it this time," he said looking toward the letter.

"Yeah, fuck Watkins and her handwritten theory bullshit."

Wayne responded to the silence by taking another sip of his juice.

"Wayne…" Liana looked away from him so he wouldn't see the pain accumulating in her eyes. "I know I don't have to, but I just want to thank you for what you did at the club that night."

Wayne waved his hand dismissively. "That's history. Don't put yourself through the pain of bringing it back up."

"I should've told the police what happened."

"And what would they have done? Trust me, his days are numbered."

The look on Wayne's face stopped Liana's next question in her throat. But she had to know the truth in order to move on.

"Wayne," she said, starting to fidget. "I really don't know how to ask you this."

"Just come out and ask it."

"Remember the night when we had that argument?"

"Which night?"

"The night I was at your house and Ron called?"

"What about it?" He turned his glass up to finish his juice.

"Did Ron show up that night looking for me?"

Wayne stopped drinking. Liana stopped breathing.

"What made you want to ask me that?"

"Did he?" Her voice tensed.

"No," he said, turning his gaze away from her. "He didn't come looking for you."

Liana closed her eyes, not wanting to believe that Wayne had just lied to her.

Wayne put his glass down on the coffee table. "He came looking for me."

Liana's head shot back up.

"A half hour after you left, he came banging on my door shouting for me to come outside. When I opened the door, I could smell the liquor on his breath. We argued for a second, and then I slammed the door in his face. That's when he yelled that I should look out the window.

Liana was listening so intently that she didn't realize her mouth was hanging open.

"When I looked outside, he was keying my truck. I ran out and we started tussling."

Liana could see the beads of sweat forming on his forehead as he re-told the story. She imagined them rolling on the ground in the driveway.

"He was too drunk to put up a fight. After I hit him a couple times, he stumbled off to his car and took off."

"Why didn't you ever tell me?"

Wayne's shoulders slumped. "I wanted to tell you about the scuffle we had, but you were already going through a lot. The last thing I wanted to do was add stress to your already stressful life. Then when I found out that Ron was killed that night..."

Liana put her hand on top of his. "I know you didn't kill him. I've known you my whole life; I know you're not a killer."

"I should've been straight up with you."

"What's done is done. *We* need to move on."

"We?" Wayne looked confused. "What do you mean by we?"

Liana picked up the letter from the coffee table and handed it to him to read. "This is the last letter I'm ever writing to the Parole Board."

Wayne took it from her, and began reading it. Every now and then, he would look up at her puzzled. "With a letter like this, you won't have to write another one." Wayne put it down. "Why am I really here, Liana? What are you really trying to do here?"

Liana looked into his eyes, allowing him to look at her soul stripped of the hatred she had for him when she lost their baby, stripped of the seething wrath she had for her father. "Whenever we broke up and we met back up, I knew we were going to get back together."

"And how would you know that?" Wayne asked, as he leaned back on the couch.

"I could tell when I looked into your eyes. You never hid how you felt about me. It's obvious to anyone who knows you."

"What do you see in my eyes, now?" He stared at her.

Liana stared right back. "I see a man who loves me even when I give him every reason to hate me." She touched the side of his face. "I just wanted to say I'm so sorry for taking your love for granted."

Wayne instinctively reached out and caught the first tear that rolled off her cheek. He then quickly backed away from her and stood up. "I have to go."

She nodded, weakly. "Maybe I'll see you around."

Wayne left without saying a word. Tears streamed down his face before he made it to his truck. He bit his bottom lip as he pulled off, fighting his nature to turn around and comfort the only person he'd ever loved with all of his soul. The road was a blur through his waterfall of tears. Twice, he almost turned around, but remembered the promise he made to Tammy—He would never put Liana before her.

He finally understood why Liana wanted to see him face to face. She wanted permission to move on. She had to look into his soul and ask his permission, something she couldn't do over the phone. He wiped his tears with the back of his hand and rummaged through the CDs Taz left in his truck. He popped in *Trey Songs* and found himself mumbling the words. *"Look at what this girl done did to me. She done cut me off from a good, good love. She told me that those days were gone. Now I'm sitting here going half crazy, 'cause I know she still thinks about me too, and there ain't no way in hell that I can be just friends with you…"*

When Wayne left Liana's, she picked up the letter to the Parole Board and ripped it in half. Wayne's expression told her what she needed to know. She printed out the alternative letter

she typed last night, and placed it in an eight by eleven envelope addressed to the Chairman of The Parole Board.

***

Liana worked the register all afternoon. The only time she left
was when she ran across the street to the drug store. JD and his
two assistants were working the floor, making sales left and
right while Rasheem worked in his office taking inventory, and
setting up a meeting with a guy in Buffalo. It seemed as if
Rasheem and Indio were in the makings of opening up a store
there, as well.

Liana peeked in his office every now and then to check on
him. As she walked towards his office, this time, it was to tell
him they were closing up. She stopped short, when she heard
Rasheem yelling at whoever was on the other end of the phone.
She decided to barge in anyway.

"JD and I are closing up."

Rasheem covered the phone and nodded, "Good looking.
I'll be down in a minute. Let me just finish up this call with
Indio."

Rasheem talking to Indio like that?

"Oh, and don't forget our date, tonight," Rasheem said as
an afterthought.

"Date? You're doing my taxes. I hardly call that a date."

"I just wanted to remind you." Rasheem saluted her, and
looked at the door.

Twenty minutes later, Rasheem came down, counted the
money, and put it into the bank deposit bag.

"I'm out," JD said, grabbing his knapsack. "It's Saturday night, just got paid, and the club is jumping. See you in the p.m."

"You mean the a.m.," Rasheem said seriously.

"If the pussy is all that, you won't ever see me again."

"Get out of here," Liana and Rasheem said at the same time.

JD pulled his fitted cap over his head, threw up the peace sign, and headed toward the bus stop.

"He's so stupid," Liana said, as she gathered her stuff.

"You got to love him, though." Rasheem started shutting off the lights.

"Yeah, like a venereal disease."

They both started laughing as they exited the store and headed to Liana's place.

***

"Okay," Rasheem said, hitting the ENTER key on Liana's computer. "This TurboTax program is what's up."

"Business must be good for Indio to be opening a clothing store way up in Buffalo," Liana said, trying to make small talk, as she stood behind Rasheem.

"Yeah, he's definitely selling his old contacts on this franchise thing."

"Old contacts?"

"Everyone you meet in the drug game isn't a drug dealer," Rasheem said matter of factly.

"Umm, hmm."

"You got those who stay just on the rim. You know, wanting to be seen with certain people, wanting to be respected by certain crowds, but never directly involved in anything illegal. So, now that Indio is legit, these *investors* want a little piece of the pie."

"And you're sure that Indio isn't using his stores as fronts for illegal activities?"

"I'm positive."

"And how can you be so sure?"

"Because I wouldn't be working for him if he was." Rasheem turned the chair around to face her. "Let me tell you something. I'm no angel, I'll be the first to admit that. I sold drugs for a long time for Indio, since we were in our teens, but I got out the game. I took my money and I invested it in an education. I obtained my Bachelor's in Business Management from the University of Maryland. My first job was at a rinky-dink sneaker store in Maryland. As General Manager, I tripled its sales in six months. Six months later, I had athletes, urban authors, rappers, and anybody who was somebody coming through. Indio peeped my skills and decided to invest into a clothing store that was going out of business and have me run it. And here we are three years later with two stores up and running, and about to open a third."

"Wow." Was all Liana was able to say.

"Indio knows that if he sold so much as a bag of weed out of any of these stores, or if I even suspected that he was using them for something illegal, I would be out. There's too much legit money out here to worry about some petty drug money that's not worth the headaches."

"I had no idea, Rasheem. I mean, I know you're good with numbers and running the business and all, but a Bachelor's?"

"I don't talk about it much, because… well, because nobody's really interested."

"I'm interested."

Rasheem blinked. *Is it me, or did her voice take on a sexy tone?*

"Maybe one day, we can sit down, and you can tell me some more things about you that I don't know."

Rasheem turned the chair back around to face the computer screen. "The feeling's mutual."

"Before you get back into accountant mode, I need you to step out of my room for a minute."

"What I do?"

"You didn't do anything. I just can't stand wearing street clothes in the house. I feel like I'm suffocating, and I have to get out of these clothes, like, right now."

"Oookay, I'll be in the living room."

"Don't look at me like that. I'm not crazy." Liana pushed him out of the room.

"I didn't say you were. And don't touch the computer—"

Liana shut the door and stepped out of her clothes. She put on a tank top and a pair of sweatpants. "God, this feels so good."

Rasheem heard her from the living room and arched his brow. *Maybe I should get comfortable.* He unbuttoned his shirt, but stopped. He didn't want Liana thinking he was trying to pull a fast one on her.

"Something popped up on the screen," she said through her bedroom door.

"Don't touch anything."

"I'm not. You can come back in, now." Liana opened the door.

Rasheem walked in and almost stumbled over his tongue. "Damn, girl. You trying to test a brother's will power?"

"Shut up and finish doing what you got to do so you can leave."

Rasheem walked toward the computer while his eyes walked up her body. He didn't even try to hide the fact that he was imagining her without her sweats or tank top on.

Liana put her hands on her hips. "Will you hurry up? I don't have all night for you to be messing around. I'm trying to go to bed."

Rasheem sat down and focused on the computer screen. "Okay here we go."

Liana stood behind him, looking at the screen.

"All you got to do is key in the numbers that each line asks for and then boom."

"Boom?" Liana mimicked.

"Boom." Rasheem winked.

"Let me see," Liana said, leaning down to enter her personal information. Her cheek was so close to Rasheem's that she could feel the razor stubble on it. Rasheem sat stiller than a statue. He figured if he moved, she would move back a little, and he didn't want that.

Rasheem was inhaling her so deep through his nostrils that he could smell the Tommy Bahama perfume Liana had put on early this morning. With each inhalation, he savored her fragrance, swishing it around his frontal lobe until his eyelids dropped half-mast.

"You're right," Liana said. "Boom! That easy." She turned to look at him and was pulled into the gravitational pull of his eyes. Her eyes automatically closed when his lips touched down on hers. His lips were soft. He gently touched them against hers and traced her lips with his tongue over and over, as if he was executing some kind of secret code to gain entry.

Liana parted her lips, and allowed him to taste her tongue. Without losing contact, she straddled him.

Rasheem palmed her butt as she dry humped him. Liana's aggressiveness brought out the beast in him as he broke the lip lock and started sucking on her neck.

"Umm, yes," Liana moaned, unsnapping her bra from the back.

As the last snap came loose, Rasheem removed her tank top and bra in one motion. His erection started to throb when he felt her nipple stiffen in his mouth.

Liana stood up and grabbed him by the waist of his pants. Rasheem stood and followed her toward the bed. Those ten steps felt like ten miles. It seemed as if everything slowed to a snail's crawl. He stared at her seductive, swaying hips, and then dropped his eyes to her jiggling booty.

When they got to the bed, Liana pushed him down onto it. That's when everything sped up. They were both naked, Liana straddled him, whispered in his ear what she was going to do to him.

"Fuck!" Rasheem shouted as he stopped Liana from grinding on his thigh.

"What's wrong, baby?"

"I don't have any condoms."

"Humph, just like a man," Liana scoffed, as she got off the bed and reached for her purse. "Never prepared." Liana crawled back onto the bed and kissed him. "Now handle your business before I change my mind." Her words came out in a whisper, but Rasheem could taste the lust on them.

He ripped the condom pack open and rolled it on, as Liana rolled onto her back and opened herself up to him. Rasheem crawled in between her legs and sucked on her nipples again, working his way up to her neck, and then to her mouth.

"You don't know how long I've waited for this," he whispered in her ear. "I'm going to make this a night you'll never forget. Umm, the things I'm going to do to you is going to—"

Liana put her finger to his lips. "If I would've known you were this talkative, I would've bought some duct tape while I was at the drug store."

Liana's forwardness was an aphrodisiac to Rasheem. He kissed her, while putting her right leg on his shoulder. When the tip of his penis brushed against her clit, Liana's heart fluttered. Her body tensed as flutters started in her stomach.

Her legs seemed to have a mind of their own as they tried to clamp themselves shut.

"You okay?" Rasheem asked, panting.

"I'm fine," Liana said in a shaky voice.

"Relax, baby. I got you." Rasheem kissed her gently on the lips.

Liana closed her eyes and tried to relax as Rasheem tried to push himself in, but just like that, she was drier than a desert.

"Damn, girl, you were soaking wet a minute ago," Rasheem said, straining to work his way in.

"I can't," Liana heard herself say.

"Huh?" Rasheem said confused.

When Liana opened her eyes, Vince was staring at her. Too shocked to move, she tensed as he licked his fingers and then began playing with her opening. "Stop acting like you don't want it bitch."

"No!" Liana screamed, striking Rasheem's chest and neck.

"Liana… what… the… fuck." He jumped off the bed and stumbled back into the couch against the bedroom wall. "What the fuck is wrong with you?"

Liana brought her knees up to her chest and was shivering. "I'm so sorry, Rasheem." She rocked back and forth. "I don't know—"

"You don't have to explain. I've been through this before, remember? I used to go out with a girl who was raped."

"Rasheem—"

"I kind of knew that's what that letter to the Parole Board was about."

Liana was too exhausted to convince him that he had it all wrong. Saliva began to pool in her mouth as Vince's devilish grin crept back into her mind. She hopped off the bed, walked quickly to the bathroom, and threw up. She got on her knees and held on to the rim of the toilet as she vomited again, and again.

Embarrassment and rage filled her heart as she emptied her guts. *I can't get this motherfucker out of my head.* Then she began to cry. *Is this how it's going to be every time I'm with a man? God, please don't do this to me.*

Liana got to her feet, still feeling faint, and washed up. She grabbed her robe and put it on before walking out of the bathroom. When Rasheem saw her, he jumped to his feet. Liana looked down at the rubber that was hanging onto his deflated manhood, and had to laugh.

"Oh, you think this is funny?" Rasheem asked, starting to laugh along with her.

Liana stared at the scratches on his chest and neck. "Rasheem, please forgive me."

He walked up to her and gently kissed her on the lips. "No matter how long it takes, we're going to work through this. You are definitely worth the wait."

Liana hugged him and felt him stiffening against her.

"I have to go." He started getting dressed.

"You can stay the night if you want."

"Nah, I need to get my shit off." He stopped fumbling with his shoes. "That didn't come out right." It wasn't supposed to come out at all. He was so focused on getting to Marissa's, his sons's mama, so she could finish off what Liana started that he just blurted it out.

"Do what you got to do," Liana said, trying to hide her hurt.

"What I meant was—"

"Don't." Liana cut him off. "I'm a big girl; you don't have to lie to me."

Rasheem didn't look at her the whole time he got dressed. He finally looked at her when she walked him to the front door.

"I was serious about what I said earlier. No matter how long it takes…"

"See you Monday." Liana closed the door behind him and plodded back to her room where she fell onto the bed and stared at the ceiling. She needed to call somebody and talk about what just happened. It was some scary shit and she wanted to know if there was something wrong with her. Did Vince's attack damage her worse than she thought? After all, he didn't actually penetrate her. So, why did her body react the way it did? And the sudden dryness. She rolled over, picked up the phone, and dialed.

"Hello?" the groggy voice on the other side said.

Liana hung up.

"Hello?" the groggy voice said again.

"Who's that?" Wayne said, blinking the sleep out of his eyes.

Tammy laid her head back on his chest. "Whoever it was hung up."

Liana laid her head on her pillow. Everyone was happy: Jenna, Reese, Elizabeth, Wayne, everyone, but her.

"God, what did I do that was so unforgivable?"

CHAPTER 15

Wayne moaned when the alarm clock went off again. He thought about pressing the snooze button, but he already did that a few times. He slid his hand over to Tammy's side of the bed and felt nothing but wrinkled sheets. She had already left for work. He opened one eye to peek at the alarm clock, thinking it had to be about seven-fifteen. When he saw eight-thirty on the face of the clock, he jumped up.

"Shit!" He stuck one of his legs into a pant leg, while hopping to the bathroom to brush his teeth. He hopped back into the bedroom while he slipped his other leg in his jeans. He snatched his cell phone off the nightstand, checking to see how many times his father must have called. *How could I not hear the phone?* To his surprise, his father didn't call at all. He sat at the foot of the bed putting on his socks and boots, bracing himself for the curse out he was going to get when he went to pick up his father for work.

He started the truck up, and then ran across the street to his parents's house. He cocked his head when he turned the knob and realized the door was locked. He rang the doorbell. No answer. He looked at his watch and then knocked. His sister answered the door with an attitude. She rolled her eyes at him and walked away.

"What's wrong with you?" Wayne asked as he stepped in.

"Go ask you mother."

Wayne rushed toward the kitchen, putting two and two together. His father didn't call him this morning because he was locked up. He prepared himself to comfort his mother, and tell her that everything was going to be okay. No preparation in the world could remove the shocked look on his face when he walked into the kitchen.

"Ma!"

His mother looked at him, and immediately put her hand on her cheek to try and hide the hand print. "It's nothing. We had an argument," she said with a sad smile.

"It's nothing?" Wayne moved her hand away from her cheek. "Where is he?"

"He left last night, to cool off."

"To cool off?"

"I'm out, Ma," Alisa said, heading toward the front door. She had on a skin-tight, mini dress that was so short her panties were peeking out.

Wayne's face turned red. "Where do you think you're going dressed like that?"

"You want to be my daddy, too? Go fuck yourself."

"What the f—" Wayne grabbed her by the arm. "Who the fuck you think you talking to?" That's when he saw the red marks on her neck that she was trying to hide with a silk scarf.

"Get off me" Alisa broke free of him. "I'm tired of people telling me how to live my life. Motherfuckers want to run the streets and do whatever the fuck they want, then go to jail, and then want to come home and tell everybody what they should and shouldn't be doing? I'm tired of the 'do as I say and not as I do' bullshit."

"You calling Dad a motherfucker?" Wayne barked.

"Dad is a hypocritical, jail bird, loser-of-a-father mother-fucker!"

"You ungrateful little—" Wayne shoved her against the living room wall. Alisa bounced off swinging.

Julie got in the middle of them. "Go!" She said to Alisa. "Get out of here!"

Heaving, Alisa picked up her purse and left.

"You're just going to let her leave like that?" Wayne huffed.

"She's not a little girl anymore. You and your father have to get that through your thick-ass heads. She's eighteen."

"She just turned eighteen."

"It doesn't matter. Fact is, your father hasn't been able to stay out of jail long enough to celebrate one of her birthdays. She turned eighteen last week, and he didn't even know it."

Wayne looked at the mark on his mother's face, and Alisa became the last thing on his mind. "What happened last night?"

"Alisa came stumbling in here at twelve o'clock, drunk, and your father lost it. Alisa didn't start going off until your father tried to ground her for the rest of the summer. That was it. She started ranting about how she was eighteen years old. Your father squinted at her and had the nerve to ask her since when? Then your sister stumbled off mumbling about he should try and stay out of jail long enough to remember when her birthday was. That's when I ran into the dining room, because I knew your father was going to try and kill her. As soon as I ran in there, your father already had his hands around her neck, choking the life out of her."

His mother's eyes began to tear up.

"I pried your father's hands from around her neck, and we started arguing. He told me it was my fault that she didn't respect him, then he called me a poor excuse for a mother. That's when I smacked him. And Nevel, being the man he is, smacked me back," Julie cracked a smile, but she was far from happy.

Wayne held his head. "And you have no idea where he is?"

"Probably lying up with one of his women."

Wayne couldn't take it anymore. "Why do you stay with him? I mean, I can understand sticking it out when Alisa and I were young, but we're grown." Wayne raked his hands through his hair. "I mean, damn, Ma, he goes back and forth to jail, and for the little time that he's free, he doesn't treat you right."

His mother's words came out in a whisper. "He's my husband, baby, and I love him."

"You love him?"

"He's trying, Wayne. He's been out for a whole year now, and he hasn't picked up a gun or a package of drugs."

"So you just ignore that he almost strangled Alisa to death and smacked you?"

His mother caressed the side of his cheek. "When you love someone, you have to take the bitter with the sweet. No one's perfect."

Wayne looked at the bruise on his mother's cheek. "Are you going to be all right?"

"Of course I am." His mother turned around and walked back in the kitchen where she went back to cutting up her vegetables.

Wayne kissed her on the cheek. "I'll call you later. If I come across Dad, I'll let you know."

"Okay, baby."

Wayne climbed into his truck and sighed when his cell phone rang. He glanced at the caller ID to see if it was his father. It was Taz. "What up," Wayne answered.

"It's going down like a motherfucker, son."

"What's going down?"

"The Feds caught up with Dexter in Texas, and that motherfucker is dropping dimes like a slot machine."

"Oh yeah?"

"Oh hell motherfucking, yeah. You better call wifey up and tell her to get her ass back up here to Albany."

"I already told you once. Stop calling Liana my wifey."

"Call her what you want, but call her now."

"Why?"

"Elizabeth's in jail."

***

Liana jumped out of her sleep when her phone rang, causing Rasheem to wake up as well. On his way to Marissa's last night, he felt guilty for the way he left Liana's. He stopped at his house, grabbed a bottle of Dom Perignon, and headed back to her place. Liana was more than happy to see him, because she was about to call Wayne's house again and make a fool of herself. They each drank a glass and fell asleep in each other's arms.

"Hello?" Liana answered, still feeling the Don.

"I got some bad news for you," Wayne said.

Liana was so happy to hear his voice that she felt herself starting to smile. Her smile quickly turned to an oh-shit face when he told her about Elizabeth. "I'm on my way," she said, staring a hole in the back of Rasheem's head.

When she slammed the phone down, Rasheem turned to face her. "Everything okay?"

"No, you lying son of a bitch." Liana picked up the whole phone and threw it at him.

Rasheem dodged it and leaped out of the bed. "Whoa, what the fuck is going on?"

"What the fuck is going on? You want to know what the fuck is going on? My friend is in jail, because of you and your snake-ass cousin."

"What?"

"Get out of my fucking house!" Liana shoved him out of the room.

"Liana you need to calm down, and tell me what's going on; tell me what happened?"

"I trusted you that's what happened. Elizabeth trusted Indio that's what happened. The police arrested her last night. They got a tip that she was transporting drugs from Queens to

Albany. They found two kilos of coke in the trunk of her car rental."

Rasheem was stunned. So stunned that Liana actually started to believe he had no idea what she was talking about.

"That motherfucker." He brushed past her and grabbed his cell phone. "I can't believe this motherfucker." He dialed Indio's home number. When he didn't get an answer, he dialed Indio's cell. When he didn't get an answer he started putting on his shoes.

"Where are you going?" Liana asked.

Rasheem grabbed his jacket and headed for the front door.

"Where are you going?" Liana asked again, snatching him by the arm.

"He better pray that the police arrested his ass, because if they didn't, I'm going to kill him."

***

Liana pulled up to Nana's at seven-thirty that night. Wayne's truck was parked outside. Jenna and Reese met her at the front door with red eyes and hugs.

"I knew that bastard was no good," Reese said, wiping her runny nose with tissue.

"What's going on with Elizabeth?" Liana asked.

"They're not telling us much of anything, right now," Jenna said. "You know Nana went down there and turned the precinct out, but they're not giving up a lot of information."

Liana followed them into the living room. She immediately spotted Wayne sitting on the sofa with Taz. When he nodded at her, she almost ran into his arms. Nana was sitting in the loveseat, looking a wreck. When she saw Liana, she stood up and walked toward her. Liana met her half way and hugged her.

"We're going to get through this," Nana said, as she held her tight.

"Nobody knows exactly what happened?" Liana asked everyone in the room.

"Dexter's talking like a motherfucker, I mean…" Taz winced, forgetting he was in Nana's house. "He got caught in Texas, trying to sell a key of coke to an undercover, so now he's trying to shave some time off his sentence by telling on every and anything."

"I can't believe this." Liana sat down, holding her head.

"I told y'all that nig… I mean Indio was still in the game, but y'all didn't want to believe me," Taz said animated.

"All of that is irrelevant, right now," Wayne said, rubbing his temples. He turned his gaze to Liana. "What's up with his cousin? You going out with him, right?"

"No! I'm not going out with him." Liana gave him a sour look.

"Is he still around?" Wayne asked.

"I don't know! And I don't care," Liana said, getting defensive.

"What you getting all upset for?" Wayne said accusingly.

"Fuck you, Wayne."

"That's enough," Nana said. "If this is telling, like Jamal's saying, then the police will know that Elizabeth was just a pawn in this thing and let her go."

"It's not that simple, Nana," Wayne said. "How do you prove to the police that she didn't know that stuff was in her trunk?"

"Dang," Nana said, shaking her head.

"What is it?" Liana asked.

"Preston retired just last year."

"Who's that?" Liana asked.

"Y'all don't remember Officer Preston?" Nana said to all of them.

Everyone in the room shook their head.

"If he was still on the Force, I could've talked to him. I know he could've pulled some strings and called in some favors. All you got to do is get one of them on your side, and the rest will do whatever he says."

Taz's jaw dropped as he looked at Wayne.

"Hell... no," Wayne said, reading Taz's mind.

"What." Liana saw the exchange between them.

"Wayne knows somebody on the Force," Taz shouted.

"Who?" Reese and Jenna asked at the same time.

"Harris," Taz blurted out.

"Thee Harris?" Reese said in shock. "The soon-to-be chief of police, Harris?"

"I don't know him," Wayne said, trying to hold his composure.

"You knew him well enough to get me out of jail."

"You need to talk to him, Wayne," Jenna said, grabbing him by the arm. "Anything is better than what we have now."

"I don't know the man like that. Besides, he's homicide, so he's not going to be interested in a drug case."

"Make him interested," Nana said, walking over to Wayne and pointing her finger in his face.

"Y'all are bugging," Wayne said. "We should be trying to get her a lawyer."

"And we are, but let's first work on convincing Harris that Elizabeth didn't have anything to do with these drugs," Reese said.

"You acting like me and this dude go way back."

"Y'all do," Taz said, snickering, "If you want to count all the years you've been cutting his mother's grass."

"You know his moms?" Reese asked surprised.

"She loves Wayne," Taz said communicating his double meaning to Wayne with a crooked smile.

"You got a lot of shit with you," Wayne said, clenching his fist at Taz.

"All I'm saying is it won't hurt for you to talk to him, and see if he can convince his boys that Elizabeth is insignificant in the whole scheme of things," Taz said.

Wayne just shook his head.

"If it'll make you feel any better, I'll go with you," Liana said.

"I don't need you going with me." Wayne stood up. "I'm out of here."

Liana jumped up and stood in front of him. "So, are you going to talk to him or not?"

"Yeah… I'm going to see what I can do."

***

When Wayne entered the precinct, he tried walking straight toward Harris's office, but the desk officer stopped him.

"Hey! Where do you think you're going?"

"To see Detective Harris."

"You just don't waltz in here and look for someone without coming through me." The officer stared at him for a moment, recognizing Wayne from the last time he was there. "Have a seat," he said pointing to the chairs, "I'll check and see if he's in."

Wayne walked over by the seats, but didn't sit.

The officer picked up the phone and dialed Harris's extension. "I got one of yours out here to see you."

"What's that supposed to mean?" Wayne said, walking toward the desk. He wasn't going to let the pudgy officer disrespect him today with that *confidential informant* bullshit.

It looked like it took the entire officer's strength just to stand up out of his chair and point his finger. "Hey! Cool it before it gets real ugly in here."

"I ain't nobody's snitch, rat, informant, or whatever other nicknames y'all got for them."

"Boy—"

"Boy? What, we back in the slavery days now?" Wayne said, refusing to back down.

"That's it," the officer said, sounding out of breath. "I'm arresting your ass."

"For what?"

"I'll make something up later. Put your hands against the wall."

"What? Hell no," Wayne said, going into a semi-fight stance.

The officer's face turned beet red at Wayne's defiance. "Why... you little—"

"Ed!" Detective Harris called the pudgy officer's name. Harris was sticking his head out of his office. He waved for Wayne to come down.

Wayne walked past the pudgy officer, not bothering to return the lethal stare pudgy was shooting at him.

"You're starting to make these visits a habit," Harris said, as Wayne walked in and closed the door. "I didn't know Nevel was your father."

The statement threw Wayne off. Before he could get a chance to say anything, Harris continued.

"We go way back, your father and me."

"Best friends, huh?" Wayne said sarcastically.

"Oh yeah, we're real close. Like Cowboys and Indians. Is that why you're here? He got himself into some trouble, again?"

"No, actually he's doing fine. Been crime-free a whole year now."

"Humph, so you *can* teach an old dog new tricks."

"I'm here for a serious matter, though." Wayne got back to the reason why he came, because he could feel himself getting upset. His father had a bad track record, but bad or not, he wasn't going to let anyone disrespect him.

"So, what's up? And keep in mind, I was on my way out."

"A friend of mine was arrested; I believe for drug trafficking."

Harris shrugged.

"She's innocent. She didn't even know the drugs were in the trunk of her car."

"Last summer, your ex's fiancé was murdered at a stoplight. Who did it?"

Wayne scrunched up his face. "What does that have to do with what I'm talking about?"

Harris ignored him. "A few months later, there was a shooting outside a club. A man used a defenseless woman as a shield. Who did that?"

Wayne shook his head.

"In Arbor Hill, also last summer, a fifteen year old was shot in the head, twice. Tell me Wayne, who was behind that?"

"You got the wrong guy," Wayne said.

"That's my point. *You* got the wrong guy. I don't care about drugs and who gets arrested for them. Homicide, Wayne. Murder. Attempted murder. That's what I do. Those three cases I just mentioned are still open, and I have no suspects."

"So what you're saying is if I can get you some leads on those cases, you'll see what you can do for my friend?"

Harris nodded.

"How am I supposed to find out that kind of information?"

"I'm sure between Taz and your father's ties to the streets you can make *all* these open cases sitting on my desk disappear, but I'm only asking for these three."

Wayne wanted to reach over the desk and smack the smug smile right off of Harris's face. Instead, he took the safer route and stood up to leave.

"If you change your mind, let me know," Harris said, as Wayne reached for the knob. "Your friend wouldn't happen to be Elizabeth Romain would it?" He knew the answer when Wayne's whole body stiffened. "Oooo, weee," Harris belted out. "She's the talk of the station. The Queens-to-Albany coke shuttle. That was an eight-month investigation headed by the District Attorney herself. You may as well put a fork in her, 'cause she's done."

Wayne turned the knob, not bothering to respond to Harris's bait.

"And, Wayne, I no longer need your landscaping services."

Wayne's face turned redder than the pudgy cop's did earlier.

"And my mother won't be needing your services, either."

Oh, hell no. Wayne turned to face him. "She has to tell me that herself."

"Oh, she will, when she finds out that you have a convicted felon working for you."

Wayne turned back around and opened the door to leave.

"You know how to reach me if you come across any info."

So this is how they turned people into confidential inform-ants? I don't know who's worst, the cops or the criminals. Wayne walked to his truck and hopped in. The heat rising from his body told Liana that things didn't go too well.

"So, what did he say?" she asked.

Wayne started his truck and pulled off.

"So, you're not going to tell me what happened?"

"That's why I didn't want you to come with me." Wayne felt a tension headache coming on. "Just don't say anything. I'm taking you back to Nana's, and then I'm going home." He took a deep breath. "Just tell Nana and the rest of the gang that nothing's happening with Harris."

Liana crossed her legs and put her hands on her lap. "Thank you for trying."

Her voice was so low and pained that Wayne decided not to tell her about the eight-month investigation, or that Elizabeth was the talk of the precinct.

Wayne pulled up to Nana's and Liana got out without look-ing at him.

"Hey," he called out to her, as she was about to close the door. "I'm sorry about snapping at you."

She looked at him for a moment and then closed the door.

Wayne pulled off as fast as he could. He had to put distance between him and Liana's pain.

***

Wayne pulled up to his house a little after dusk. Nevel was sitting on Wayne's porch reading the paper. Wayne flashed back to the marks on his mother's face and around Alisa's neck. "Something wrong with your porch?"

"You want to fuck with me, too?" His father looked up from the paper.

"What were you thinking when you put your hands on Mom and Alisa? You talk all that Muslim stuff, about the importance of family and patience and gratitude then you turn around and do that?"

"And now you want to judge me?" Nevel closed the paper.

"We're judged every day."

"No, we're only judged when we do something wrong. Nobody's congratulating me for being home for more than a year, nobody's noticing how I'm not moving weight or puffing trees—"

"Welcome to the real world, Dad. No one's going to praise you for doing what you're supposed to be doing."

"Yeah? Well, if that's the case, it should work both ways. People shouldn't be coming down on me when I fuck up."

"Not for nothing, Dad, Alisa isn't a little girl anymore, and I don't know if you realize it or not, but she has a lot of resentment toward you."

"Yeah, I know she does; but that doesn't give her the right to disrespect me."

"Look beyond the disrespect and you'll see why she rebels against you every chance she gets."

"Rebels?"

"I bet you if you complimented her instead of 'judging' her, she would start to respect what you have to say."

"I'm her father. I shouldn't have to compliment her in order for her to respect me."

"Dad, just listen, please. Just because you took part in the baby making process doesn't make you a father. A child needs more than just a sperm donor."

Nevel flipped his hand, dismissing him. "I'm not trying to hear that bullshit."

"Dad, you haven't been here for her or for me. You watched us grow up through pictures and prison visits. You come home, swearing to us that you'll never leave us again, and two months later, mom's telling us that you won't be coming home for awhile." Wayne saw the lines in his father's face soften. "I recognize the change in you, and I know that you're trying your best to do the right thing. I know it's not easy knowing that you can make a phone call and make more money in one minute than you do mowing lawns with me in a week."

His father nodded.

"And you were the last person on earth I thought would become Muslim."

"That's the same thing people said about Malcolm X."

There was a moment of silence between them.

"Did you talk to mom, yet?"

"Nah, your mother and I need some space between us, right now."

"Some space?"

"Yeah, some space. You know, time away from each other like you and Liana do from time to time."

"Liana and I are history."

"Again?"

"It's for real, this time."

Nevel unfolded his paper, and turned to the sports section. "You know what song you two remind me of?"

"Here we go," Wayne said, putting his head down.

"It's before your time, but it's a classic so you probably heard it before. It's by the Stylistics." Nevel cleared his throat and started singing. "Break up to make up, that's all... we do... first you love me, then you hate me, that's a game for fools. Break up to make up..."

"I'm out." Wayne left his father to finish reading his paper and singing his song.

***

Liana sat at Nana's kitchen table eating her chocolate ice cream straight out the box when her cell phone rang. She looked at the caller ID and debated on whether or not to answer it. When Rasheem hung up and called right back, she answered.

"What do you want?"

"Indio lied to me, Liana," Rasheem said. "Believe me when I tell you, I had no idea he was still in the game."

"Umm, hmm." Liana slurped on a spoonful of ice cream.

"The cops picked Indio up this morning. They called me down to the precinct and the DA asked me a few questions then they let me go." Rasheem sucked his teeth. "He really fucked shit up. The DA closed down the stores, and froze all the business accounts."

"Humph, that's all you care about? What about Elizabeth who's sitting in jail because of your grimy ass cousin?"

"That's the reason why I'm calling. The charges they're filing against Indio are serious."

"How serious?"

"Twenty to life serious. And I know Elizabeth had no knowledge of what Indio was doing. My lawyer said the DA down here was working with the DA up there on this investigation for about eight months. They have wiretaps and all kinds of shit. They got phone conversations with Indio and a dude in Albany named Shatiq Miller."

Fat Sha, Liana thought.

"He would call Indio and tell him what he needed, and Indio would send it, via Elizabeth's car rental. Then Maurice, the dude that's in charge of cleaning out the cars when they're returned to Hertz, would retrieve the package and deliver it to Shatiq. And from what my lawyer is saying, Maurice is trying to cut a deal, too."

"If they know all of this, why are they still holding, Elizabeth?"

"I don't know, but she may need a lawyer, and a good one. I'm just trying to right a wrong here. I got some money tucked away that I want to bring to you to assist in retaining a lawyer for her."

"How soon can you get up here?" Liana asked.

"Tomorrow evening."

"I'll be waiting."

***

The next morning Wayne was parked in front of Mrs. Levinson's house, taking deep breaths. She left seven messages on his cell, telling him it was urgent he come by; they needed to talk. He tried getting her on the phone, but she wouldn't answer. Which told him whatever she had to tell him she wanted to say it to him face to face.

I have to be professional about this. Don't get upset, be understanding. She may try to run some bullshit about me not being honest with her, and that I should've let her know that my father is a convicted felon. The important thing is I can't lose my cool. I don't want her trying to poison my other clients.

He got out of his truck and headed for the front door. As he stepped onto the porch, Mrs. Levinson opened the door.

"I was wondering when you were going to get out of your truck and make your way up here. Come in." She stepped to the side for him to step in. "Have a seat," she said, pointing to one of the dining room chairs.

Wayne sat down and twiddled his thumbs.

Mrs. Levinson sat down, and placed her hand on his twiddling thumbs. "My son called yesterday and told me he didn't feel comfortable with you doing my lawn, because your father, who works with you, has been to jail a couple times."

"Mrs. Levinson—"

She put her finger to his lips. "Your father is a hard working man, and although a lot of people would hold his past against him, I don't. I trust *you,* and I know that you wouldn't put me in any kind of danger."

Wayne was freaking out on the inside, because Mrs. Levinson still had her finger on his lips.

"And how many times do I have to tell you to call me Carol?" She removed her finger.

"I really appreciate you giving me the benefit of the doubt... Carol. I would love to continue doing business with you, but I don't want your son making it his business to make things hard for me."

"Please, if he gives you any trouble, you let me know. I'll straighten his behind right the fuck out, excuse my French," she said putting the same finger she had on his lips to hers.

Carol had on a baby blue Polo shirt and the way her hard nipples were stretching the fabric, it was obvious she wasn't wearing a bra. Wayne looked away a second too late. She caught him staring and smiled.

"Uh... Carol, I don't want to overstep my bounds, but I need to ask you for a favor."

"Anything for you, honey."

Wayne felt his breakfast coming up. He swallowed hard, trying to keep it down. "I have this friend who got arrested a couple days ago, and she had nothing to do with what the police arrested her for."

"What did they arrest her for?"

"Her boyfriend, unbeknown to her, has been smuggling drugs to Albany in the trunk of her car."

"That's terrible," Carol said, putting her hand on Wayne's.

"She really had no idea what this guy was doing. She has so much going for her, and I would hate to see her go to jail for this grimy dude. It would just destroy her career."

"So, you need me to talk to Marcus and get her off the hook?"

"Can you do that? I mean just get her off the hook?"

Carol leaned closer to him and whispered. "I can do lots of things."

Wayne smiled and leaned back, trying not to make his nausea look too obvious.

"What's her name, baby?"

"Elizabeth, Elizabeth Romain."

"Pretty, light-skinned, valedictorian Elizabeth Romain?"

Wayne forgot Mrs. Levinson was a teacher at Albany High, like, forever. "Yeah, that's her."

"Oh my God. How did she get involved with someone like that?"

"Like I said, she had no idea. If she did, she wouldn't have messed with him."

"Don't you worry. I'm going to get Marcus on the phone and find out what's going on."

"Thank you, Carol. I really appreciate anything you can do to help."

"Not a problem."

"I have to get to work," he said standing up, and heading toward the front door.

"It seems like you owe me a favor, huh?" Carol said, behind his back.

"If there's anything I can do for you—"

"Oh, I'm quite sure I'll figure something out."

Wayne could see her reflection in the glass of the front door window. She was biting her lower lip, as she stared at his butt. He headed out the front door and hopped in his truck, feeling like he just got violated. A shiver shot up his spine when the thought of him in bed with Grandma Dynamite flashed across his mind.

***

That afternoon, Wayne was at the Johnson's house mowing the lawn, while his father was trimming the hedges in the back when he saw Taz sitting on the hood of his truck. He cut off the lawnmower.

"What's up?"

"I'm chilling," Taz said, hopping off the hood.

"No," Wayne said, "I mean how do you always know where to find me?"

"You're not hard to find. Just follow the sound of lawnmowers, and the scent of fresh cut grass, and there you will find... Look up in the sky! It's a bird... It's a plane... No it's... Lawnmower man. Dat, dah, dah, daahhh."

"You got jokes, huh?"

"Just figured I come by and give you the inside scoop."

"The inside scoop?"

"Yeah, the inside scoop from my homies in Albany County jail. Dexter's giving everybody up, son. The DA is adding attempted murder to Indio's indictment."

"What!" Wayne said.

"Dex is saying that Indio was one of the guys shooting at him and Reese that night in front of the club."

Wayne looked confused. "Why would Indio want to get at Dex?"

"Use your head for something other than cutting grass. Remember when Nana had that cookout/baby shower for Jenna, and Indio was kicking it with Dexter about opening up his own business? Well, Indio gave him a jump-start with a kilo of coke, but Dex fucked it up. You can fill in the rest."

"And you just used your head to figure all that out?"

"Nah, Dexter's little man, Shorts, put me on."

"So, there were two guys shooting at them." Wayne cocked his head. "So, the other one had to be his cousin, what's his name?"

"Of course, it was. I already told you how he was getting down in Maryland."

"No, Taz, you didn't."

"Yes, I did. That night when I was released from jail over that Vince situation and we were… pardon me, and I was putting some purple haze in my system."

"No, you didn't. You started to then you changed the subject."

"I didn't?"

"What's up with Indio's cousin?"

"The dude did some time in Maryland. He was running a business, kind of like what Indio was doing up here. Dudes said he ran up in one of his competitor's crib and sprayed him right there on his sofa while dude's wife and kids were in the other room."

Wayne reached into his overalls and pulled out his cell phone.

"Who you calling?" Taz asked.

"Liana," Wayne said into his phone. "I'm going to swing by later on tonight. I have to talk to you about something."

"What's it about?"

"I'll tell you when I get there."

"Yeah, Wayne. Whatever."

***

That night, Rasheem pulled up to the curb of Nana's house at ten o'clock. Liana was leaning on the front yard fence. She pushed away from it and headed up to the porch, assuming Rasheem would follow. When she didn't hear him get out of his car, she turned around. Her stare of confusion made him step out. She waved for him to come on, and come inside. He walked to the porch, but he didn't follow her when she stepped through the front door.

"What's wrong?" she asked, looking back at him.

Rasheem looked at his watch. "I don't have much time. I just came by to say what I have to say and then I have to go."

Liana blinked, trying to understand the nervousness in his voice. "Can't you come inside and tell me what you got to say?"

Rasheem slowly walked up to her until there was nothing between them but air. "I just want you to know that I'm really sorry Liana... I really had no idea—"

"I believe you, Rasheem. Don't ask me why, I just do." Rasheem surprised her when he tilted her head up and kissed her. She felt the pain that his words couldn't convey. She stood on her tiptoes, put her hands around his neck, and let him know she understood.

Rasheem gently broke the connection and opened his eyes. He swept away the strands of hair that the night breeze had blown across her face. The way the moonlight blended with her dark complexion had him at a loss for words. The trance was broken when they both heard the roar of an engine speeding down the block. Wayne's truck hadn't even come to a full stop, and he had already opened the door and was stepping out.

"Let me guess," Rasheem said. "That's Wayne."

"Wait here." Liana walked down the porch steps and met Wayne at the curb.

"What's up?" She said when she got into talking distance.

"Did you know that Indio's also being charged with attempted murder?" Liana looked back at Rasheem. "Dexter is saying that Indio was one of the individuals who shot at him and Reese that night in front of the club."

Liana's head snapped back around to Wayne.

"Yeah, and word is your man over there was the other shooter."

"Wha…what? Wait, wait. Reese said they had on masks. It all happened so fast. Indio knows Reese why would he… Why would Rasheem—"

"Because that's how they get down. When it comes to that drug money, they don't care who gets in the way."

Liana shook her head. "But they came to the hospital—"

"This dude has you so open that you don't want to believe he shot Reese."

"You know what, Wayne? You better slow down. You're making a whole lot of accusations. Where did you get this information from anyway?"

"Taz."

"Taz? You need to stop treating everything that Taz says as the gospel. Dexter got caught with a kilo of coke in Texas, so it's obvious he's trying to give up some names, so he can work out some type of deal."

"So you know about him being arrested?" Wayne said.

"Elizabeth told me. That's old news."

"Well the new news is your boy over there did some time in Maryland for murder. Did you know that?"

"Let me guess, Taz told you that, too?"

"So because Taz told me, it's not true?"

"Why are you telling me all this, Wayne? I mean what are you trying to do? You like to see me miserable? You don't want me to be happy if I'm not with you?"

"You talking real reckless, Liana."

"Am I? I'm not the one standing in front of your house telling you all kinds of shit about Tammy now am I?"

"You think I'm jealous?" Wayne spat, as if his words tasted like vomit. "Jealous of that dude?" His animated hand gestures got Rasheem's attention.

Wayne sized him up as Rasheem walked toward them. Liana turned around when she saw Wayne looking behind her.

She turned to face Rasheem. "Give us a second, please."

"You know what?" Wayne threw his hands up in defeat. "I don't even know why I bother."

"That makes two of us," Liana said, putting her hands on her hips.

"I'm done with it. Do you, do him, do whatever you want."

"Damn right I'm going to do whatever I want," Liana said emphatically.

"Fine!" Wayne said, as he turned to walk away.

"Fine!" Liana shouted back. With Wayne gone she focused back on Rasheem. "Did you know the police are saying Indio was one of the gunmen who shot at Reese and Dexter in front of the club last year?" Liana watched him carefully, trying to uncover the truth from his reaction more so than from his words.

"That's one of the things I wanted to talk to you about, Liana. I didn't want to tell you over the phone, because I know how close you and Reese are. Dexter is on some bullshit. I don't know why he's trying to put Indio's name in all this. He's probably hoping that Indio's past will validate some of the shit he's feeding the police."

"You said you went to the University of Maryland, and then you went on to get a job in a sneaker store."

"Yes."

"Somehow, you forgot to mention that you did time for murder." Rasheem looked away. "It's true then? You killed somebody?"

"Liana, that was a long time ago, before I got out of the game."

"But you did kill somebody?"

"I did, but it was a stupid decision on my part. And when people find out about it, they look at me the way you're looking at me now; they forget all the positive things I've done in my life, and they just see a murderer. So can you blame me for not telling you? Killing a man is not the sum total of who I am. Rasheem took a step toward her. "Indio may be a lot of things, but a murderer isn't one of them. He didn't shoot at Dexter or Reese, and I definitely didn't' either. You got to believe me."

"I don't know what to believe, now." Liana folded her arms. Rasheem tilted his head as far back as it could go and focused on the stars directly above him, then looked back down at Liana with moist eyes. "I have to go." He handed her an envelope with twenty-five hundred in cash and, then headed to his car.

"You said you had two things to talk to me about. What's the second?" she called after him.

He thought of the two plane tickets to Bermuda in his pants pocket. "It was nothing." He opened his car door, and looked at her one last time before getting in and driving off.

***

"Yes, Wayne, yes," Tammy moaned, as Wayne put her legs on his shoulders and he plunged into her as deep as he could. Twenty minutes later, he was still pounding away, and he wasn't any closer to coming than he was twenty minutes ago.

"You almost there, yet?" Tammy cooed in his ear.

"Yeah, baby, almost," Wayne said, panting. "Wrap your legs around my waist." After that shit Liana pulled tonight, he wasn't going to pretend he was making love to her, not tonight. But it was evident that if he didn't he wasn't going to come, and if he didn't come, that will open the door to a whole lot of questions and suspicion from Tammy. He closed his eyes and Tammy's legs became Liana's legs. Tammy moans became Liana's moans. He could hear Liana's moans in his head getting louder as he got closer to climax.

"I feel you, baby," Tammy moaned. "I feel you about to explode."

"Suck on my chest," Wayne said. Liana always sucked on his chest when she knew he was about to come.

When Tammy's lips formed a suction cup on his nipple, the fantasy was complete. He buried his face in a pillow, while his body twitched and spasmed.

He got up and headed to the bathroom.

"Baby, where are you going?"

Wayne didn't answer. He looked in the bathroom mirror and shook his head. So much for being in love with Tammy.

CHAPTER 16

"Yo, dad," Wayne called out to his father, who was sitting in the air-conditioned truck. "This is it." He waved his hand back and forth under his chin.

His father rolled down the window.

Wayne cut the lawnmower off. "I said this is it. It's too hot. We'll get to the other houses tomorrow."

"Hot? Boy, don't you know that it was three times hotter than this when our ancestors were in them fields picking that cotton, and they were in the heat three times as long?"

"So, come on out here, and help me do some of this work."

"You want me to get heatstroke? Don't play with me."

"What about the ancestors?"

"They *had* to be out there. I'm fine right where I'm at."

"Well, like I said, this is the last house."

"Fine by me." Nevel rolled up the window.

"So, you straight with Alisa?" Wayne asked on their way home.

"I took your advice. I spoke to her like she was a grown woman, and I apologized for treating her like a kid."

"Whoa, somebody call the Guinness Book of World Records. Nevel Dupree apologized," Wayne joked.

"Yeah we had a long talk, me, her, and your mother. I had to bite my tongue this morning when I saw her leaving the house with a tight ass button up shirt. I can't believe how fast she grew up. One day, her chest is flatter than mine. Then, I'm watching her breasts damn near tumbling out of her shirt. She'd better not be fucking. That, I'm not going to tolerate."

"Okay, Dad. I don't' need to hear what my sister may or may not be doing."

"If you see her hanging with anyone of these dingy-ass, pissy-ass motherfuc—"

"Dad! I'm hot, I stink, I just want to get home and take a shower. I just wanted to know if you and Alisa are on speaking terms,"

"Yes, we are," Nevel said, and then got quiet.

"Glad to hear that."

They got out of the truck and started heading their separate ways. "See you tomorrow, Dad," Wayne said, locking the truck doors.

"Yeah, tomorrow," Nevel grumbled.

Wayne was so engrossed in the conversation that he didn't see the unmarked car parked three houses down, nor did he see when Detective Harris stepped out of it.

"Nice house you got here," Harris said, walking up on Wayne.

Wayne spun around. "What are you doing here?"

"Went crying to my mother, huh?"

"Crying?"

"Yeah, snitched me right out."

"I don't know what you're talking about Detective Harr—"

"Spare me the bullshit. Here's the deal. I don't care which lawyer your friend gets to represent her; she's going down. It's tough as fuck to beat a conspiracy charge. So, not only is she going to do time, but whoever she gets for a lawyer is going to suck her bank account dry."

The hairs on the back of Wayne's neck bristled as Harris reached into his jacket pocket, and handed him a piece of paper. As Wayne started to unfold it, Harris stopped him.

"Before you look at that, keep this in mind. It's a onetime offer, and it's non-negotiable."

Wayne unfolded the piece of paper and almost passed out. "Ten thousand dollars?"

"In my hand by Friday morning, and the charges against your friend will be dropped just like that." Harris snapped his fingers.

"How do I know you're not trying to scam me or—"

"I didn't come here to play games. What's it gonna be, yes or no?"

"I'm going to have to get back to you."

"Give me an answer, now, or we're done."

Wayne closed his eyes. There was no way he could get ten thousand dollars by Friday. Then again, between him, Taz, Jenna, Reese, Liana and Nana it might be possible. *Nah, fuck that. I'm not giving my hard earned money to this corrupt pig.* Wayne shook his head, knowing that, in spite of how Elizabeth felt about him, he would never be able to live with himself if he didn't do all that he could to help her. "Okay."

Harris smiled. "See you Friday morning, ten o'clock."

"Where?"

"Where are you supposed to be Friday at ten o'clock?"

"Humph." Wayne shook his head. "Cutting your mother's lawn."

"See you then."

***

"He wants what?"

Wayne had to pull his ear away from the phone. "If I repeat it, I'm going to throw up."

"Fuck that cracker motherfucker," Taz spat into the phone.

"How much can you give me, Taz?"

"Not a fucking dime."

"I'm going to pay you back."

"Fuck that motherfucker. He couldn't get the sweat off my balls if he was in the middle of the Sahara desert dying of thirst."

"It's not about him, Taz. We're talking about getting Elizabeth out of doing prison time. This shit has to be serious because the judge refused to grant her bail."

"I tried to tell her that motherfucker, Indio, was no good, but she swears she's a know it all. Maybe she needs to do some time to humble her high yellow ass."

"How much can you give me, Taz?"

"I'll let you know tomorrow."

"Tomorrow? Why can't you tell me now?"

"Because I don't have anything, right now! I'll call you tomorrow." Taz hung up, leaving Wayne more stressed out than when he called.

"Wayne!" Tammy called his name as soon as she walked through the front door. She jumped into his arms and kissed him. "Oh my God, I'm sooo happy." She hugged him as hard as she could.

"Had a good day at the gym, huh?"

"Good isn't even the word. Try great, stupendous, the best. I got a call from Ursula Mack. She's Akirah's manager."

"Who's that?" Wayne asked.

"Who's that? Akirah, the model/actress?"

Wayne shrugged.

"God, Wayne, you're so out of touch. Anyway, she's going to be starring in a movie where she's going to be a female assassin."

"Okay, that's great, stupendous, the best."

"No, silly. What's great is Ursula wants to hire me to be Akirah's personal trainer." Tammy wrapped her arms around his neck again, and hugged the life out of him. "They're shooting most of the movie in Florence."

"Florence? Florence, Italy?" Wayne stated, wondering if there was a Florence in New York State that he didn't know about.

"Where else, silly? The job's for six months, all expenses paid for two."

"Two?"

"You didn't think I was going without my man, did you?"

"I'm not going to Italy for six months, Tammy."

"But—"

"But nothing. Six months? Who's going to run my business?"

"Your dad can—"

"For six months? No, I don't think so."

"But Wayne, you said you would always support me when it came to my career."

"And I will, but I don't have to go to Italy to do it."

Tammy started walking toward the phone.

"Who are you calling?" Wayne asked.

"Hi, can I speak to Miss Ursula Mack please? Yes, I'll hold."

Wayne walked toward her. "Tammy hang up the phone and let's talk about this."

"There's nothing to talk about. If you're not going with me, I'm not taking the job."

"Whatever. Don't take it," Wayne said, pretending not to care.

"Hi, Miss Mack," Tammy said when Ursula came on the line. "Yes, I'm calling about the job you offered me. I—"

"I'll think about it," Wayne blurted out.

Tammy's face lit up. "Uh… yes, Miss Mack about the job. I just wanted to thank you again. Thank you so very much."

"I didn't say yes," Wayne said, as Tammy covered his face with kisses.

"You went from no to I'll think about it." She ran her finger along his jaw. "If there's anything I can do, and I mean *anything*, to convince you to say yes don't hesitate to ask. Your wish is my command." She bowed her head before him.

"Anything, huh?"

Tammy opened her arms, "Anything."

I wonder if this is how guys get their girls to agree to three-somes? Wayne's wicked side questioned. He imagined being in bed with Tammy and Liana. He blinked away the fantasy when he felt himself starting to rise.

"What's on your mind, dirty man?" Tammy said in a low seductive voice.

"You don't want to know," Wayne said, heading to the den to watch TV.

***

When Tammy went upstairs to take a shower, Wayne called Liana.

"What do you want?" Liana said in a hostile tone

"Who you think you're talking to like that?" Wayne responded just as hostile.

"Nobody, because I'm about to hung up if you don't tell me what you want."

"I got some good news and some bad news about Elizabeth."

"What is it?" Liana sat up straight in her chair.

"I can't talk to you about it over the phone."

"Why not?"

"I'll be there around eight o'clock," Wayne said, looking at his watch.

"Should I call Jenna and Reese over?"

"No! This is for your ears only."

"You're freaking me out, Wayne."

"Just be on the porch at eight o'clock."

***

"He wants what?" Liana shouted.

"Shh, you trying to let the whole neighborhood know our business?" Wayne said, moving closer to her.

"I can't believe it. You only see that type of shit in the movies."

"This ain't no movie."

Liana thought for a moment. "You know what? If I had it, I would pay it."

"I know you didn't go through all that money that Ron left you."

"No, I allowed Derrick to invest it for me."

"How much did you allow him to invest?"

"All of it."

"Damn! Everything?" Wayne asked.

"It's a good investment. I walk away every month with no less than a grand."

"So, what can you get your hands on by tomorrow?"

Liana sighed. "All I have is the twenty-five hundred Rasheem gave me for Elizabeth's lawyer. But I know Jenna and Reese—"

"No! No Jenna and Reese. The last thing we need is them running their mouths, and putting me under the gun with Harris, literally."

"So, how do you expect us to get the rest?"

"I got four, Rasheem gave you twenty-five, so that's sixty-five. Taz is going to call me tomorrow."

"Taz isn't going to have thirty-five hundred dollars, Wayne."

"Try and hit Rasheem up for another thousand. It's the least he can do."

"I don't know," Liana said. She somehow felt that she was never going to hear from him again.

"Why not?"

"I've been calling him since yesterday, and he's not answering his phone."

"Keep calling him."

"I will."

Wayne raked his fingers through his hair and then clasped his hands behind his neck.

"What's on your mind?" Liana asked feeling just as frustrated as Wayne.

"I'm trying to figure out how the hell I got dragged into this."

"I'll get the money back to you, Wayne, don't worry about it."

"I'm not just talking about the money. I'm talking about everything that's happened to me. I've had more fights in this past year than I've had in my whole life. I've gotten myself involved with a crooked cop, I'm with a woman who I can never love the way she loves me, and now she wants me to go with her to Italy for six months."

"Italy?" Liana said stunned.

"She's got a job being some movie star's personal trainer."

"Are you going to go?"

"If I had to choose, hell no, but it's not just about me."

"So, when I suggested that we move out of Albany when we were engaged, you were saying that I was just thinking about me?"

"Not tonight, Liana, please."

"And it just so happens that you didn't get into all of this drama until I came back to Albany."

"Yeah, that's it. Blame yourself, carry the cross, be everybody's scape goat."

"You know what's funny? You wouldn't leave Albany for your *fiancée,* but you're willing to go to a whole other country for your girlfriend."

Wayne took a step back. "Number one, it's not permanent. It's for six months. Number two, if I choose not to go, she's not going to hook up with somebody else and take off."

"That's what I did? I *hooked* up with somebody and just took off? Fuck you, Wayne."

"No! Fuck you, Liana. I'm out of here. I'll come by tomorrow afternoon to take whatever money you can scrape up."

"Fine!" Liana stormed off, not bothering to look back.

***

"How much you got?" Taz said, after he took a pull off the blunt he had camouflaged in his hand.

"I got four Grand, plus the twenty-five I picked up from Liana earlier this afternoon," Wayne said, sitting down on his porch steps.

Taz clipped the blunt, stuck it behind his ear, and dug into his pocket. He pulled out a knot bigger than Wayne had ever seen him with and peeled off thirty-five crisp one hundred dollar bills, which didn't even make a dent in the knot. "Here," Taz said, holding the money out to him.

"Where... in the hell did you get all that from?"

"Does it make a difference?"

Wayne didn't move to take the cash out of his hand.

"Being that my boy, my homie, my man didn't want to put me on his funky car insurance, I said fuck it and sold my ride that's been sitting in my driveway since last year."

"You serious?"

"That's what Cee said when I called the garage and gave him a sweet deal he couldn't refuse."

"You sold your car to help Elizabeth?"

"I sold my car, because *you* didn't want to put me on your insurance. So, it didn't make any sense to have it sitting in my driveway. Here, take this before I change my mind."

Wayne grabbed the money. Taz quickly lit his blunt back up, and took a long pull.

"You need to give that shit up," Wayne said.

"This shit is the only reason why you got that thirty-five hundred in your hand, because if I was in my right state of mind, I wouldn't give my *mother* thirty-five hundred."

Wayne slapped him five. "I just can't believe you're coming through for Elizabeth like this."

"And don't tell her or nobody else, either," Taz said, pointing his finger in Wayne's face.

"Don't worry, your soft side is safe with me."

"I'm out." Taz started walking off.

"All jokes aside, Taz, Good looking. I'm going to get this back to you."

Taz waved his hand at him. "Don't even disrespect me like that. You don't have to give me anything back. I borrowed twice that from you over the years."

"Yo," Wayne called out to him. "Before you go, you know who Akirah is?"

"The model?" Taz asked.

"Yeah."

"What about her?"

"She's supposed to be in a movie that begins filming real soon."

"Umm, you know I'm going to be first in line for my tickets. The ass on that girl is like… Gawd damn!"

"Well, Tammy's going to be her personal trainer for the movie and—"

"Get the fuck out of here. Our Tammy? Oh shit." Taz started jumping up and down. "Yo, son, she gots to introduce me. I can take it from there." Taz punched the palm of his hand. "Now, that's a chick that'll have a man wanting to have her babies."

"It's not that easy, playa. They're filming the movie in Italy." Wayne could see that he busted Taz's bubble.

"Italy?" Taz said.

"Yeah, six months. Tammy wants me to go with her, but—"

"But? But? Are you out of your fucking mind? Do you know how hot and horny those Italian chicks are?" Taz tapped his pocket. "I should have just enough money to accessorize my summer and fall wardrobe."

Wayne looked at him like he was crazy.

"If you ain't going, I am," Taz said dead serious.

"If I'm not going, she's not going," Wayne said.

"Fuck is wrong with you? How you not going to go with her? When was the last time you took a vacation?"

"Never."

"Exactly. And now you got the chance to take a six month vacation. You paying?"

"No, the production company is."

"You stupid mother—How... in the hell... can you pass something like this up? You'll be spending time with Tammy on the breathtaking beaches while I'm fucking Akirah in between filming. Shit, I'm going to lay the pipe game on her so official she'll demand I be in the movie. Boy, you better stop thinking of Liana and start thinking of Tammy and *me*."

Wayne sucked his teeth. "Don't play yourself. It ain't even about her."

"It's over, Wayne, get it through your thick ass head. If y'all were meant to be, it would've happened already. It's time for us to move on. Time for us to pack our shit and move the fuck on to Italy," Taz said, throwing an uppercut and a right hook in the air. "Don't fuck this chance of a life time up for me."

"How did this become all about you?"

"You see, that's your problem, you're always thinking about yourself."

"How you figure that?" Wayne said, utterly confused.

"When your right hand man needed some car insurance, you told me no, forcing me to sell my ride. And now, Tammy has a chance to rub elbows with influential people who will put her on the map, and you're going to ruin that for her. And why? Because all you do is think about yourself."

"If I thought for a second you were serious, I would punch you dead in the head."

"If that's what it's going to take, then huh," Taz said, bowing his head. "I'll take a punch to the head if it will get me a chance to make Akirah wifey and a chance to fuck all the Italian pussy in Italy."

"I'm out of here." Wayne stood up. "I have to get up early in the morning and deal with a lot of shit."

"Let me know how it goes down."

"Sure."

"Hey, Wayne," Taz called out to him just before he closed his front door. "Hasta la vista… baby."

"They speak Italian not Spanish you retard."

"Spanish, Italian. Tomato, tomahto. I bet they understand this." Taz tapped the knot of money in his pocket.

"Later, Taz," Wayne said, shutting the door.

***

Friday morning, Wayne pulled up to Grandma Dynamite's house. *What if this motherfucker is setting me up? I hand him the money, and then the whole precinct jumps out of nowhere and arrests me for bribery. I can't put it past him. He locks me up, and he doesn't have to worry about me being around his mother.*

Today, Carol didn't wait for Wayne to get out of the truck and knock on the front door. She knocked on his. Wayne looked up from his daze when he saw her at his truck door.

"Did I scare you?" she said innocently.

"Nah, I was in another world," Wayne said, opening his truck door.

"I talked to Marcus about Elizabeth. He's going to take care of everything. She's going to be all right," she said, resting her hand on his shoulder.

"That's wonderful," Wayne said, forcing a smile on his face. As he turned to walk to the back of the truck, Carol let her hand slide down to the deep grove of his back before pulling it away. Wayne wished his father was here. Carol would never be so bold with him around. But today was Friday; his father would be at the Mosque all day.

Wayne pulled the lawnmower out of the back of his truck. "You're in the way, Carol."

"No, I'm not," she said, reaching into the back of the pickup and grabbing a rake. "I'm giving you a hand today. See,

I got my work clothes on." She showcased her short shorts, and her button up shirt with the sleeves rolled up.

"I don't know, Carol. It's a lot of work, and it's only eight-fifteen and the sun's already beaming."

"Please. I don't have a problem with working hard, and I definitely don't mind a good sweat."

"If you insist." Wayne grabbed the other rake. "We can start from the front and then work our way to the back."

"Umm, I like the sound of that."

Wayne's face turned red as he pretended Carol's sexual innuendo went over his head.

***

"Wooo," Carol said, wiping her brow with her handkerchief. "I haven't worked like this in years."

Wayne turned off the hedge trimmers. "You can take a break if you want. We've been going at it for almost an hour."

"Yes, a break is a good idea. Let's go inside and get something cold to drink."

"You go ahead. I'll finish up out here."

"Put those hedge cutters down and come and get something to drink." It was evident she wasn't taking no for an answer.

Wayne put the trimmers down and allowed her to lead the way. Wayne got the chance to get a long and hard look at her butt. Her behind was just a big and round as Tammy's. He got a warm sensation in his groin as he watched how Carol put a little sway in her strut.

As they walked into the house, Wayne sighed as the air conditioner dried the sweat off him. He pulled out a chair at the kitchen table and sat down.

"That air feels good, huh?" Carol asked, as she stripped out of her button up shirt. She pulled the bottom of her tank top out of her shorts and fanned herself with it. Every time she lifted it, Wayne couldn't help but stare at her taut stomach, and the silky, flat trail of wispy hairs that disappeared below her shorts.

I must be really losing it. Wayne felt himself stiffening.

She reached into the fridge and grabbed two bottles of Coke. "Marcus said he was coming over at ten to see you," she said, as she sat down at the table and handed Wayne his soda. "What do y'all have to talk about?"

"He wants to give me an update on Elizabeth, I think?"

"How much did he want?"

"Huh?"

"I said, how much did he want?"

"What you mean?" Wayne said, as he put the bottle of soda to his lips.

"Don't play dumb with me."

Wayne focused on the soda bottle when he put it back on the table. "Ten thousand."

Carol shook her head. "Just like his father. He was a cop, too, you know."

"Was?"

"He's dead."

"I'm sorry about your husband."

Carol flipped her hand at him. "He wasn't my husband. I was fucking him behind my husband's back, God rest his gentle soul. And there's nothing to be sorry about when it comes to Marcus's father. Those thugs got tired of him shaking them down. They lured him into an alley one night, and shot him thirty-two times."

Her straight forwardness about her extramarital affair, and the death of a cop left Wayne speechless.

Carol slapped her hand on the table, causing him to jump. "Marcus will be here any second. So, I'm going to stop playing games. You know what I want, Wayne." She looked down at his crotch and worked her way back up to staring him in the eyes. "You. Here. Next Saturday."

"Carol—"

She put her finger to his lips. "After all is said and done, you'll walk out of here a whole lot more experienced *and* with your ten thousand dollars."

Wayne's eyes widened.

"Yeah," Carol said, "You got the money in your truck?"

Wayne nodded.

"Go get it."

Wayne got up without saying another word, and headed for his truck.

What in the fuck did I get myself into? Wayne grabbed the tote bag off the passenger seat and headed back to the house.

Carol was waiting by the side door for him. She held her hand out for the bag. "Grab your stuff and leave," she said, as she looked in the bag.

"Leave?"

"I'll see you next Saturday. That is, if you want this back." She held the bag up.

"Carol, I'm not leaving. Harris is expecting me to be here to give him this. I already feel uncomfortable doing this, but now you're making things worse. The last thing I want to do is get on his bad side."

"Baby, I'll deal with my son." Carol patted him on the cheek twice with an open hand. "And don't worry about Marcus doing anything to you. Trust me, *he* doesn't want to get on *my* bad side."

The look in Carol's eyes let Wayne know who really was in charge.

CHAPTER 17

Outside of Albany County Court, a small entourage awaited Elizabeth's release.

"There she is," Reese said, pointing and running to greet her.

Elizabeth's eyes immediately filled with tears as Reese hugged her hard.

Reese refused to let her go. "God, girl, I'm so happy to see you." Elizabeth cried on her shoulder. Liana, Nana, Jenna, Efran, and Wayne, one by one, gave her a hug and a kiss. When Taz opened his arms to give her a hug, Elizabeth ran into them and embraced him like a long lost lover, and kissed him on the cheek.

"Thank you, Taz."

Everybody looked at Taz, while he laughed nervously, and shrugged.

"You actually thought LaKeisha wouldn't tell me that you put money in her account to make sure I had food and cosmetics?"

"What?" Taz said, acting surprised. "I always look out for LaKeisha. If she looked out for you, she did that on her own."

"LaKeisha also said you sold your car and some of your jewelry to help bail me out."

"And you believed her?" Taz said, his face turning red. "You know you can't believe that girl; she's a crack head."

"Stop it, Taz," Elizabeth said, staring him in the eyes. "As much as you run the streets, you know you can't lie for nothing."

Taz put his head down. When he picked it back up, Wayne was looking at him with the you-know-you're-rec-when-we're-by-ourselves look.

"Girl, I know you want to get home, and take a hot shower, without having to worry about dropping the soap," Reese said.

Everybody started laughing.

"You so stupid," Jenna said.

Elizabeth kissed little Efran on the cheek. "He's getting so big."

"So, what's going on with the case?" Reese asked. "They're just going to drop it?"

"Whoa," Wayne cut in. "She just got out, Reese. The last thing she wants to talk about is jail, courts, or anything related."

"You're right about that," Elizabeth said. "Thank God it's over. DA Watkins said she was dropping the case against me, and that's all I needed to hear."

"Let's get you home, baby," Nana said, putting her arm around Elizabeth's waist. "I cooked you something real special." Elizabeth followed her to Liana's truck. Liana hung back a little.

"I just wanted to thank you for what you did," Liana said to Wayne.

"Don't thank me, she's my friend, too. Just remember, this Harris thing stays between us."

"No problem."

"You hear anything from Indio's cousin?"

"No, I don't know what's up with Rasheem."

Wayne looked at his watch. "I have to go. I'm meeting Tammy at the Gateway diner for lunch."

"Enjoy yourself," Liana said in a tone that let Wayne know that she really didn't mean it.

"I'll see you around, I guess," Wayne said.

"Yeah," Liana said, nodding. "I guess."

"Oookay." Wayne stared at her like he had so much more to say.

"Oookay." Liana stared back at him like she was eager to listen.

Wayne headed to his truck. He wanted to turn around so bad to see if Liana was looking at him, but he didn't. When he hopped into his truck, he looked over at Taz, who was sitting on the passenger side, and started humming the Mr. Softie jingle.

"Fuck you," Taz spat out.

"And here you were, talking all that smack about how you can't stand Elizabeth with her stuck up ass."

"You're going to make me tell you something real foul," Taz threatened. "So, drop it."

"Drop it? Like how you dropped money in LaKeisha's account to make sure Elizabeth was all right?"

"No drop it like you better be dropping something in Grandma Dynamite Saturday night," Taz retorted.

"Ain't happening."

"The fuck you mean it ain't happening? You get to wax that old ass *and* get your ten G's back? You bugging. Well, I want my four G's back."

"What? You told me don't worry about it."

"That was before I knew you had a chance to get it back. You acting like you too good to fuck some seasoned pussy."

"Seasoned pussy? I'll get your money back to you. Don't even worry about it."

***

"So, everything work out?" Tammy asked, before biting into her sandwich.

"Yes, we met her at the court steps and welcomed her home."

"That's some crazy shit. I don't know what I would've done if something like that would've happened to me."

"You would've made bail and kicked Indio's ass."

"You damn right." Tammy sipped on her juice, and then stared at him.

"What's on your mind, Tammy?"

"You know what's on my mind."

Wayne sighed. "I told you I was going to think about it."

"How long does it take for you to think about it?"

"We're not talking about a weekend vacation or even a summer vacation. We're talking six months. That's half a year. When we leave, I'll be twenty-seven, and when we get back, I'll be twenty-eight."

"And when we get back, I'll be twenty-four, with half a mil in my account, and we can do whatever we want. You wouldn't have to do any more landscaping."

"No more landscaping?"

Tammy grabbed both of his hands. "No more, baby. This is it. The big break I've been waiting for. Let me take care of you."

"I don't need you to take care of me. I happen to like the landscaping business."

"Well then, let me help you expand it. We can rent one of those big warehouses, and make it an office/garage for your trucks and supplies. You can lock down Albany, Schenectady, and Troy."

"That's a pretty big dream you got there," Wayne said, taking a bite of his sandwich.

"I wouldn't be where I am today if I didn't dream big. You wouldn't have your own business if you didn't dream big." Tammy looked at him, awaiting a response.

Wayne closed his eyes. "Something's telling me I'm going to regret this."

"I swear you won't," Tammy said, clutching his hand.

"And when are we supposed to be leaving?"

"In six weeks." Tammy tensed up, waiting for Wayne's answer.

"All right, I'll let my father know and—"

Tammy grabbed both sides of his face, leaned across the table, and covered his face with kisses. "Yes, yes, yes, I knew you were going to say yes. I knew it."

"Tammy," Wayne said, in between her kisses. "You need to calm down. We're in public."

Tammy sat back in her seat and took a deep breath, as she looked around. "I'm calm," she whispered. "I'm calm. Your dad's going to be okay with this right?"

"Of course."

***

"Hell motherfucking no!" Nevel said, as he stomped his foot for emphasis. "Six months? Way on the other side of the world? And I have to run this business on my own? What are you trying to do, force me back into the drug game?"

"Dad, it's not that hard. I ran the business for years by myself."

"You were young; I'm not. The only way we're going to have a business when you get back is if you let me hire somebody before you go."

"And who's that someone?"

"Jerome and David."

"That's two people, and they both did time with you."

"So, you discriminating?"

"Yeah, I'm discriminating. The first thing that comes up missing from one of those properties or the first one of them that gets broken into, they're going to try and hold us responsible, because we got ex-cons on the payroll."

"I'm an ex-con."

"But you're my father."

"What's that got to do with—"

"No! The answer is no. We can hire somebody, but it's not going to be one of your homies you did time with."

"You cold, son. And people want to know why a brother goes back to the game."

"Spare me the guilt trip, Dad. As a matter of fact, I got the perfect person. What about the Muslim kid you introduced me to that one Friday when I went to the Mosque with you? He asked me for a summer job, back then."

"You talking about Hameed? Short, stocky?"

"Yeah."

Nevel shrugged. "He's a good kid, and I know he'll work, and he's Muslim."

"Well, talk to him; see if he wants to get down. We got a month and a half to show him the ropes."

"You told Liana you're going to Italy?"

"Why would I tell her?"

"I'm just asking. Six months is a long time."

"Dad—"

Wayne's cell phone rang, interrupting his train of thought. "Hello?"

"Wayne this is Reese."

"What's up?"

"Me and Elizabeth are at Jenna's apartment. We need you to come over like right now."

"What's up?"

"We have a situation and we don't know what to do."

"What kind of situation?"

Reese whispered into the phone. "Elizabeth knows who killed Ron."

***

Wayne walked into the apartment out of breath from running up all the stairs. Elizabeth stood up from the couch when she saw him, and walked to the window. Wayne watched as Jenna and Reese walked over to her, and each put a hand on one of her shoulders.

"What's up, Elizabeth?" Wayne asked, walking toward them. Elizabeth shook her head.

"Tell him," Jenna said to Elizabeth.

"This is crazy," Elizabeth said. "I mean, you know how people talk. You don't know what or who to believe. That's why I didn't want to say anything to Liana."

"Say what?" Wayne asked, getting antsy. "Tell me what you heard."

"There was this woman in the county jail. Her name was Janay, she's a straight up crack head. The day she got moved to the cell block I was in, she walked up to me all happy to see me and what not. I had no idea who she was until she started naming all these people we both knew from back in the days. A few days later, she asked me if I knew Ron. I told her yeah I knew him. So, she got to talking about how she was there that night, on the corner, when that bitch ran him over."

"Bitch?" Wayne was lost. "Who's the bitch?"

***

Liana rubbed her eyes as she pulled up to Nana's house. She brought her right fist to her chest and pulled on her elbow with her left hand, trying to stretch the tension out of her arm. After holding it for twenty seconds, she did it to her other arm before getting out and heading inside. She walked toward her bedroom, stripped, and put on a pair of sweats.

"Nana," she called out, as she walked into the living room. Her mouth dropped when she saw Nana face down on the living room floor. Liana caught the reflection off the television screen of someone running straight for her. Before she had the chance to turn around, the assailant bashed her across the head with an iron pipe, knocking her out cold.

***

Way in the back of her mind, Liana heard a tearing sound. As she slowly drifted back to consciousness, she could also feel a throbbing pain on the side of her head. She felt a pair of hands on her, holding her upright. Then again she heard the tearing sound.

Her eyes fluttered. She tried to focus on something, anything to give her a clue as to what just happened. The tearing sound got louder, and was now accompanied with a voice.

"Slow, bitch. Real slow. You hear me?"

Liana could feel the person's lips on her ear.

"I'm going to kill you reeeal slooow."

Liana's eyes popped open and focused on the hands duct taping her to one of the kitchen chairs.

"There we go," the intruder said from behind Liana's back. "All done. Comfy?"

"Nana!" Liana screamed out, remembering how she saw her last.

"Nana can't save you." Liana recognized the voice all too well. "Bridgette why are you doing this?"

"Why?" Bridgette walked in front of her. "Why?" Bridgette smacked her. "Why?" Bridgette started choking her. "You know why!"

Liana gasped for air when Bridgette released her grip from around her neck. "You're crazy," Liana said, still gasping for air.

"I'm crazy? No, you're crazy. Did you think you could take my man from me? I was willing to share him, I even told him I didn't have a problem with him marrying you, but then you turned him against me. You..." Bridgette mushed her, "Turned him against me."

***

"She's not answering her phone," Wayne said.

"And Nana's not answering the house phone," Jenna said, hanging up and dialing again.

"Why are you such a rush to tell her?" Elizabeth asked, folding her arms. "You don't even know if it's true. Janay's a crack head. She could've been talking just to be talking."

"That's not the point!" The bass in Wayne's voice made her jump. "What if it is true? She's saying that a dude she didn't recognize, pulled Ron out of his car window and started beating him down. Then when Ron broke free and tried to run, Bridgette ran him over, got out, and kicked and punched him until the dude pulled her off him."

Wayne hit speed dial on his phone again. "Fuck! This doesn't feel right. Something's wrong," He headed for the front door.

"Where are you going?" Jenna grabbed him by the hand.

"I'm going to swing by Nana's and tell Liana what Elizabeth just told us."

"Hold up," Reese said, snatching her jacket off the couch.

"I'm coming, too," Jenna said, grabbing her jacket out the closet.

"It's not that serious, y'all," Elizabeth said with a nervous laugh. When she saw them leaving, she grabbed her purse. "Wait up."

***

"Bridgette, I don't know what you're thinking, but I didn't have anything to do with Ron's death."

"You had *everything* to do with his death. If you wouldn't have left him, he wouldn't have left me, and if he didn't leave me, I wouldn't have had to kill him."

Liana's eyes widened, as she began to feel sick to her stomach. "What are you saying?"

"Why didn't you just get with Rasheem? He was doing everything for you. He even wore your favorite cologne."

"How did you know he wore—"

"I told him to wear it!" Bridgette smacked her on the side of the head. "Ron would've seen you with him, and that would've been that, but no, you wanted to play hard to get."

"Where's my grandmother, Bridgette?"

"I convinced Rasheem to scare Ron up a little, you know? Just to let him know that you were off limits."

"Bridgette where's my grandmother?"

"But then Rasheem fucks that up. He allows Ron to wiggle out of his headlock and talk shit. Ron started yelling how he's never going to stay away from you and how he loved you, and no one was going to keep him away from you. I couldn't take it. I had to shut him up. You brainwashed him!" Bridgette mushed her. "You made me kill him."

"Nana!"

Bridgette ripped off a strip of duct tape and stuck it over Liana's mouth. "Now," Bridgette said, retrieving a knife from the kitchen drawer. "Let's get started."

***

"Look!" Reese said. "There's Liana's truck parked out front."

Jenna had her cell phone to her ear. "She's still not answering her phone."

Wayne shut his engine off. "Wait here."

"Nah ah," Reese said, "We're coming with you."

"Just wait here, and be quiet," Wayne said, getting out. He walked up to Nana's front door, straining to hear some kind of sound coming from the house. All the lights were off from where he could see. *Maybe I'm overreacting, I'm bugging the fuck out.* Then he heard a noise from behind him. He spun around.

"Didn't I say wait in the truck?" he whispered.

"Reese made us come," Jenna whispered back.

"Man, fuck this," Wayne said, walking up to the front door and knocking as hard as he could.

***

Both Bridgette and Liana jumped when they heard banging on the front door. Bridgette put her finger to her mouth, pulled out a .25 automatic, and whispered.

"If you make a sound, I'll put two in you, and then put two in Nana."

Even if Liana wanted to scream, she couldn't. She was duct taped to the chair so tight that she could barely breathe, much less make a sound. Bridgette placed the barrel of the gun against Liana's temple when Wayne knocked again. Bridgette reached over and flipped off the kitchen light.

***

"You saw that?" Reese whispered.

"Saw what?" Elizabeth asked.

"The side of the house just went dark, like somebody inside just turned off a light."

"Get the fuck out of here," Wayne said. "Anybody else see that?"

Elizabeth and Jenna shook their heads.

"I know what I saw." Reese walked toward the side of the house.

"Reese," Jenna whispered as loud as she could. "Get your behind back here."

Reese stopped at the side door and peeped in.

PAP! PAP!

"What the fuck was that?" Wayne whispered.

Reese came flying back around the house screaming. "Oh my God, Oh my God, someone's in there with a gun. They shot at me!"

"Liana!" Wayne screamed, as he started kicking in the front door. On the third kick, it gave in, and he ran in not knowing what to expect.

***

Bridgette jumped when she heard the front door bang open. She opened the side door and then hid behind the kitchen door.

From the living room, Wayne could see the side door was wide open. His heart was beating fast. *Whoever it was must've run out the side door and took off.* He ran into the kitchen and froze when he hit the light and saw the horror in Liana's eyes. As he ran toward her, she shook her head hysterically.

PAP! PAP!

Fire shot up Wayne's legs as he fell to the ground. He turned around and saw Bridgette bringing the butt of the .25 down across his head.

"Motherfucker!" she yelled, as she hit him over and over. "You ruined everything!"

Liana wiggled and rocked in the chair pleading for Bridgette to stop. Seeing Liana cry for Wayne only intensified Bridgette's barrage of blows.

Bridgette flashed a devilish grin at Liana as she took aim at Wayne. "He's fucking pathetic." She focused her gaze on him and began to pull the trigger. "Ungh," she moaned as Reese bashed her in the back of the head with a poker from the fireplace. Bridgette spun around disorientated, aiming at the screaming voices of Jenna, Reese, and Elizabeth, as they ducked and ran for cover.

Wayne hoisted himself up and fought against the pain in his legs as he stood.

"You fucking bitch!" Bridgette yelled as she held the back of her head and pointed the gun at Liana and squeezed the trigger. Wayne threw himself on top of Liana, toppling the chair she was in. On their way down to the floor, Liana felt Wayne's body jerk as bullets entered his back. Bridgette stumbled toward them. She aimed at Liana's forehead and squeezed the trigger. Nothing happened. She squeezed again. Nothing. She noticed the gun was out of bullets the same time Elizabeth, Reese, and Jenna did. Elizabeth picked up a glass vase and threw it at Bridgette. Reese charged her swinging the poker like a baseball bat. Jenna worked her way around her and was able to grab a handful of her hair. Then it went down like a WWE handicap match. Jenna, Reese, and Elizabeth screamed at the top of their lungs as they stomped, kicked, and beat the shit out of Bridgette.

The pool of blood spreading around liana and Wayne caught Jenna's attention.

"Oh my God." She ran over to Liana and Wayne. "Oh shit." She pulled out her cell phone and dialed 911.

***

"Ahhh," Wayne yelled as the sharp rocks bit into his fingertips. One of his hands slipped. "No!" he yelled as he looked down into the dark chasm. He looked up at the lip of the cliff he was holding on to. His grip was slipping. He clenched his teeth and swung his other hand up. He yelled in pain as his hand slipped off the edge. It was raw and blistered.

"Let go," a voice down in the chasm whispered.

"No!" Wayne yelled again, starting to cry. He closed his eyes and with a grunt, he tried getting a better grip on the edge of the cliff with both hands.

"Give me your hand."

Wayne's eyes popped open as he looked up. There was a little girl on her stomach with her hand outstretched, reaching for his. She couldn't have been no more than five years old. He shook his head.

"Reach for me. I'll pull you up," the little girl said, her fingertips grazing Wayne's. The last thing Wayne wanted to do was pull her into the dark pit with him. He shook his head again.

"Give me your hand, now!"

A vein bulged from Wayne's forehead as he swung his hand up to the little girl's. He couldn't believe how strong she

294

was as she grunted and pulled him up inch by agonizing inch. When the top half of his body got to the flat surface, the girl stopped pulling. She cradled his face in her arms, and rocked with him.

Wayne was breathing hard, trying to figure out where he was and what had happened.

"Where am I?" he asked the little girl.

She ignored him and kept caressing his face.

"Where am I? What's going on?" Wayne's voice got a little louder.

"Anna!"

Wayne and the little girl looked in the direction from where the female voice came from.

The girl got up and ran in the direction of the voice. "Coming, Grandma." Wayne tried to get up, but his legs wouldn't move.

The little girl stopped running and turned back to face him. "I knew you weren't going to let go. You love mommy too much."

"Wait!" Wayne's eyes filled with tears, but the little girl ran off.

"Wait! Annaaa… Annaaa!"

Liana sat up from the hospital chair when she heard Wayne mumble. When she saw his mouth move, she ran to get the doctor.

***

"You can go in, now," the doctor said to Liana. "But only for a few minutes. He needs his rest. I called his parents, and they're on their way."

"Thank you, Doctor." Liana walked into the hospital room not knowing what to expect. Wayne was lying there staring at the ceiling. He didn't look at her until she was standing right next to the bed.

"Hey," Wayne said.

"Hey. How you feeling?"

"Like shit."

Liana didn't respond.

"I was in a coma for thirty-two days, huh?"

Liana nodded.

"And you've been here every day of the thirty-two, huh?"

Liana nodded again.

"What about Tammy?" Wayne asked half-heartedly.

"Tammy's... working."

"Working?"

"In Italy." Liana could see the pain in his eyes. "She couldn't seeing you like this. She said she had to move on."

"Can't say I blame her. What would she want with a man paralyzed from the waist down?" Tears welled in his eyes as he looked away.

"Don't say that. There's so much you can do—"

"Please, Liana, spare me the look-on-the-bright-side speech."

"So, this is how it's going to be? You're just going to feel sorry for yourself? This is what I hung around for?"

"Nobody told you to hang around."

"And nobody told you to jump in front of those bullets. What were you thinking? You could've died that night." Liana's voice cracked.

She grabbed him by the chin and made him look at her. "You're not going to push me away. I'm here." She mustered up a smile. "Whether you like it or not, you're stuck with me. You know we're meant to be together." She caressed his cheek. "Tell me honestly that you don't believe that."

"If we were meant to be together, then how come we weren't? Why'd you break off our engagement? Why'd you get engaged to someone else? Why'd you move to Queens and just forget about me?"

"Listen to me," Liana said, trying to hold it together. "I'm not the same twisted, bitter, woman you once knew."

"How much could you have changed in a month?"

She reached into her purse, pulled out a Polaroid picture, and handed it to him.

"Get the fuck out of here," Wayne said, looking more closely at the picture. "You went to see your father?"

"After they hit him at the board, he wrote me thanking me for the letter I wrote to the Commissioners advocating his release."

"You're not talking about the letter I read, right?"

"Nah, I tore that one up and drafted another one."

"I'm proud of you, Liana, really I am."

"If I can forgive my father, and give him another chance, I know you can find it in your heart to forgive me, and give me just one more chance. I promise you won't regret it."

"What happened with Bridgette?" Wayne asked, changing the subject.

"She's too through. Watkins is charging her for Ron's murder, attempted murder on you, and for assault on me and Nana."

"What about Indio and that whole situation?"

"He copped out to twenty to life for drug trafficking and attempted murder on Reese. Rasheem *was* the second gunmen, by the way. Indio gave him up, but Rasheem is nowhere to be found."

"What's up with Taz?"

"He's good. He bought himself a car, and got his driver's license."

"Where'd he get money to buy—"

"He told me to tell you that being the true friend that he is, he filled in for you and took care of that business, whatever that means, and he said to tell you it was dyno-mite."

Wayne couldn't help but laugh. "Good ol' Taz. Where would the world be without him?"

"I like the way you changed the subject, and avoided giving me an answer, Wayne."

"I got one more question for you," Wayne said.

"No! Answer my question first."

"I will, but I just need you to answer one more for me, please."

Liana shook her head. "What is it?"

"The doctors told me I was lucky to be alive. I don't believe luck had anything to do with it. I was about to give up and let go, but Anna didn't let me."

"Anna?" Liana questioned. "Anna who?"

"You named her after your mother, didn't you?"

Liana gripped the bed. "Why are you bringing this up?"

"I have to know." Wayne held his breath as he stared at her.

Wayne's question opened up a floodgate of memories and tears. Liana hugged herself as she tried to stop herself from breaking down. She looked in Wayne's eyes and couldn't keep it together any longer. He opened his arms and she buried her face in his chest.

"Don't ask me how, but I just knew we were having a girl. I knew if I had that baby, it would mean the world to all of us. Nana would have a great granddaughter named after her daughter, your parents would've had a grand baby to spoil, and we... we would've had a daughter. We would've been the perfect parents. I know we would have." Liana cried harder. "Why didn't God allow me to have her?"

Wayne felt himself tearing as he remembered Liana's mother calling out for the little girl. "I think, No, I know that Anna's in a good place and she's being looked after by a very special person."

Liana found some comfort in Wayne's words. "Regardless of what I did in the past, I know that we're meant to be together."

Wayne kissed her on the top of her head. "What are you going to do with a man paralyzed from the waist down?"

Liana gently kissed him on the lips and looked into his eyes, allowing him to see into her soul. "I am going to love him with my heart, my body, and my *soul*."

COMING SOON!

DARKEST BEFORE

DAWN

ARLENE BRATHWAITE

Author of *Youngin', Ol' Timer, Paper Trail,* and *In the Cut*

COMING SOON!

Brathwaite Publishing
P.O. Box 38205
Albany, NY 12203
Phone: (800) 476-1522
www.BrathwaitePublishing.com

Order Form

Title	Price	Quantity
Youngin' by Arlene Brathwaite	$15.00	_____
Ol 'Timer by Arlene Brathwaite	$15.00	_____
In the Cut by Arlene Brathwaite	$15.00	_____
Paper Trail by Arlene Brathwaite		
Shipping/handling (via U.S. Media Mail)	$ 3.95	_____
	Total:	_____

Purchaser Information

Name: _____ Reg. #:_____

Address: _____

_____

City: _____ State: _____ Zip: _____

Total Number of Books Ordered: _____

We accept Credit card payments, money orders and institutional checks.
No personal checks will be accepted.